RISK MANAGEMENT

ROY CHESNUT

Copyright © 2015 Roy Chesnut

All rights reserved. No part of this book may be reproduced without written consent of the author.

This book is a work of literary fiction and should not be construed as real. The names, places, characters and events are a product of the author's imagination. Any similarities to persons (living or dead), actual events, locations and organizations are entirely coincidental.

Full Moon Publishing, LLC

Glade Spring, VA

Website http://www.fullmoonpublishingllc

Edited by Jamie White and CP Bialois

Cover image by Ryan McCarron

ISBN: 0692470468
ISBN-13: 978-0692470466

ACKNOWLEDGMENTS

I would like to give special thanks to my wife, Nadine Chesnut, and friends Greg Stefanek and Steve Corn for reading my work and encouraging me..

Part I

Chapter 1 – The Hook

Jack Hooker preferred cocaine for the fraternity party Saturday night. A little cocaine would sharpen his wits, helping him battle a small faction of frenemies he'd encounter there. He knew the conflict was childish, but couldn't resist it and looked forward to prevailing over them, outwitting them with the thrust and parry of verbal repartee. He called them 'The Brotherhood of Evil'—— a name reminiscent of superheroes struggling against sinister forces.

Jack used cocaine infrequently. His previous dalliance had been many months before, but tonight he decided to indulge to soothe the welts left on his psyche by his father that evening at dinner.

Curled up in the black beanbag chair in his room at Sigma Chi, he reflected on dinner with Dad. They had sat in an Italian restaurant nibbling bread dipped in oils seasoned with garlic and basil.

A waiter arrived and Jack ordered, “Calamari and a shot of vodka, neat, with 2 olives. Need to get me vegetables, Dad.”

George, his father, smiled warmly but corrected him, “Olives are actually fruit.”

Jack grinned but took mild offense.

Melanzone, a bottle of Super Tuscan, and happy chatter followed. While they ate, George waxed on about Pinchus Zuckerman performing in San Francisco. “We had front row seats. It was trance-like.”

“Trance-like? Sounds like a Rave. You should try a Rave, Dad,” Jack said.

George raised his eyebrows. “Rave?”

“Let’s not go there. By the way, did you know Zuckerman means Sugar Man?”

“I didn’t.”

Got you that time, Jack thought.

They chuckled, reminisced, shared anecdotes and vulgarities until the wine washed away a layer of George’s self-control and barring the teeth of his disappointment. Tonight, he disparaged Jack’s career choice.

“Accounting, right? The Dismal Science,” George said.

“Economics is the Dismal Science. Accounting is just plain dismal.”

“Bean Counting! How do you like it, counting beans? You

must like it, counting the musical fruit. There's something septic about it," George said. In contrast, George researched science at a Stanford Research Institute, where he sorted through the mysteries of the universe with the same faith and certainty as a priest studies God.

"Sooooo, what's so great about what you are doing?" Jack retorted.

"Particle Physics is a little more novel than accounting. Don't you agree?"

Jack didn't reply, but he did agree. He would count other people's money to earn a living. *A little like counting holes in Blackburn, Lancashire*, he thought. *But it pays a hell of a lot more!*

The problem was that life offered Jack too many worldly pleasures like partying, a high paying career, romance, and occasional love. He'd been lured away from the disciplined priesthood of science, rejected its grey austerity, considered the sacrifice too great and its payoff too paltry. In spite of this, the banality of his upper-middle class future pained him and he tightened the ball of his constricted posture in the bean bag chair, alone in the darkness of his room.

Yeah, a little cocaine will soothe the pain, he thought.

The crackle and pop of guitars plugging into amplifiers distracted him, ending his self-pity and bringing him back to the present.

The band is warming up downstairs, he thought as he listened to the rising murmur of celebrants who gathered for yet another drunken Saturday night at Sigma Chi. The idea of more partying bored Jack. By his senior year, he had seen it all. What didn't bore him about frat world embarrassed him.

While he lamented the twin hoods—the Brotherhood of Evil and his father's scientific priesthood—his neighbors cranked up their stereo, flooding the floor with the sickly sweet lyrics of insipid pop music; a chorus of high soprano singing a teenage love fantasy.

"Lady Gaga? Oh my god" he gasped and bolted from the chair, grabbed a wad of cash, and began his journey to the 3rd floor of Sigma Chi to purchase.

Chapter 2 – The Tunisian Port City of Souse

Mikhail Kazaki sat in a dust-covered Land Rover studying a languid marina in the Tunisian port city of Souse. He watched a crew of men in tunics heave burlap bags onto their shoulders, totter onto a ship, and leave them in neat rows. A fishing boat slipped into the harbor, its crew throwing snatches of fish to a swarm of jeering gulls. Its engine chugged through the green water leaving puffs of exhaust, each round like a period, each ending a moment. The bells and horns of buoys and boats punctuated the ambient chorus of sea birds; the air smelled of brine, seaweed and diesel.

He started his car, drove to the light house on the far side of the marina, parked, and continued his watch until sunset. Then he left.

He returned to the docks in the small hours of the night to find fog nestled in the harbor, blocking stars and deadening sounds. He watched for minutes, the silence broken only by the groans of boat hulls rubbing dock pylons. Suddenly, he left the car, tip-toed towards a speed boat, freed it from the dock, and jumped on. Once on board, he froze and scanned the marina for sound or movement. There was nothing in the deep fog. He started the boat engine and motored out of the harbor.

The fog cleared, revealing a starry moonless night. Microbes of the sea fluoresced his wake.

Hours later, he reached the coordinates, cut the engines, and drifted in the whistling wind. From maybe a quarter of a mile away, the running lights of a vessel flashed on. He motored to within shouting distance and waited until he heard, in accented English and through a bull-horn, “Who are you?”

He shouted back, “Eve Marie Saint”

“What is your bearing?”

“North by North-West.”

“Approach the barge.”

Mikhail pulled a ski mask over his head, motored toward the lights, and pulled alongside. He threw his ropes up to the deck to be tied. A walkway extended from the barge to his boat, which he crossed. Once on the barge someone shined a search light into his eyes, blinding him. Someone else kicked him in the stomach. He collapsed.

“Take his mask. Search him.”

Hands slid over his body. “He’s clean”

“Take him inside.” The men pushed him into the main quarters of the barge where he stood before four masked men. The man pulled the ski mask from Mikhail’s head, revealing his face.

One spoke to him, “So, it’s Mikhail Kazaki. It’s been a long time. Twenty years?” “Mikhail, it’s me, Anton, from the Army.”

Chapter 3 – Buying Cocaine

Jack stepped into the hallway and walked towards the stairs, dragging a finger along the dirty beige wall. His footfalls stuck to the carpet, making faint ripping sounds as each tore away. The frat house still donned its original fixtures, like a stone fireplace with mahogany mantel, worn porcelain sinks, balusters made of dark wood, and rumors of secret passageways. It all conspired together to create an eerie feeling of a dead era.

A Mister Littleton built the mansion in the 1920's after striking it rich. He lost it all, including his mind, in the crash of 1929. His wife disappeared without a trace and he murdered his daughter, leaving her bloody corpse sprawled in the third floor bathroom. The spot was memorialized in the oral history of Sigma Chi. No one ever stepped on the spot.

The steps creaked as Jack climbed to the third floor. The fixtures, rumors, odors, and sounds made the third floor a perfect inner sanctum for fraternity secrets and lore; a place where the brothers gathered in the wee drunken hours to tell and retell gossip, news, and tales.

The lore included a story about Jack who, as a freshman, retaliated against a feuding fraternity by stealing their Moose Head; a grotesque heirloom they displayed with pride. Frat world ignored the felonious nature of Jack's prank and, instead, elevated him to hero status.

As he reached the third floor, he noticed that Bob, the Insolent Voice of the Brotherhood of Evil, had posted an advertisement for an upcoming party. He stopped and read. *Oh...yeah...the Heidelberg Beer Party is in a couple of weeks, Jeezus, grow up,* he thought.

Jack had a special scorn for theme parties and their stupid rituals. Before continuing down the third floor hallway, he recalled passing Bob earlier in the day, downstairs, on his way to the main hall for lunch. Bob stood with a cloister of frenemies and said, “Oh look, here comes the whore, I mean Hooker.”

Jack replied, “Not very original, Bob. Speaking of sex life, picked up any nice boys recently?” Jack’s politically incorrect insult evoked a groan and chuckle from the cloister, and entitled Jack to a small victory over the Brotherhood of Evil, but it didn’t represent his feelings about gays. Unfortunately, homophobia was a reality in Sigma Chi, so Jack used it to his advantage.

As the memory of Bob faded away, Jack reread the posting, summoned his talent for insulting nonsense, and scribbled graffiti across the page.

Bob, Next time please embrace your penis envy in private.

The depths of the third floor led to Kit’s room, a second year medical student and the fraternity’s supplier of illegal substances. Jack once joked that Kit studied anesthesiology because of his interest in drug abuse, to which Kit replied, “Why not? Oliver Sacks made it legitimate, right?” Jack had his doubts about that.

He reached Kit's door, knocked the secret knock and a voice from behind the door spoke, "Passphrase?"

"It is now time for the lies behind the truth and the truth behind those lies behind that truth."

The door opened. "Well, I'm glad someone knows what time it is around here. Hey, it's the Hook! Welcome"

Marijuana scented the air. The Sigma Chi President, Steve and his friend Mark sat on the floor blinking with glazed eyelids. Kit commented, "The boys wanted to play a little before the party downstairs." Pot stimulated in them a riot of behaviors Steve and Mark thought creative and tonight Steve expressed his creativity by wearing a motor cycle helmet, which he pretended was a space helmet. He drifted about the room as if floating in zero gravity while making bleeping sounds.

Jack froze awkwardly. *They're playing make belieeeeeeeeve! These guys are really idiots...*

"What brings you to my humble abode?" Kit asked. Jack pointed to his nose. "Ah yes, a wee bit of white powder. One half gram, one hundred dollars." Jack produced a C note. "Don't snort it all in one place!" Kit handed Jack a tightly folded paper packet.

Steve pulled off the helmet and said with authority, "Aren't you going to share with your brothers?"

Fraternity etiquette required that Jack accommodate Steve, the President. Besides, Jack liked the idea of lowering the Sigma Chi President to the level of cocaine. "Aye, Captain." Jack opened the packet and spilled out enough for the four. The stimulant re-energized Steve and Davey, who disappeared into pantomime while Jack escaped into the hallway.

Chapter 4 – Business as Usual

Mikhail recognized Anton's rodentia of yellow teeth that poked through his lips. In a previous life, they'd served in the same military unit in Chechnya. Over the years, he'd aged into a repulsive bundle of fat and nerves; twitching, rocking impulsively. He hadn't shaved, he smelled, and his un-tucked shirt fluttered behind like a piece of toilet paper clinging to an oblivious host.

The tall, clean-cut Mikhail had short grey hair, grey unblinking eyes, and a calm, controlled demeanor. He wore black leather gloves, a black shirt, and jeans that clung to his muscular body.

Anton spoke, "Well, well, well. It's been a very long time. How many years? Twenty? Twenty-five? You look good. A drink? We can toast the Army. Remember those days and our comrades?"

Mikhail answered with silence.

"No drink, eh? You haven't changed. Still very quiet. You never had much to say, as though something was missing. We all wondered about you, Mikhail. Well, now isn't the time to catch up."

"Where's the cargo?" Mikhail asked.

"Now that's the Mikhail I remember. All business, no pleasure. No, no, no. The cargo? Do you mean the payment or the product?"

Mikhail's job was to pick up the payment and deliver it. One hundred kilos of gold, worth more than five million dollars. The rest didn't matter. "Payment. We will count it," Mikhail said.

Anton objected, "We don't have time to count."

Mikhail's vacant eyes stared through Anton as he calmly repeated, "Get the gold. We are going to count it."

Anton wringing his hands, backed down, "Ok, get it." Two of the men disappeared.

"Do you know the merchandise?" Anton's chuckle bared his brown, rotting teeth. "White girls, seventeen, eighteen years old. Four of them. Want to play with one? I can tell you, they're really sweet. Each in her own way. How about this one?" Anton nodded to the remaining man who pulled on a cord.

A drapery dropped, revealing a nude woman, arms bound over head. Anton's abuse left marks on her abdomen, thighs, and face. One eye was swollen shut.

Anton spasmed as he spoke, "We made a film, a gang bang. It is making a little money for us to spend."

Chapter 5 – Remain Calm at All Times

Jack stepped away from Kit's room lightened by a nostril full of cocaine when Amy Hanover, his girlfriend, called and began to rant, "WHERE ARE YOU? Everyone is here. I've been looking for you forever. You're not in your room. You're not in the bathroom. WHERE ARE YOU?"

Shit! Amy's about to go off the deep end AGAIN! Now, be nice, he thought.

"Hi, Sweetie. I'm just running a little late. I had an early dinner with my dad."

"WELL, HURRY UP. Susan and Ben are here, the band is about to start, and I am halfway through a margarita, so GET THE HELL DOWN HERE!" She hung up.

Great! Ben! My favorite person. At least Susan's nice, he thought.

As a senior member of the Alpha Phi sorority, Susan held sway over the people in frat world and Amy clung to her for status and security. Ben was not a nice person. He was a short, homely outcast whose own mishegoss fed his narcissistic self-hatred. Jack understood Ben's self-loathing, but thought, *acting like a jerk sure doesn't help.*

Descending the stairs, he passed his friend Greg who led a young blonde by the hand. "Jack, Jack, Jack," Greg crooned, "Where have you been? Amy Hangover, I mean Hanover, is looking for you. She's pissed."

"I know she is. I'm working on it. Who is this beauty?"

"Anya Gustafsson from Sweden. Anya is studying Computer Science," Greg said.

Jack took her hand and looked into her eyes. "Computer Science, you must be as brainy as you are pretty. Enchanté."

"What is brainy?" she asked with an adorable accent.

"It means smart, beautiful. And yes, she is smart. Speaks English, Norwegian, and Swedish."

Anya then said in perfect English, "Well, I speak a little English. It is so difficult to express myself properly in your language."

"You know, the Angels came from Sweden to Denmark then to England, a long time ago. They brought English to England," Jack said.

Greg said, "Jack is one of the few guys who actually learned something in college. It makes him boring. Don't hold it against him." He shifted his attention to Jack, "By the way, is Kit in?"

Jack knew what lay ahead for them; a little pot followed by some vigorous, but healthy, physical exercise in the form of sex. "Yeah, he's there. With Steve and Mark," Jack said.

"Ah, a little pre-party?"

"A little pre-party fupidity."

"Yeah, I know what you mean. Hopefully they've left," Greg said.

"What is fupidity?" Anya asked.

"I'll tell you later. Come with me, my dear." Greg kissed her hand.

"You give me duck pimples when you are doing that," she emoted with faux drama.

"I think you mean 'goose bumps'," Greg replied.

"Anya, beware my friend Greg. He has a corrupting influence on the weak."

Greg rolled his eyes like a madman as he spoke with the calm, evil voice of Hannibal Lecter, "Come with me, my little pretty."

"Oh, no! Stop! Stop! Please help me!" Anya feigned.

Jack thought, *Kool. I wonder if she means, 'don't stop'. I wonder if she likes to role-play?*

Jack arrived at his room, unlocked the door and stepped inside just as his phone beeped a text from Amy: *WHERE ARE YOU?*

He texted back, *5 minutes more.*

He threw on a black silk shirt with floral prints and blue Levis. He snorted two more lines of cocaine, watched his pupils dilate in the mirror, and began to feel like a demigod, ready to confront the raucousness at the party below.

Chapter 6 – Liability

Mikhail cast a pitiless eye on the bound woman, registering her agony but feeling nothing. Instead, he was alarmed over Anton's reckless stupidity. Without masks they were exposed. *Now she can identify us, but she won't escape, so we're safe. Anton cannot make any more mistakes,* he thought.

"Get her out of here, now!" Mikhail said with a calm, deliberate voice.

Mikhail's speech carried a gravity that Anton either missed or ignored, because he taunted and chuckled. "What's the matter with you, Mikhail? Don't you like women?"

Mikhail's eyes dissected Anton like an insect.

"Okay, okay. Suit yourself. Take her away." Anton said.

The man hustled the woman out of the main quarters. The two other men returned carting a number of crates into the room.

"Open them." Mikhail ordered. He inspected random bars from each crate.

"Satisfied?" Anton asked.

"I want a complete weighing and counting."

"Weigh each one? We will be here all night. Forget it. We have to get moving. Don't you trust your old Army pal?" Anton said.

Mikhail looked at the men and repeated, "Weigh each. If

any are light, set them aside."

The men weighed and stacked the bars into piles of ten. When they finished counting, one man said, "These five are light."

Mikhail took one and peeled away the thin golden surface with a knife to reveal the dull grey metal beneath. Mikhail's inscrutable look returned to Anton and found him pointing a gun.

Chapter 7 – Amy Hanover

Noise, people, and music whirled about the first floor as the partiers gathered into bunches, gossiped, laughed, and drank—commotion in constant motion. Amy, Susan, and Ben stood clear of the social tides and eddies, huddled away by the fireplace in the living room. Amy sipped a margarita while studying her phone, knitting her eye brows. A pale blue cotton blouse and black wool pants hugged her svelte body. Her coiffed brown hair flipped upward at her shoulders. She had brown button eyes, beige skin, and a cute Parisian face.

Susan scanned the party with pursed lips and a critical eye, her arms folded in judgement. She was pale, brunette, tall and gaunt. She had a long face and oversized jaw. Her Macy's ready-to-wear dress, white with floral prints, clung lifelessly to her skinny body. She was bland.

Ben stood safely behind Susan, peering out from behind, wearing a mask of superior disapproval as if to say, 'I may not be like you and I may not be liked by you, but I am still better than you.' He really believed it too.

Pangs of abandonment tugged at Amy as she read Jack's text. "Five minutes more. Why am I always waiting for him? He said he had dinner with his father, that's why he's late." Amy lost her balance, wobbled, and sat.

“Amy, have you had too much?” Susan asked.

Ben frowned at Amy as though he thought he was better than her, too.

“Not too much. Just about right,” she said and thought, *I’m not supposed to mix Xanax and Tequila. Bad Girl.* Before guilt could set in, she recalled Jack’s enabling statements, “Here’s to self-medication, Luv.”

She did self-medicate, too often, sometimes excessively. This resulted in collapsing several times and emergency trips to the hospital. Her friends all knew about her problem.

Susan craned downward and looked Amy directly in the face. “Are you okay? Do you need to lie down?”

“Okay, Susan, stop it. Right now.” Amy slowly rose and stood. “See? I’m just fine.”

The overdoses and other traumas had scarred her psyche, haunted her thoughts, and poisoned her moods. This endless cycle led to more substance abuse, which caused more trauma. She had a good teacher; her mother.

One lesson began at her family home near Canon Drive in Beverly Hills. The doorbell rang. Amy came to the landing on the second floor to see who it was while Estrella, the maid, answered the door. A young, stylish brunette stood there. “Is Missus Hanover home?”

Mother came to the door. “I’m Missus Hanover. How can I help you?”

“We need to talk about Frederick, Missus Hanover. May I

come in?"

Frederick Hanover was her husband and Amy's father. "No, you may not come in. What do you want to say?" Mother snapped.

"All right…I have been seeing Frederick for months. I think you should know," She said.

"I don't believe you," Mother said.

"Well it's true. We're in love, but he's afraid to leave you."

"Listen, you stupid gold digger, you need to know this: Frederick doesn't have a cent. He lives off of me, so you can get lost." She slammed the door shut.

Later, Frederick arrived home pale, shaken, and drunk. He went to the living room and poured a drink.

Estrella entered the room. "Good evening, Mister Hanover, Missus Hanover is waiting for you in her bedroom."

Frederick climbed the stairs and disappeared. Amy heard her mother ranting and raving, and her father shouting and things breaking. Frederick bolted from the room with blood on his cheek. Amy's mother chased him to the top of the stairs and threw a paper weight that missed him by inches and hit the wall, leaving a mark. He stumbled down the stairs and out the door.

That night, Amy heard her mother weeping, pacing, and shouting. Amy awoke early in the morning to find paramedics taking her mother away. She had overdosed on prescription pills.

Chapter 8 – The Gun

Anton pointed his weapon at Mikhail. “Five Bars? It is a small discrepancy, Mikhail. My advice is to let it go. Ignore it. Forget about it. Look, we are old army pals. You can let this go.”

Anton is stealing. A deadly sin, Mikhail thought, *that's a line the others won't cross.* Mikhail looked Anton in the eye and waited for the others to respond.

One of the men said, “Drop the gun, Anton, you piece of shit.” The man turned to Mikhail and said, "We knew nothing about this. Anton acted on his own.” Although this was true, Anton's action was everyone's liability.

The men pointed their weapons at Anton. He dropped his gun. “Raise your hands.” One of the men searched him. “Hands behind your back.” They handcuffed him.

“Where are the five bars?” Mikhail asked.

“Mikhail, this is such a little nothing. Five bars…”

Mikhail nodded at one of the men, who smacked Anton in the face with his gun, knocking Anton to the floor.

Mikhail calmly repeated, “Where are the five bars?”

“In the safe,” Anton said.

“Where is the safe?” Mikhail asked.

One of the men said, “I know where it is. It's a floor safe.”

“What is the combination, Anton?”

Mikhail and the man descended a staircase into the dank belly of the ship where the floor safe lay beneath a clutter of boxes and crates. They cleared the area revealing the door and dial of the floor safe. Mikhail stood by as the man knelt and spun the dial, paused, changing the direction of the dial, paused again, and finally stopped. He yanked open the safe and looked inside. Unable to see due to the shadows, he searched his pocket for a light just as a sliding sound began overhead. Mikhail saw a huge crate crashing downward. He shouted, "Watch out" and ducked, but it was too late. The crate crushed the kneeling man with a wham, popping his skull like a gourd.

The men and Anton heard the muffled crash of the crate and even the skull popping.

"Did you hear that?" one said. "What was that?" He directed his question at Anton, who lay still and silent on his side on the floor, hands cuffed.

He brought his boot toe up to Anton's face, raised it, and poked his lips. "What was that?" the man asked.

"I don't know."

"You're sure you don't know?" he gestured to another man. "Go see."

The man nodded and left.

Mikhail took cover and waited. *Anton set this trap,* he thought.

He gradually stood, looked around, and when he thought it was safe, moved towards the crate, pushed it aside, and examined the man. His eyes had come out of their sockets, coming through the eye holes of his mask and lay by his face like broken eggs; blood trickled from his mouth, nose and ears. Mikhail knelt and checked his pulse. *Nothing, he's dead.*

He saw one of the men enter the hold and got to his feet.

"A trap," Mikhail said. "The crate fell when he opened the safe. He's dead"

"Who is he?" the man asked, looking at the crushed, masked head and eye balls.

"I have no idea."

In the safe, they found the five bars, a stash of heroin, and a handgun. They took the bars and returned to the main quarters of the barge.

The cuffed Anton lay on the floor looking up sheepishly.

"What was the noise?" one of the men asked.

"A trap. Your comrade is dead. We have Anton to thank for that."

After a moment of silence, one of the men shouted, "FUCK YOU, ANTON!" and walloped him in the chest with his boot. The man menaced over Anton, raised his boot to his crouch, pointed the boot toe at his temple, and took a step back as though preparing a drop kick the flinching Anton.

Mikhail spoke, "I am going to leave now. I will take Anton."

The masked man kicked Anton in the stomach and then in the head.

Chapter 9 – Coyote Women

The small dose of coke set Jack aflame, poisoning him with euphoria. His heart pounded, beads of sweat appeared on his forehead, his mouth went dry and tongue prickled. *Time to go. Charge!* He shot out of his room and careened towards the party on the first floor.

He heard a pack of women cackle away, huddled in the bathroom, verbally ripping someone's reputation to shreds. "Yes, I heard all about it. Oh my god, what a slut she is."

"She's such a whore."

"That is *sooooo disgusting*."

Just like a pack of coyotes, Jack thought and then said, "She sounds like my kind of girl."

"Shush, someone's listening." The door popped open and a brunette peaked out. "Oh, it's Amy's beau. Hi, Jack." She waved and giggled.

"Hi." He waved back and the door shut.

"It's Jack Hooker. You know, Jack and Amy."

An authoritative voice followed, "Jack, you better find Amy. She is looking for you and she is peeved."

"She's such a brat," one of them said.

"Shush, he might hear you."

Jack fled entanglement with the coyote women, glided down the stairs to the first floor, and rounded a blind corner, just missing a couple sipping drinks. “Woops, ‘scuse me”

I need to slow it down. He shifted into low gear and ambled into the outer envelope of the party. The dimmed lights of the hallway, which led from the front door to the main hall, hid faces, and provided cover for couples who necked.

“Stop,” murmured a girl, whose boyfriend buried his face in her neck.

“Let’s go,” he said.

“Upstairs? I can’t.” She pushed him away.

Once in the main hall, Jack passed an insecure looking group of four men, one of whom toasted Jack and spoke. Jack smiled and nodded, but couldn’t hear a word and moved on. He scanned the main hall. No sign of Amy. He wandered into the living room and scanned the crowd.

Amy’s face rose above the commotion. She saw him and waved. A smile spread across her face. In a moment, he was by her side.“Hi, Love.” He gave her an affectionate embrace and kiss on the cheek, then turned to the others. “Hi Susan, Ben.” He bowed slightly.

“Hi, Jack,” Susan said.

Ben managed a supercilious grunt. “Hi”

“At last you appear. Where have you been? Your hair is a mess.” She combed his hair with her fingers. “And your shirt is horrible.”

His affection for her became self-defense. “Do you want me to change?”

"No. You're already late."

He kissed her cheek. "Sorry I'm late. Didn't mean to keep you waiting."

"Are you stoned?" Amy asked.

"No." Jack kissed her on the mouth to shut her up.

Just then, the band began playing Nirvana. He grabbed Amy's hand and led her to a scrum of bodies on the dance floor. They joined and undulated to the adagio of Kurt Cobain, her head on his shoulder. Everyone staggered through the thick, dark music. When the song ended, the dancers applauded and the band set their instruments aside to take a break.

Jack and Amy strolled to the deck outside and joined a crowd whose bodies cooled in the night air, releasing a fog that floated above their heads. Someone lit a joint and passed it around. They both hit the joint and the THC created a feeling of rapture. Free from the grip of anger, Amy became the person Jack liked; affectionate, silly, sexy, and playful.

She wrapped her arms around him and pulled his body to hers. "When does my master want to carry me off and have his way with me?"

It's a complete change, Jack marveled, unable to grasp the forces that changed her from angry bitch to playful kitten. He played along with her mood swings, stepping away as it swung by while embracing her when she was warm. "Let's go," He replied. She purred.

Chapter 10 - Lobster Trap

Anton's eyes opened to stars that spun round overhead. He heard the loud drone of a boat engine. He shivered uncontrollably in the freezing wind and was totally confused. *What the hell? What the fuck is going on!* He rolled onto his side and through the netting saw Mikhail Kazaki piloting the boat. *On a boat, in lobster trap?? Mikhail Kazaki! That bastard.*

The recent past flooded his mind: the gold, the girls, and the murder. *I'm trapped.* His blood-shot eyes opened with terror as he grasped his predicament. *Oh my god, oh my god. I'm trapped. HE'S GOT ME!*

He began to recall the army years with Mikhail and an incident in Chechnya when the soldiers went on a drunken rampage and the rowdiest, Vladimir, raped the daughter of a village leader. A riot ensued and Vladimir was jailed for his crimes.

When calm prevailed, Dmitri Chesnakov, the captain of the unit, and Mikhail Kazaki met secretly with the village leaders. The crime of rape carried a punishment of death under Chechnyan Law. The strategic value of the village for trade in arms, drug imports, and people required that Dmitri make peace with the villagers. That meant sacrificing Vladimir. Dmitri ordered Mikhail to carry out the execution in the presence of the village leaders hours before dawn.

That night, Anton snoozed through his shift at the jail watching Vladimir until a neatly uniformed Mikhail appeared, startling him awake. “Handcuff the prisoner.”

“He is already handcuffed.”

“Open the cell.” Anton did and Mikhail ordered Vladimir out into the oblivion of night.

Later, Anton heard a shapeless mumble of voices rise and fall like a chant. The mumbling came to an abrupt end when one final voice spoke with certainty as though making a decree. A quiet followed that ended with silenced gun shots. The mumbling began anew, rising, falling, and slowly dissipating into the chilly silence of deep night.

Mikhail reappeared at the jail. “Vladimir has been shot.” He ordered Anton to retrieve and bag the body. “Then police the area. It must be immaculate.”

Anton went with a lantern, cart, and body bag to find Vladimir’s corpse, which he discovered a kilometer from the jail. Most of his head had been blown off. The stench of blood and brain tissue sickened him and he gagged uncontrollably. As he lifted the body bag, he felt shards of skull scrapping along the bag’s fabric, making his skin crawl. He scrapped bits from the ground with a trowel, which he later tossed into the bag and returned to the jail.

Mikhail showed Anton a death certificate which stated that Vladimir had been killed in the line of duty. Dmitri Chesnakov, the captain, had signed it. Mikhail then clarified the situation to Anton. "It is not in your interest to mention anything you have seen or heard to anyone. Do you understand what I am saying?" The terrified Anton understood the message very well and nodded.

Anton kept the secret and his loyalty earned him a position in a sinuous web of criminals that led him from that night in Chechnya to now, this moment in time, trapped like a lobster and prisoner of a psychopath. He tried again to sit up, but could not. *I'm fucked!* he lamented.

Anton watched Mikhail perform his duties with robotic detachment. *Maybe his executions are quick and painless like with Vladimir, or maybe I can make a deal.* Anton began to scheme.

The Mikhail Anton knew was essentially unknowable. Mikhail had distanced himself from the others, never eating, drinking, or whoring with them, and only speaking with them about official business. Mikhail's physical toughness and mental acuity frightened Anton. Mikhail held higher rank. His privileges, like a private bunk and shower, created jealousy among the men who gossiped hatefully, speculating that he molested young boys and had deformed genitals.

Maybe money, that's the only thing. I can offer him a lot of money, he mused. "Hey, hey, Mikhail!" Anton shouted above the engine and wind. "Mikhaaaaaaail!" Mikhail looked back at Anton. "Hey, Mikhail! Hey!"

Mikhail stopped the engine, walked over to the trap, and stared downward at Anton. "Do you want to make a deal?" Anton asked.

Mikhail stood still, eyeing the cage. "What?"

"I have money. I can pay you," Anton said

"How?" Mikhail asked.

"Wire transfer. We can do it now. It takes twenty-four hours to clear."

"How much?"

"Ten million rubles. I pay you and you let me go. Drop me on shore. Somewhere, anywhere. No one will know. It will be our little secret, Mikhail."

Mikhail walked aft-ward into the darkness, to contemplate Anton's offer. He wondered if it was a trap. Minutes passed. He suddenly decided, *take the money.* He walked back to Anton. "Okay. How?"

"You have a phone?" Mikhail pulled a cell phone from his pocket. "Dial this number." Anton dictated a phone number. An automated voice response answered in Swiss-German. "What do you hear?"

"It is asking for an account," Mikhail said.

"Okay, enter this account number and press the pound key." Anton dictated a series of numbers. "Now wait."

The voice asked for an amount.

"What currency are we using?" Mikhail asked.

"Francs. Swiss Francs. Ten million rubles is around three hundred thousand Swiss Francs. Enter it."

Mikhail heard, "Wire Transfer. Please enter the Destination

Account number."

"It says, 'Destination Account'."

"Do you have an account you want to wire to? Enter it," Anton said. Mikhail entered an account number.

Mikhail completed the transaction and hung up. A few seconds later, a text message arrived with the transaction id.

"So?" Anton asked.

"The transaction is completed."

Anton believed he could buy time by repeating, "It takes twenty-four hours to clear."

Mikhail stared through Anton and then dialed another number. He held the phone to his ear and walked to the stern of the boat.

"Hey, Mikhail. HEY, MIKHAIL! GET ME OUT OF HERE!"

Mikhail turned his back.

Chapter 11 – Overdose

The cocktail of booze, pot, and Xanax sedated Amy, who teetered as they descended the Sigma Chi steps to the tree-lined street. They stopped in the shadow of Sigma Chi while Jack helped Amy on with her coat. Amy fumbled with her purse while Jack surveyed the house, looking up at its grey slate roof, brick chimneys, and gabled dormers that ran the length of the third floor. A friend called out to them from the deck above. Amy and Jack waved and then shuffled away, hand in hand. As they walked between street lights their shadows slid along the uneven sidewalk, catching them from behind and then racing ahead. The roar of the party faded into a soft background din. She grabbed Jack's arm for balance.

"Little tipsy tonight, eh, Luv?" He asked.

She put her head on his shoulder and slurred, "The kinnnndnesssss of sssstrangers."

He steadied her as they strolled towards his car. "This way, Miss Dubois."

She asked with vulnerable naivety, "Who's Miss Dubois? Another old girlfriend?"

"No, no, no. You know, Blanche Dubois, the kindness of strangers?"

"I don't get it, Jack," she emoted dreamily.

"Yeah, that's okay. Forget about it."

"So, again you were late. You're always late. I'm always waiting and I looked like a fool standing there alone," Amy said.

"You were with Susan and Ben."

"Even worse. I was humiliated in front of them," she said.

"I'm sorry. I already told you. I had dinner with my dad."

"Where did you meet Georgie for dinner?" she asked.

"Carpaccio's"

"I love Carpaccio's. Why don't we ever go there?"

"We can anytime you want," he said.

"What's Georgie up to these days? Still searching for that big Scientific Truth?"

"Yeah, still searching. At least, he has something to keep his mind busy."

"Nonsense! He just never learned how to enjoy life properly. How was dinner anyway?" she asked.

"It was good for a while. And then it wasn't so good."

"Another lecture on the meaning of life?" She asked.

"No lecture. Just the usual put downs. This time was my career choice."

"Well, at least he sees you. I haven't heard from Daddy since Tahoe in July."

Jack and Amy had vacationed at Amy's place in Zephyr's Cove near South Lake Tahoe that July. Her father and mistress joined them for Amy's twenty-second birthday. The trip was a disaster.

“Maybe that’s a good thing,” Jack said as they arrived at his car. He opened the passenger door for Amy.

“Thank you, Jack.”

He climbed into the driver’s seat, shut the door, and started the engine. As he pulled away from the curb, he asked, “Who was that woman he was with again?”

“Margie, his current mistress bitch whore.”

Amy and Jack had travelled to Amy’s place near Zephyr Cove at Lake Tahoe. They stood on the porch watching boats bob on the lake at sunset when they heard Margie raise her voice. “She is such a self-centered, spoiled psycho-path. I can’t stand the sight of her, Frederick. And why couldn’t I bring Danny?” Danny was Margie’s twelve-year-old son.

“I’m sorry, Margie, really sorry. We can come back with him another time. I can get another place during the winter. We can ski,” Frederick said.

“Get another place? What’s wrong with this place? Why can’t we stay here?”

“This is Amy’s place,” Frederick said.

“Oh, I get it. Danny can’t be under her roof. I want to leave, now. What am I doing here anyway?” Margie said.

“You insisted on coming. We can’t leave. Tomorrow is her twenty-second birthday,” he said.

“And where were you on Danny’s twelfth birthday? Away, with her! If birthdays were so important where were you then?” She asked.

Amy ran to their room and confronted Margie. “Leave then. Now! I am sick of you and your son leaching off me and Daddy. NOW GET OUT OF HERE! AND KEEP THAT UGLY, STUPID KID OF YOURS AWAY FROM ME!”

“Fine,” Margie said. “Frederick! Call a cab. We’re leaving.”

Jack hid in the TV room surfing channels.

A few minutes later, Amy entered the TV room sipping vodka, tears streaming down her face. She collapsed on the sofa next to Jack and began to rant. “Why is she here? Why is she always with him? I hate her. If he remarries the money stops. Does she know? Probably not. Maybe I should tell her. Maybe she’ll disappear.” She buried her face in her hands.

The doorbell rang. . “Must be the cab” Jack said.

They heard Frederick’s shoes descend the wooden stairs and cross the marble entryway to the door. Frederick spoke to the cabbie, “Oh good. Here are our bags. Cab’s here, Margie.”

The sound of Margie’s lighter footfalls on the steps followed. “I can’t wait to get away from that spoiled little bitch.”

The door slammed shut and a minute later the cab drove off.

Amy pulled two Vicodin from her purse and washed them down with vodka.

“Self-medication is better than no medication, Luv,” Jack said.

She took a mirror from her purse. Her makeup was

smeared. “I look awful. Jack, I need to clean up then let’s go to Evan’s for din din.”

About an hour later, they pulled up in front of Evan’s, a small restaurant that sat around thirty and served gourmet meals with wine pairings. Evan’s was a modest house converted into a small restaurant on Route 89 near South Lake Tahoe. It was painted a creamy light green that blended into the forest.

“Go in. I’ll park,” Jack said.

“I wish Daddy was here. Why is he always with that bitch, or another bitch? If only Mother hadn’t—”

“Come on, let’s forget about them and have some fun.”

She left the car and wobbled towards the restaurant.

Jack parked, entered the restaurant, and found Amy seated, sipping a martini.

“What are you drinking?”

“Washington Apple.”

“Sounds good. Waiter, Washington Apple for me, too.”

She downed hers. “Waiter, one more for me, too.”

“Serious drinking tonight, eh?”

“It’s my birthday. I want to cele…” She burped quietly. “I want to cele…brate…excuse me…”

He took her hand, “Amy, Happy birthday. You look beautiful tonight.”

“Oh, that’s sweet, Jack.”

The drinks arrived. Taking one, he held it up.

“Cheers,” She said and took a big gulp.

“Don’t overdo it. You’ll be sick in the morning.” He studied the menu. “Let’s see here. What looks good? I think I want Hoisin orange glazed prawns for starters. What about you?”

“I’m not hungry. I’ll just have desert.”

Jack ordered the appetizer. “So what’s the story with your parents, anyway?”

Amy hung her head and looked away. “Mother died when I was seventeen and Daddy’s always gone. Mother left me everything. He gets something from the trust fund. That’s all.”

Jack gasped quietly with surprise. “I am so sorry, Amy. I didn’t know. What did she die of?”

“Breast cancer.” She finished her drink. “Waiter! Another!” Breast cancer was a lie. Her mother committed suicide on Christmas day after a violent fight with Frederick. Amy and the maid found her mother in the bathtub. The image of her pale face, dead, starring eyes, and a bathtub full of blood made Amy turn towards the window, away from Jack, and into the snow and cold darkness.

“What’s a matter, Luv?” Jack asked.

She starred out through the window onto the quiet, white snow while dramas of Mother replayed in her mind: her mania, her sobbing, and pacing footsteps in the middle of the night. The shock of her mother’s face made Amy nauseous and dizzy. Her thoughts began to race.

“Jack, I don’t feel good.”

“What’s the matter?”

The nausea intensified and her peripheral vision faded, forming a tunnel around his face. Beads of sweat collected on her face. She knew what was next, but it was too late. She collapsed. Her face dropped to the table, hitting it with a bang, breaking the bread plate and opening a gash on her chin. She then fell to the floor, taking the table cloth, plates, and drinks with her. Blood poured from her chin. Everyone in the restaurant turned to look. Women gasped.

Jack rounded the table and knelt down by her. "Oh my God!"

Two waiters stood over him. The other diners looked on in shock.

"Her chin is bleeding like crazy." Jack pressed a napkin against the cut. "She's still breathing."

Then he heard sirens and paramedics appeared dressed in white.

"My name is Jose Lopez and this is Jim White. Are you with this woman?"

Jack nodded.

Jim White, an African-American, crouched down by Amy while Jose questioned Jack.

"Can you give her name, address, age?" Jack did. Jim asked, "Any idea what happened?"

"It's her birthday. She's had too much to drink."

"Did she take anything else? Is she on any medication? Does she have any medical conditions?" Jose asked.

"None that I know of."

"Her pulse is thirty and blood pressure is forty-six over twenty-six," Jim White said.

"Forty-six over twenty-six? Jeezus!" Jack said.

Amy's eyes opened and shut, her eyeballs rolling back in their sockets as she tried to wake up. Eventually, she came to.

Jim White spoke calmly, "Hi luv. How are you feeling?"

"Dizzy."

"Your blood pressure is very low. What happened?" Jim asked.

"I drank too much," Amy said.

"Anything else?"

"Vicodin."

"Ouch. Not a good combination. You cut your chin pretty badly. You need stitches," Jim said.

"I'm going to give you some fluids to hydrate you. You'll feel a little prick." Jim inserted a needle into her arm with an IV bag. "We're going to the hospital."

As Jack drove with Amy through Palo Alto the recollection faded away and he glanced over at the scar on her chin. "Yeah, that was quite a time we had at Tahoe...How are you feeling tonight, Luv. Didn't drink too much, did ya?"

She took his hand and squeezed it. "Yes, I did and I'm so vulnerable when I'm under the influence. Are you going to take advantage of me?"

"Full advantage of you."

“Promise?” She said.

“ Another promise to keep, before we sleep.”

Chapter 12 - Risk Management

From the stern of the boat, Mikhail stared into the night sea, holding his cell phone to his ear. From behind him, Anton shrieked like a caged animal. “WE HAVE A DEAL, MIKHAIL! WE HAVE A DEAL! LET ME OUT OF HERE!”

At NovoRisk Bank headquarters in Moscow on a small office desk amid a landscape of tidy cubicles, a phone rang. A young man answered in Russian, “Da?”

Mikhail Kazaki spoke to the employee. “I want a wire transfer to clear now.”

The young man hesitated. “What is the account?” Mikhail read the account number. “Password?” Mikhail gave the password. The young man consulted a computer. “I see a transfer pending from Switzerland for three hundred thousand Swiss Francs. Can you tell me the transaction number?” The young man scribbled onto a note pad and then said, “Can you hold?”

He left his desk and walked to a large office with a glass wall that faced the cubicles. Several men and women in business attire watched a slide presentation. He gingerly opened the door.

“Leena,” he said quietly, shrinking, becoming as invisible as possible. They all looked at him and he turned red. “I need to speak with Miss Leena.”

An annoyed blonde woman rose and walked to the door.

The two stepped outside. “What’s the problem, Philip?”

“We have a wire transfer coming into one of the G accounts,” Philip said.

“What?”

“A transfer from Switzerland into a G account.”

She poked her head into the glass office and said, “I will be back in a moment.”

“It is for three hundred thousand Swiss francs,” Philip said.

“Three hundred thousand Swiss francs? Which account?” He showed her a paper with the account number. G accounts were used for ‘special’ transactions and required CEO approval. She’d seen such transactions, but had never cleared one. She couldn’t disrupt the meeting either. “Can this wait?” Philip shook his head no. “Okay, Can you confirm it?” Leena asked.

“Yes. I have the transaction number.” Philip replied.

She hesitated. “What do they want?”

“Immediate confirmation,” Philip said.

“Accept the money, move it to the Belgrade branch, keep the currency in Francs, and delete the transactions from the logs.”

“Can I get something in writing from you on this?” he asked.

“No. Just do it. Be sure to clean the audit trails,” she said and kept the account number.

“Are you sure?”

She snapped, “Just do it.” She returned to the meeting.

Philip returned to his desk and picked up the phone. “The

transaction is confirmed. We have the money."

Chapter 13 – Confession

Jack parked in front of Amy's apartment. "We're here." They jumped out of Jack's car and ran to her door. As she fumbled with her purse for the keys, he reached around her and placed his hands on her belly, nuzzled her neck, and slid his hands up to her breasts. She purred, dropped the keys, turned, and kissed him.

"Let's get inside. Hurry," he said and picked up the keys. They staggered inside and fell onto the bed. He stripped her naked and then tore off his clothes.

After making love, they laid in each other's arms. She brushed the hair from his face and kissed his cheek bone, then forehead. Jack arose and disappeared into the bathroom. Amy turned on the TV and surfed channels, stopping on an old classic, *Play Misty for me*.

He returned to bed and cuddled with her as they watched the movie with dopey, glazed eyes.

"How old were you when you lost your virginity?" Amy asked.

"Around sixteen. Why?"

"What was she like?"

"A cheerleader. Her name was Laurie Petersen. In a car. We made a mess. Later, I figured out I could climb through her window at night. That was much better," Jack said.

“Was she pretty?”

“You are much prettier, Luv. How about you?”

“I don’t want to tell you,” Amy said.

“Aw, come on. I told you.”

“Well, alright, it was Fernando. He was our pool boy, or should I call him a pool man? He was a man, after all. Twenty something. He cleaned our pool.”

“How old were you?” Jack asked.

“Sixteen, like you.”

“How did it happen?”

“Well, I found out that whenever he came to clean he met with Estrella, our maid, in the guest house,” Amy said.

“Wow! Pretty sneaky of them. Sounds like the guy got around.”

“He was good looking, nice body. He took off his shirt when he cleaned the pool.”

“So, who did he do first that day? You or Estrella?” Jack asked.

“Oh, I put an end to him and Estrella. I threatened to tell Mother. The next week, I waited for him in the guest house. We met a few more times.”

“How did it end?”

“Mother fired him,” Amy said.

“How come?”

“She found out. Estrella told Mother.”

“Wow. Did you tell your mum about Estrella?” Jack asked.

"Yes, she didn't care about that. After Mother found out, I had to go to therapy for a while."

"I'll bet you were angry at the maid."

"Oh, I got even with her," Amy said.

"How?"

"That's a secret." She stopped talking and began recalling her revenge.

"Oh my GOD" Amy heard her Mother exclaim. "AMY! AMY! COME DOWN HERE RIGHT NOW!"

Amy found her mother and Estrella sitting in the living room.

"Estrella claims she caught you and Fernando in the guest house having sex."

"That's a lie. She didn't catch us doing anything," Amy said.

"They were in the guest house, Miss. I saw them leave. The bed was a mess," Estrella said.

"You little spy. And what did you and Fernando do in the guest house? Tell Mother about that," Amy said.

"That doesn't matter," Mother said. "He could have AIDs. You could be pregnant. He is guilty of statutory rape. I could have him arrested."

"She's a whore." Amy pointed at Estrella. "How long have you been fucking Fernando?" she shouted, red-faced.

"Shut up, Amy. I am firing him and you are going back to see Doctor Strassman. Estrella, I am extremely disappointed with you. You may go back to your work now."

"Yes, Missus Hanover," Estrella said as she left.

Amy was furious. That Saturday night, Estrella was off and Mother was out; passed out, high on pills and booze. Amy went into Estrella's bed and bathroom.

Estrella decorated her room with pictures of her family in Mexico, a crucifix, rosary beads, *Dia del los Muertos* figurines, and a picture of Ricky Martin. There was a stack of Junior College text books on her desk. On the bookshelf was a cage where she kept her pet hamster, Chiquita. A blooming cactus accompanied a book of poetry by Octavio Paz on a table by the bed.

Amy shuffled through her things. What could she take? *Books, Cactus, how about Ricky Martin? No, they're replaceable,* she thought.

She found an album of photographs. She set it on the bed and continued looking. There were some letters in Spanish. She set them next to the album. *They would suspect me*, she realized.

The squeak of the hamster wheel caught her attention. *And then there's Chiquita. She could escape,* she thought.

She put the cage on the bed, opened it and reached inside. "Come here, Chiquita." She raised the warm furry creature to her cheek. "That's a good girl." She set it on the bed. Chiquita preened herself, wetting her paw and running the paw across her head. "What a cute little girl you are."

Chiquita crawled to the cage, stood, putting her upper paws on the cage peering inside. She then circled the cage and settled next to it. "You're supposed to run away."

Amy put Chiquita on the floor. Chiquita disappeared under the bed and nested in the corner. It became clear Chiquita wouldn't run off, but would instead stay close by.

Amy climbed under the bed to retrieve the tame creature who waited patiently to be picked up. She scooped up Chiquita and shimmied out from beneath the bed. "Sorry, Chiquita," she said and took Chiquita to the bath room, filled the sink with water, and then held the creature under the water. Chiquita struggled and squirmed, burrowing into Amy's palm but Amy held firm. The sensation of the struggling creature gave Amy a queer thrill of power and the satisfaction of revenge. It was almost sexual.

She held Chiquita there until she stopped moving, then laid her on the counter and watched water drained from her mouth. She took a blow dryer and brushed and dried the animal and put the corpse back in the cage.

She often thought about Chiquita. The memory always made her hand tingle. She rubbed her hand as she looked at Jack. He had fallen asleep.

Chapter 14 - Loose Ends

Mikhail stood at the stern of the boat, his back to Anton, peering into the abyss of night.

"MIKHAAAAIL! MIKHAAAAIL! GET ME OUT OF THIS CAGE!" Anton howled.

He walked back to Anton.

"Is everything okay?" Anton said.

"I have the money," Mikhail said.

"Good. Get me out of this cage. I need a fix."

"There are no drugs here."

Anton's eyes, wild with withdrawal and terror, peered from the cage. "SHIT! Get me out of here. LIKE NOW! You crazy fuck!"

Mikhail fastened a cable to the trap and began turning a crank which lifted the trap from the deck. He cranked until it rose above the gunnels of the boat and then swiveled the trap out over the water.

"Hey, what are you doing?" Anton shouted. "We have a deal! We have a deal. What are you doing? You son-of-a-bitch! WE HAVE A FUCKING DEAL! YOU HAVE THE FUCKING MONEY. ARE YOU CRAZY?"

Mikhail's empty stare fixed on Anton's eyes.

"Mikhail, let me go, please let me go. We have a deal.

NOW LET ME GO NOW, GOD DAMN IT!"

Mikhail's serene face projected neither gleeful triumph nor regret. He hit a button on the crane.

"Nooooooooo!" Anton howled like an anguished animal as the trap sank into the dark water. "YOU MUTANT FUCKER! WE ALL LAUGHED AT YOU!WE ALL LAUGHED, YOU DISGUSTING MUTANT! NOOOOOOOO!" Anton took one last gulp of air before sinking into the freezing brine.

Mikhail watched the bubbles as he pondered the money left in Anton's Swiss account. *The money will sit there for the rest of time,* he decided. He stared up at the stars and calculated the interest at two percent for a thousand years and thought, *Is that really four hundred million? What do Swiss banks do with all that money?*

One last belch of bubbles popped to the surface, disturbing Mikhail's mathematical reverie. He raised an eyebrow. *The bubbles have stopped, but he's still alive. He's inhaling sea water now. Soon his suffering will cease. One, maybe two minutes more,* he thought.

Mikhail returned to the controls and piloted the boat through the darkness.

Chapter 15 – After the Meeting

The meeting in the glass office broke up. Leena gathered her papers and walked towards the door when an older, fiftyish man asked her to stay. She waited while the others filed out of the office.

"Close the door," he said.

"Yes, Dmitri."

Dmitri had brown hair with grey temples and large predatory brown eyes. He was dressed immaculately in a suit. He was handsome, muscular, and tall. "What did Philip want?" he asked.

"There was a transfer to a G account. It required immediate confirmation."

He paused and looked at the svelte Leena who stood by the table. "Do you know who it was?"

"We never know who with the G accounts."

"Yes, yes, I know, I know." He sighed and drummed the table with his fingers.

"Which account?" She put the paper with the account number on the table. He picked it up and studied the number. "All right, is this being managed properly?" She nodded. "Good." He wrote a number on a slip of paper. "Move the money into this account, close the G account, and clean the audit trail."

He changed the subject. "When do you leave for California?"

"In three days."

"Lucky girl. When I was your age, we were at war with America. Now you are going there to study."

"Stanford University! It is going to be such fun." Leena was around twenty-six, thirty years his junior. "I want to thank you again, Dmitri. You have been so kind to me." Leena had been a brilliant student and now climbed the corporate ladder at NovoRisk bank with the sponsorship of the CEO, Dmitri Chesnakov.

"Yes, I know." He studied her shape while his thoughts turned from finance to the prurient. "Can we meet for dinner tonight?"

She smiled and rolled her eyes in a knowing way. "Of course." She giggled.

"How about nine? Café Pushkin?"

"I look forward to it." She smiled, tipped her head to one side and turned to leave.

"Oh, Leena." She stopped and faced him.

"Yes, Dmitri?"

"Wear something pretty." Which meant, 'don't wear any underwear'.

"Yes, Sir." She blushed, clearly smitten and under his control.

"Oh, one more thing. There will be a transfer tomorrow, for Sovcomflot. It will be gold. One hundred kilograms."

“That is a lot. Sovcomflot?” She queried.

“You know. Sovcomflot import/export. I will email details. Please close the door on your way out, Leena. Thank you, dear.” He studied the sway of her backside as she walked away.

When she was out of sight, Dmitri picked up a cell phone and dialed Mikhail.

Mikhail cut the boat engine and answered, “Da?”

“Did you get it?” Dmitri asked.

“Yes,” Mikhail replied.

“Did you count it?”

“Yes. I got it all.”

“Was it smooth?”

“No.”

“What happened?” Dmitri asked.

“The point of contact, he tried to steal. He killed a man.”

Dmitri frowned and comprehended the rest. “Terrible! He always worried me. Unreliable. Did you manage it?”

“Yes, everything is under control.”

“No loose ends?”

“Nothing. Not a trace.” Mikhail confirmed.

“What was this wire transfer all about?” Dmitri asked.

“A small bonus,” Mikhail said.

“It wasn’t expected?”

“No. Nothing is amiss. Everything is in place.”

“I don’t like surprises,” Dmitri said.

“Understood,” Mikhail acknowledged.

Dmitri hung up the phone. Mikhail continued through the darkness and fog.

Chapter 16 - Luv?

The next morning, Jack awoke to hear Amy whine, "I'm still horny," while she strutted naked across the bedroom.

She climbed onto him, straddled his chest, grabbed his wrists and held him down. "Now you are my slave," She giggled. "Kiss me! I order you." Then she noticed the time. "Oh my God, I'm late," She said and began rushing around, opening and shutting drawers, putting on underwear, leaving for the bathroom, and returning from the bathroom.

"Where are you going?" Jack asked.

"Where are *we* going you mean?"

"What?" Jack protested.

"I'm meeting Susan at the Barn to ride and then we are all going out to brunch, including you." She meant the Stanford Barn which is by the Stanford Campus, a place for the wealthy to keep their horses since the beginning of time.

"You gotta be kidding me. You never told me about this. What if I had plans?"

"What if you had plans? Simple, you'd break them."

"That's just great! I don't want to go."

"That's too bad. You're going anyway!"

"You, my dear, are a spoiled, rotten brat."

"That may be true, but I make up for it by being good in

bed…" She smiled slyly. "Have you ever had a better lover?"

She had him there.

"That shut you up. And Mother said the way to a man's heart is through his stomach. What a joke. She must have been lying."

"Well, have you ever had a better lover than me? Perhaps we're even," Jack said.

Her hand tingled as she said, "Are you sure you want me to answer that question?"

Jack joked, "Oh my God! I am wounded. I'll kill him! Who is he?"

Her mind released endorphins that soothed her unrelenting insecurity. "It was Professor Kittridge…Do you know him?"

He sat straight up in bed and reeled. "WHO?"

"Doctor Kittridge. You know, that young, handsome, sexy, and kinky professor of French Literature."

"Oh nooooooooooooooo!" He collapsed, hitting the bed and pillow with a plop. "He's a friend of Goldman's. James Kittridge. Young? He's ancient, at least thirty-two. You slept with him?" Howard Goldman, Jack's best friend, never mentioned Kittridge and Amy.

She murmured breathlessly, "He's older than that and… yes… I slept with him often."

Her words flogged his self-esteem and he howled, "Ohhh man! You've got to be KIDDING ME. WHEN THE HELL WAS THIS?"

She turned to the mirror and calmly applied makeup. “Before I knew you. I was a freshman.”

“What? You were only eighteen and he was twice your age. That’s statutory rape!”

“No it’s not. He was merely robbing the cradle. But even if it was…” She paused in mid-sentence and leaned towards the mirror continuing with mascara. “I used to play doctor with Doctor Kittridge. In fact, he taught me everything I know about French Literature and sex.” She turned and coyly pouted. “I wasn’t very good at French Literature.” She then returned to the mirror and makeup. “Anyway, you have been the beneficiary of his training.”

“Training?” Jack squirmed. “What are you, some sort of circus act that needed to be trained? I don’t want to hear anymore.”

“Well, I was his student and he was the professor,” She said.

“I hate him.” He pulled the pillow over his head.

“I never did anything with him that we haven’t done.” She paused with the mascara, rolled her eyes as she said, “Hmmm, well, perhaps there are a couple of exceptions.” She chuckled and then continued applying make-up.

“Oh my God! I hate him so much!” He gasped.

After dressing, she sat down beside him on the bed and took his hand in hers. Her eyes opened wide like a curious child as she spoke with a soft, apologetic voice, nearly blushing, “I have been such a bad girl, and I am so ashamed. He took advantage of me. I was so young, so innocent. It’s not my fault. Perhaps later you should punish me for being such a bad, bad girl. Do you want to try those other things he taught me?"

He cried out, "YOUR'RE CRAZY!"

She laughed wickedly, "I am not crazy." She kissed him again. "Meet us at the Bistro at eleven-thirty. And don't be late or I'll sleep with him again!"

The door slammed behind her.

Did Goldman know about this? I can't believe it. I wonder if Kittridge has any naked pictures of her. Shit! He punched his pillow, rolled over and tried to go back to sleep, but couldn't. He rose from the bed, stretched, belched, and scratched in one continuous motion. *Does she have any pictures of him?* He searched the room for clues. In a collection of pictures above the couch he saw pictures of Amy with her horse, with her parents, a picture of her with the Eiffel Tower, Amy skiing, and many with friends, but none of Kittridge.

He went to her desk and searched the drawers until he found one filled with photographs. He riffled through and found a smoking gun: an envelope with a couple of photos of Kittridge and one naked picture of Amy. She lay on a bed, nude, arms at her side, looking seductively into the camera. At first, he thought, *Wow. She looked really great at eighteen.* Raging jealousy immediately followed, stabbing him repeatedly in the abdomen. He trembled with psychic pain as he put the photos back in the drawer, slammed it shut, shaking the bureau, and overturning a lamp. He let it lay.

Chapter 17 – eMail from Dmitri

Leena settled into her chair behind the large desk in her comfy corner office. Diplomas for BS and MS in Mathematics from the University of Moscow hung on one wall. Her bookshelves were full of books and trophies; awards for ice skating and academics. A Bonsai Tree decorated her desk. She logged into the G account number and performed the clerical chore of transferring monies and cleaning the audit. When she finished, she peered out at the grey buildings of Moscow and thought about what she would wear on her date with Dmitri that evening.

Dmitri promoted her rapidly, groomed her for the executive suite, and sponsored her trip to Stanford. In spite of her copious talent, none of these things would have happened without Dmitri's help. When they first met two years earlier at the Executive Christmas party, the fiftyish CEO dazzled her with his charm, wit, and power. Her thoughts drifted back to the evening they met.

On that night, before the party, she waited for her date in her apartment which overlooked Moscow's Clean Pond (Chistiye Prudi).She watched ice skaters glide across the pond amid Christmas lights and snowflakes longing for the talent to paint what she saw.

Her date, Alexi Andreovich, was Executive Vice President of Accounting, a position achieved after years tracking down fraud and keeping the books in order. Driven by nationalism and paranoia he would say, “Fraud has ruined Russia. It is everywhere. I can never relax.” He was one of the few really honest men she knew, and she thought him naive.

His slight paunch, pasty white skin, and stringy brown hair repulsed Leena, making romance impossible. Thick round lenses framed his feelings which moved between anxiety, disdain, and sadness. She agreed to see him because he opened doors, like to the party that night.

His obsession over minutia turned conversation into a water torture of words. Her attempts to end his monotonous monologues failed, resulting in terse replies, like, “May I please finish?” or “Will you please stop interrupting me?” She planned to end things after tonight.

A text on her phone announced his arrival. She put on her jacket and hat, rode the elevator to the street, walked to his Mercedes, and climbed in. She gave him quick look in the eye and ambiguous smile. She said, “Hi, Alexi,” and then looked away, avoiding the perfunctory kiss that always left her cheek disgustingly wet with his drool.

Alexi noticed her reserve and tried flattery to warm her up. “What a beautiful outfit. You look like a model.”

Surprised that Alexi would even notice a woman’s clothing, she perked up and answered. “It’s Slava Zaitsev.”Slava Zaitsev was a famous Russian designer. She’d scoured thrift shops for the discards of wealthy women and found a black skirt and top embroidered with dazzling paisleys, turnstiles, flowers, and leaves, brightly colored in red, green, and gold.

"They're beautiful and expensive. Where did you get them?"

"No Comment."

"Did you come by them honesty?"

"That is an insult, Alexi. I bought them."

Awkward silence followed.

Alexi broke the silence by saying, "The party is at Mindovsky House, in the Arbat district."

Lev Kekushev designed the Art Nouveau Mindovsky house in 1903 in the style of Art Nouveau. Often used as an embassy, it sat empty, so the Bank rented it for the party.

Arbat Street is among the oldest streets in Moscow. *Arbat*, is not a Russian word and linguists debate its possible Arab origin, but no one is sure. Leena briefly imagined a village of middle-eastern traders in the Arbat over a thousand years before: brown skinned merchants importing goods up the river from Byzantium.

"Did you have a good day?" he asked.

"Yes Alexi, it was a good day."

"What did you do?"

"Nothing really. What about you?"

He seized the opportunity to pontificate. "I spent the day reviewing reports from the Kiev office, with Pavel and Danislav. All day! What a mess. That bank is always late. There are some unusual inaccuracies, as though someone is laundering money."

"Laundering money?"

"Yes. Not that surprising. Little bits…here and there. We will find out what's going on. It's nothing new. When we acquired the bank, I don't remember the exact year, sometime in the 1990s,it was run by thieves and politicians. Two species of the same ilk, in my mind."

He waited for her to chuckle at his feeble joke, but she did not. He shrugged and continued, "They reported assets that disappeared or were never there at all. A cabal of government officials took loans that they never repaid. Dmitri took care of it. Everything! Some went to jail, a few just disappeared. Dmitri has connections that you don't want to know about, believe me."

Leena had never met Dmitri Chesnakov, but she'd seen him. He was in his mid-fifties, tall, and good looking. She asked, "Wasn't he in the Army? Do you think he is KGB?"

"Army yes. KGB maybe. He was in Chechnya, an officer, Captain. A very sharp guy. Very impressive. And tough, doesn't take bullshit from anyone."

Alexi returned to the subject of accounting. "Now the problems in Kiev are mostly management and accounting. Once assets were one hundred million rubles over liabilities. It took three days to find the errors. It was very interesting how we found it."

Alexi droned on and on in excruciating detail. Soon, she stopped hearing him and peered out the window, her mind disappearing into the Christmas lights on Christmas trees, the nutcrackers, sleighs drawn by horses, and snow.

Eventually he turned off Leningradsky highway into the Arbat, arriving at a block of mansions all lit for Christmas. "Here it is. Mindovsky House."

Mindovsky House was several stories tall, white with bay windows at the corners. Dormers ran the length of the building with pilasters and proud work in between. Strings of colored Christmas lights clung to its sides like vines. A balcony overlooked the semicircular driveway where the guests arrived, leaving their cars with valets.

Leena and Alexi sat in silence in the queue of cars waiting for a valet. After a couple of minutes, valets opened the doors. Butlers greeted them with flutes of champagne and shot glasses of vodka. Alexi grabbed vodka, which he downed immediately. Leena took Champaigne and sipped.

They hurried through a small portico and into the antechamber where they checked their jackets and hats. The purr of the party poured forth from the ballroom. Alexi reached for a second vodka that he spilled on his crotch with a grunt. Leena looked askance and moved away as he cussed and fussed. A third vodka quickly arrived which disappeared down his gullet with a gulp. He ordered a fourth while vulgarly wiping his pants with a napkin.

Leena left Alexi and drifted into a spacious ballroom which buzzed with chatting voices and the strains of a string sextet. Foliated molding and Christmas festoons decorated walls that vaulted upward to a high ceiling. The room sparkled with the lights of Christmas and chandeliers. Leena admired a Christmas tree, adorned with a rococo of bulbs, figurines of Russian Guards, sleighs drawn by reindeer, and Father Christmas (Dyed Moroz). Memories of Christmas trees in her childhood filled her with warmth.

She felt a tap on her shoulder and turned. It was her friend Tatiana, holding a Champagne glass. “Leenaaaa,” she emoted and hugged her. “How are you? You look beautiful.”

Tatiana worked at NovoRisk and dated Nikita, the Director of IT and Telecommunications. Tatiana was taller than Leena, skinny, and not a great beauty, but she was a brilliant computer scientist who graduated near the top of her class from Saint Petersburg University. She managed a small group of programmers who produced reports on the state of bank finances.

”So good to see you, Tatiana. Let me look at you.” She took a step back. “You look beautiful.”

“Thanks! Your outfit is amazing.”

“The outfit? It is Slava Zaitsev.”

“Oh my God. Where did you get it?” Tatiana asked.

“It’s a secret. I can’t tell you.”

Tatiana raised her eyebrows and curled her lips into a smirk. “Was it a gift from an admirer?”

“No… I bought it myself.”

Tatiana put her hands on her hips. “I don’t believe you… you can’t afford something like that.”

“I found it at a thrift shop. Don’t tell anyone.” Leena raised a finger to her lips.

Tatiana hissed, “You’re kidding.”

“It is true. How are things going with Nikita?” Leena said.

Tatiana looked away. “They’re fine.”

“Where is he? I’d like to meet him.”

Tatiana pouted. “He’s about. Are you with Alexis?”

“Yessssss. Well, sort of.” Leena smiled. “I am hiding from him.” She toasted her friend. “He is so boring. I don’t think I can stand anymore of him. He’s a slob and a drunk. Do you know what he did?”

Tatiana shook her head.

“Oh, well,” Leena sang. “You wouldn’t believe it. He spilled vodka on the crotch of his pants, like he peed. He finished two more while wiping his crotch. He’s drunk by now. I left him.”

Tatiana chuckled.

“So, what about Nikita? Have you fled him too?” Leena asked.

She scanned the room. “No, he’s around here somewhere.”

“How are things going with him?” Leena asked.

Tatiana pouted. “I don’t know.”

Just then, Nikita sneaked up behind and tickled Tatiana.

“Yikes!” Tatiana jumped.

“There you are, my love,” Nikita emoted and kissed her on the cheek while Tatiana’s eyes sparkled. “My name is Nikita,” he introduced himself.

“I am Leena Kiraskaya. Tatiana and I have been friends for

years. I have heard much about you from Tatiana."

"And what has she told you about me?"

Although Nikita was a Director, dating Leena's good friend made him more of a peer than a superior. She played with him. "Oh, the usual. That she is dating some handsome and powerful man, witty, charming. You know."

"The usual?"

"Yes, the usual *romantic* stuff." Leena emphasized romantic stuff by moving her head quickly toward him and then away, as though pecking at him. Her comment poked Nikita's self-esteem like a stick in the eye. He blinked. She coolly lit a cigarette. "Tell me about your position at the bank." She exhaled in his direction.

"I will tell you about my man," Tatiana interrupted, taking hold of his arm. "He is Director of IT and has a staff of sixty. He is very important."

"Very nice. She never mentioned you had such a big position at the Bank," Leena flattered.

He studied her face and then gave a quick look downward to examine more. His pupils dilated. "Tatiana, you never told me you had such a beautiful friend," he articulated slowly. An uncertain look returned to Tatiana's face. "And what an outfit! You look like a model." Leena's knitted eyebrows protested his advances, a signal noticed by Tatiana, but lost of Nikita. "Where have you been hiding your friend from me, Tatiana?" he joked.

"Nowhere," Tatiana said meekly.

An awkward silence followed. "I work in Risk Management," Leena finally said.

"Really? How long have you been with the bank?" Nikita asked.

Leena took another drag on her cigarette and gave Nikita a supercilious look. "A couple of years."

"So, you're still new. We should have lunch sometime."

Leena and Tatiana exchanged glances. "I am sure that will not be possible." Leena exhaled smoke in Nikita's face. "Nice to meet you, Nikita. We will talk later, Tatiana." She moved on.

As Leena drifted through the crowd she saw Alexi trapped by underlings who competed for his attention. As he listened to them his eyes followed her. She glanced at him briefly, noting the rectangular cave of his mouth encircled by wet lips that glistened with spit. *He is revolting. This is definitely the last time. Thank God I never slept with him,* she thought.

Yuri, her peer in the Risk Management group, emerged from the crowd. "Hello, Leena."

"Yuri! What are you doing here?" Yuri didn't belong to the executive class.

"Connections." He moved his eyebrows up and down mysteriously.

"Oh, well, we all have our secrets, don't we?" Leena asked.

"You and Alexi are no secret," Yuri said.

"I have nothing to hide about that. Here's a secret. He's a creep."

"That's no secret, either. Why are you with him?"

She blew smoke at him and said, "Simple. I was curious." She leaned towards him and stared wide-eyed into his face. "Now I am bored of him." She resumed her normal, relaxed pose, and continued, "And besides, I don't know him that well, if you know what I mean. Look at him." She threw her head in Alexi's direction. "He is disgusting."

Yuri looked at Alexi. "Don't look now, but he is staring at us. I think he's jealous"

Leena shrugged. "I could not care less."

Just then the lights dimmed and a female vocalist joined the sextet. They began playing the Beatles' *Back in the USSR*.

"Want to dance?" Yuri asked.

"Sure." They moved on to the dance floor.

When the music ended, Leena and Yuri found Alexi standing right behind them. "Where have you been?"

"What do you mean? You know where I've been. You have been watching me like a bird of prey," Leena said. Yuri stood behind her, not wanting to mix things up with a senior executive.

"You are with me and I expect you to stay with me," He said harshly and grabbed her wrist roughly. A number of people turned to look at the commotion.

"Okay, but you will have to excuse me while I run to the bathroom." She peeled his fingers from her wrist. Yuri disappeared into the crowd. *What a coward*, she thought as she trotted away. A line at the lady's room thankfully postponed her return.

When she re-entered the Ballroom, Dmitri Chesnakov, the CEO, stopped her. He towered over her. He was stylish, immaculate, and good looking. “May I introduce myself? I am Dmitri Chesnakov, CEO of NovoRisk.”

Her usual wittiness had fled, leaving her stumbling and awkward. She gulped. “Uh, nice to meet you.”

“Do you have a name, young lady?”

“Um, yes, of course. I am Leena Kiraskaya.” She bowed slightly.

“I saw you were here with that drunken accountant of ours, Alexi. I think he has had too much to drink tonight. One of my men is taking him home.”

She saw Alexi being escorted out of the main gallery by a tall, well-dressed man. “Who is that?”

“One of my men,” Dmitri said. Alexi paused and glared until his escort nudged him along. The escort was tall, muscular, and grey haired. They disappeared.

“It would be my privilege if you stay and accompany me this evening. Will you?” Dmitri smiled warmly at Leena. She nodded yes and Dmitri offered his arm. “Come with me.”

As they walked across the floor, the crowd parted, turned, and nodded at Dmitri and Leena. Dmitri introduced Leena to several that stopped to speak. This is how the next chapter of Leena’s life began, at age twenty-four with the CEO of NovoRisk.

Chapter 18 – War

Damp leaves and wisps of chimney smoke seasoned the grey October air, soothing Jack's sizzling wound as he walked to his car. The nude photo of Amy hurt until he realized he'd done the same, more than once. More than twice. In fact, he had a small collection of similar photos. Soon he forgot about it.

At the Bistro, the chatter of people and savory aromas billowed onto the sidewalk. He scanned the crowd and saw students embroiled in debate, families with screaming children, and retired folk poking sullenly at their food, but no sign of Amy, Susan, or Ben. A hostess sat him at a table for four. He bought a *New York Times*, ordered a double espresso and sat.

Jack heard a voice say, "Ah, espresso and the *Sunday New York Times*. Reminds me of home."

He looked up from the paper. "Hi, Ben, pull up a chair. Where're the ladies?"

"They stopped to clean up," Ben said.

Jack noticed a small cut on Ben's forehead. "What happened to you?" Ben looked away ducking the question. "Here, sit down. Get an Espresso. Relax. You want part of the paper?"

Ben sat. "Thanks. Yeah I fell. I'll take the Book Review."

"You fell off the horse?" Jack asked. Ben nodded. "Poor fellow! Anything broken? Perhaps a bruise to your pride?"

"Don't condescend to me," Ben sneered in defense and rocked back and forth in his chair.

Jack was a little confused by Ben's sharp reaction and managed to mumble, "Uh, right."

They both buried themselves in the *New York Sunday Times*, avoiding additional petty arguments.

"Boys!"

Ben and Jack looked up. Susan and Amy waved from across the Bistro.

At last, I'm rescued from this schmuck! Jack thought as he rose and walked over to greet them.

"Hi, Luv." Jack kissed Amy on the cheek. "Hello, Susan, how are you?" He gave her a perfunctory hug. "Come, sit."

"Oh, how cute. The boys are having coffee and reading the paper, just like real men," Susan said.

Jack looked at Amy and rolled his eyes. Amy returned an angry glance. The women sat down. Jack waved to the waiter who arrived with menus while Ben stood awkwardly.

Susan said, "He rode my little grey mare and then he fell off. But he just got up and walked away." She took Ben's hand in hers and squeezed it. "He wasn't hurt at all. Except for this little cut on his forehead."

"Falling off horses? Not my idea of a good time," Jack said.

"He's afraid of horses," Amy taunted Jack.

"Well, yeah, but it's mainly the stench of it that keeps me

away," Jack said.

Everyone stopped and looked at Jack.

"Sorry, didn't mean to say exactly that," he said. *Yes, I did,* he thought.

The others let it go. The women ordered coffee and Jack ordered a second espresso and a croissant. The girls chatted while the men sat in frozen silence. To Jack's relief, the women took over the conversation and he became their prop, listening with one ear, nodding, smiling, and tossing in occasional comments. He watched their reflection in the Bistro window as the women chattered away, emoting, gesticulating, hands rising into the air, with one landing on Amy's heart or Susan's cheek as embellishment.

Chapter 19 – Oblivion

A curling bank of fog enveloped Mikhail and the boat, blotting out the stars and further blackening the oblivion of the night sea. The violence of the evening had no effect on him. Any ability to react emotionally had been ground away in the crucible of his youth, a time when he suffered in a dusty village called Vyazovka on the banks of a small tributary of the Volga River, south of Volgograd. His childhood left him with an inert face, monotone voice, and a vacant, piercing stare that made others uncomfortable.

As he piloted the boat across the dark void of the sea, images of his early life rose in his mind, and became palpable, painting over the night. He saw the white washed orphanage and treeless soil where he lived with his sister and forty or so other abandoned children, all twelve years or younger, except Vadim, a special case, who was around eighteen. It was downstream from a landfill whose garbage littered the river banks for miles, filling the air with the stench of fermenting garbage.

Was I eleven? No one knew exactly…and you, Sasha, were you only four?, he thought.

They had no last name and no date of birth and other basics missing from their identities. The only remnants of a former life were Romanian accents.

The daily routine, waking at six in the morning, making beds, oatmeal breakfasts, gathering for roll call, and being dispersed for chores varied unnoticeably day by day. Orderlies clubbed the orphans for invisible infractions. Unchecked bullies ruled the playground, terrifying the smaller orphans. The scarce food lacked nutrition. The showers were cold. Bugs fed on the sleeping children leaving itchy welts they scratched into scabs. In this barren landscape, Mikhail and Sasha found sanctuary with each other, each providing the other with the only kind human contact they had known.

"Mika, Mika, Mika. He is hurting me. Stop him. Don't hurt me." Sasha curled up in Mikhail's arms.

"Shhh, shhh, Sasha. It is only a dream." Mikhail and Sasha shared a bed in a dingy dorm room with ten others, including Vadim. Their ragged bed was a cot, sheets, a coarse blanket, and an old chair cushion Mikhail found on the banks of the Volga they used as a pillow.

"Ilya was coming. He wanted my bread. He hurt me and took my bread."

"It is only a dream."

She curled up into him like a puppy seeking the warmth.

"I have to pee."

"Okay, come." Mikhail took her hand and felt their way through the darkness to the bathroom. He saw shapes in a corner of the bathroom, one standing, one kneeling.

"Mika, I see Oleg. Hi, Oleg" Oleg was an orderly.

"Shhhh, Come peepee here." Mikhail led her to a toilet.

Oleg was abusing that girl. I was too young to know, he thought.

They returned to their bed. "Mika, I am hungry."

"Here, Sasha." Mikhail took some bread from his hiding place, a hole in their mattress. Sasha munched while Mikhail held Sasha like a teddy bear. Sleep carried them off.

The play yard was several acres of hard brown dirt and a patch of crumbling black top. There was a rusting jungle gym, a few soccer balls, jump ropes, and broken toys. Lines scratched into the dirt made a soccer field where boys endlessly dribbled soccer balls. Ilya tossed a stuffed animal into the river and laughed sadistically as it floated away.

The orderlies attached Vadim to a pole with a harness and chain, to keep him from running off. Vadim rocked feverishly while reciting radio programs verbatim, over and over and over, oblivious to everything. Playground bullies preyed on him, throwing rocks or taking his pants, leaving him half naked, bleeding, and ignored by the indolent orderlies who smoked, played pinochle, and talked.

Vadim refused to come in at night and was beaten to comply. His 'bed' was a cage, the only way to control him. At night he howled, waking the others until the orderlies sprayed him with cold water.

Mikhail felt little pity for Vadim. He had problems of his own, like getting enough to eat and defending himself and Sasha from bullies and abusive orderlies like the orderly who insisted on bathing Sasha. She resisted, but the orderly would force her, carrying her off. Mikhail could do nothing to stop it.

Once, Ilya stripped Sasha, blooded her nose, and crushed her doll with his boot. Sasha ran naked through the play yard. "Stop hurting me! He is hurting me!" A group gathered round and taunted the naked four-year-old. Ilya ruled the play yard.

When Mikhail saw Sasha and Ilya, animal hatred overcame his fear. He reflexively pulled a picket from the fence, charged Ilya, holding the stick over his head as he galloped towards him. He jumped in the air and slammed the stick down onto Ilya's blonde head. The picket broke into pieces and Ilya fell to the ground, his head bleeding. The children gathered and watched. Mikhail came at him again, hitting him over and over until Ilya cried.

"You want me to stop?" Ilya nodded. "Say, 'please stop, Mikhail'." He did. "Say it louder, so all can hear."

"PLEASE STOP Mikhail!" he shouted.

He pointed the broken stick at Ilya. "Remember this day Ilya." From then onwards, Mikhail became the anti-bully of the play yard. Even Vadim was safe.

Sasha retrieved a piece of the broken stick. A cleft at one end made a mouth and a burl near the mouth made an eye. The piece of wood became Sasha's pet dog, Milosz. Milosz became her talisman.

Chapter 20 – Plague in the Orphanage

Mikhail and Sasha spent bleak winters in the orphanage. Winter brought lice and shortages of food, medicine, and toilet paper. Hunger drove them to bark and wood. The heating stopped and everyone huddled inside beneath bed covers for warmth.

Flu infected Ilya, who vomited, splattering bed sheets and walls. He filled the pot by his bed with dark liquid until that stopped as well. Mikhail emptied the pot to clear the air.

The flu became a plague and infected everyone including the staff, Mikhail, and Sasha. Within a few days, all medicines disappeared. Diarrhea backed up the toilets, causing flooding and covering floors with a brown ooze that froze. They choked on the un-breathable stench. The orphanage became a hell never before conceived, even by Dante.

Some orderlies revived in a few days and began making rounds checking the children and feeding them gruel. They stepped around the messes on the floors, too fatigued to clean them.

Milan, an orderly, brought food to the children. He poked at Mikhail and Sasha who huddled in a warm cave of blankets. They peered out like cubs and emerged. Milan smiled as he served porridge to the children.

Mikhail devoured his paltry portion, licking his lips, wanting more, but Sasha was too sick to eat. The cool air soothed

Sasha's fever and Milan gave her water.

Milan moved on to Ilya. He poked at Ilya. Waited, and poked again. "Ilya?"

Ilya didn't move. "Ilya." Milan poked again. He was inert.

A startled Milan stood up, chest heaving. "Ilya!"

He stooped over Ilya, rolled back the blanket and felt Ilya's neck. *Cold, Dead.*

He felt faint and fled, returning with two other staff members. One had a stethoscope. He put the scope to Ilya's back, listened, then shifted position and listened again. He placed a hand on his neck; two fingers feeling for a pulse. "Nothing. He's dead."

Deaths from flu were rare. There had been suicides, deadly accidents, a murder in the dead winter, but this wasn't expected and the staff didn't know what to do about it.

They wrapped his body in sheets, put it on a cart and parked it outside where the moon cast tormenting shadows on the playground. Frozen ground made burial impossible. The staff considered disposing of him in the river, but realized he would freeze and then thaw in the spring to rot. They decided to burn the corpse and dispose of the ashes in the river. They couldn't wait till morning as the body would freeze, so the staff lit the refuse furnace and prepared to cremate Ilya.

The cremation's grey smoke twisted and turned in the dark night air, sprinkling grey bits on the snow, smelling like cooked meat. His ashes colored the snow drifts shades of grey. Ilya's burning corpse filled Mikhail's dream life with terror, making sleep impossible. Days passed, another orphan died, then another. Their ashes mingled in the snow, making a mass grave.

The end game of the plague in the orphanage returned and he recalled the very day he permanently changed.

In the morning, Oleg came, bringing soup and bread. He tapped Mikhail on the head. Mikhail looked up. “Here is some bread and soup.” He placed them on a chair near Mikhail. “Sasha.” Oleg put his hand on her head. “Sasha…wake up…Sasha…” He stopped and looked at Mikhail.

“She’s asleep,” Mikhail said.

“Sasha wake up. Sasha.”

“She’s asleep,” Mikhail repeated.

Two others joined Oleg. “She’s dead. We have to get her out of here.”

Mikhail’s eye’s opened wide. He tightened his grip on his sister.

“No,” Mikhail said and wrapped his arms and legs around Sasha. “She is alive. You are lying.”

“Mikhail, I’m sorry. She is gone. Let go.”

“NOOO!”

The orderlies wrestled with Mikhail, overturning the soup and bread. They couldn’t pry him loose. An orderly beat his legs and arms with a rubber club to no avail. Then there was a blow to his head.

Mikhail’s body swirled in space, floating, mass-less. His eyes fluttered open to a blinding white light that drew him towards it, appearing like a portal to another place. Grey shadows passed before the light on the other side, as though someone waited for him. He glided towards the light like a mist. There was no sound, no feeling. Only the blinding light. He didn't breathe as he approached the portal. He approached it, wanted to pass through it, but it became smaller. Too small. He couldn't pass through. He pushed up against the portal, but he couldn't pass through. He couldn't breathe until he passed through. He began to panic. He couldn't breathe, as though he was drowning.

He inhaled, taking a long, deep breath, and then gradually let it out. He took a second breath. His face prickled and limbs tingled. He took a third breath. The prickling left as feeling returned to his face. His breathing stabilized and the portal came into focus. It was the light on the wall by his bed in the orphanage. A moth circled the light, casting shadows.

After a moment of wakefulness, he sank back into sleep and dreamt that he stood high on a river bank overlooking the tributary behind the orphanage. A litter of fetuses dotted the river, rotting in the sun. A pipe jutting from the river bank spewed brown and yellow sludge, bringing more fetuses. On the far side of the river, he saw Sasha struggling in the muck. She fell over and became stuck, stopped struggling, and died. He watched her corpse turn to ash and blow away in the wind.

He crumbled in despair, falling to his knees, and burying his head in his hands. He wept until he was unable to breath and became catatonic. Everything turned black.

And then he felt a presence emerge. A separate presence. Part of him, but alien to him, having a will all its own. The presence called itself Anomie. Anomie spoke, "They were never alive…merely tissue, organic matter."

Mikhail opened his eyes to the horror of fetuses. "Nothing is alive…it's just complex chemistry…moving…reacting to events. Everything is this way…the earth, the sea, minerals washed together, zapped by lightening, becoming self-replicating molecules, evolving into bacteria, then insects, then rats, and eventually you. Organic matter, secretly dead. Life is an illusion."

He looked at the birds pecking at the fetuses. Anomie spoke again, "Everything preys on everything. Germs preyed on Sasha until her chemistry broke down. She feels nothing now, is nothing now. Why suffer? Why feel? All decays into oblivion."

Anomie became quiet and Mikhail felt Anomie leave.

Over the next week, Mikhail endured sickness and the horror of cremated orphans until suddenly his strength returned. He left his bed and explored, venturing outside into the freezing cold. Howling wind lashed his face with frozen rain. He looked at the grey ash in the snow. *They are dead, but I am not dead.* He savored the stinging wind, sensing his strength against it.

Chapter 21 - The Proposal

"Jack? Jack?"

Jack emerged from his day dream.

"Jack, listen, Susan and Ben have something to announce," Amy said.

"Huh? What? Oh? Something to announce? That sounds important. I am all ears," Jack said.

"You tell him, Ben," Susan said while Ben flushed and hesitated.

"I asked Susan to marry me," Ben said.

Jack feigned surprise. "Really? That took courage. I'll bet she said no."

"No, I am afraid I said yes." Susan laughed.

"Now, that's a mistake," Jack joked. "Wow! When's the wedding?"

"Late June. Amy is my maid of honor."

"Well, congratulations to you both." Jack's sincerity belied his true feelings.

Mission accomplished. Now, I want to get out of here, he thought.

Jack took the first, socially normal step towards a quick exit. "Check," He flagged the waiter.

The women conspired to prolong their pleasure at the

expense of the men's agony. "Oh wait, Jack. I just want to see the menu again," Amy defied, admonishing him with an obstinate look. The men waited patiently while the women wiled away the next fifteen minutes, waiting for menus that never came.

After brunch, the couples strolled back to the cars moving to the rhythms of feminine harmony and unspoken masculine dissonance. "Well, it was nice to see you, Jack." Susan pecked Jack on the cheek. "When will we see you again?"

"I leave those plans to Amy." Jack smiled. "Nice to see you both. Goodbye." He took Amy by the arm hustled her away. "I'm meeting Howard for a run after this. Got to hurry."

They arrived at Jack's car and climbed in. Amy settled into her seat. Smug contentment spread across her face. Her friend had found commitment and a stable relationship. "I'm so happy for Susan and Ben. Aren't you happy about it?" She gave Jack a side long glance.

"Not exactly. A little terrified, I guess."

Her contentment turned to anger. "And what exactly do you mean by that?"

"They're too young for one thing. And he's crazy."

Amy folded her arms and snapped, "What a critical, insulting thing to say. You're just jealous. You feel inferior to Ben. That's why you don't like him."

Jack replied sarcastically, "I am deeply wounded by your remark. Look, Ben is a loser. He is short, ugly, insecure, arrogant, and mediocre. He has the intellect and the values of a Nouveau

Riche Radiologist."

"Ben comes from a good family and he is smart and he is—

"Why do you say that? Because his father is a surgeon?"

"He's a well-known surgeon. Makes big bucks and—"

"His father is a self-important name dropper and third rate conspicuous consumer. Ben's parents hate each other. They throw things at each other when they fight. His mother's bipolar. Wasn't she in rehab a couple of times? You call that a good family?"

*Throw things when they fight? Rehab? S*he thought. It sounded like her family. It sounded like her. A tidal wave of bad chemistry flooded her central nervous system, causing her pulse to sky rocket and her normally beige complexion to turn bright red. She gasped for breathe for a moment and then gathered enough composure to shout, "LISTEN, YOU UPPER-MIDDLE CLASS SNOB.WHAT DO YOU KNOW ABOUT BEING RICH?"

He shouted back, "DOES BEING RICH MAKE YOU MENTALLY ILL? IS THAT HIS EXCUSE FOR BEING A DOUCHE BAG?"

"HOW DARE YOU SHOUT AT ME!PULL OVER!PULL OVER, NOW!"

"WHAT?"

She pounded on the car door. "LET ME OUT!LET ME OUT!PULL OVER!I'M GETTING OUT!"

Jack pulled over to the curb. She jumped out and stormed away. *Shit! What just happened?* She wondered.

Chapter 22 – Leena and Helena

Leena's computer sounded again, retrieving her from thoughts about the Christmas Party. It was an email from her mother, Helena. Emails from Helena usually covered the minutia of her life with enthusiasm, reporting lists of small pleasures, like the fragrant flowers in spring or hot mugs of chocolate warming hands in the winter. This email brought heart-rending details about her new brood of Borzoi pups.

Leena opened a picture Helena attached to the email that showed Leena and her mother cuddling with Borzoi puppies. The picture reminded her of the warm fuzzy puppies who licked her hands with unconditional affection and stirred unconscious memories of her mother's tactile love.

They admired the long narrow heads and slender bodies of theBorzoi that had been why they were used for hunting wolves by the Russian Aristocracy for hundreds of years and then fell from favor under the Soviets. Helena and Leena loved them anyway, as a symbol that was Russian to the core.

The image of her mother warmed Leena's heart, bringing tears. Helena's face had weathered into a quilt-work of decades; a scar here, a patch there, a dimple in her chin, and a contented twinkle in her oily blue eyes. Her body was crooked and arthritic, but strong and she hiked up and down the stairs to her small apartment many times a day without so much as a groan.

Both Helena's parents died during the Battle of Stalingrad. She lived in the orphanage until twelve, after which she began work in a steel mill. She learned at a young age that the company of men and vodka allowed her to escape the barren monotony of Soviet Life. She had many lovers, some of whom opened doors for her. She used her good looks to get what she wanted; choices she felt no remorse about. It was a lesson Leena understood very well.

Helena had promised herself never to bring a child into her concrete, cinder block world, but to her surprise, she conceived and bore Leena in her early forties. Leena created meaning for Helena. She cherished Leena as the only love she had ever known, except for the puppy love of Borzois.

Chapter 23—Socrates

Jack fled his drama with Amy to the other side of town where he sought the cool-headed reason of Howard Goldman, Jack's best friend. By choosing a path less taken, Howard Goldman had completed a Ph.D. program at Stanford in Russian Studies. While waiting for a review of his thesis, he sought a position with liberal policy think tanks in Washington DC. Goldman knew what he wanted; everyone else could be damned.

Howard exorcised Jack's demons with medicinal marijuana and long-slow jogging. Always before the exercise, they discussed their recent triumphs, tribulations, and weird topics like different types of infinities, some of which were larger than others.

Jack screeched to a stop in Goldman's driveway, parked, scooped up the newspaper, and then galloped towards the backdoor of the guest house. He knocked on the door.

From inside, Jack heard Howard say, "Oh, shit!" He's early!"

An annoyed female voice complained, "Not again. Howwwuurrd!" It is Rachel.

"Hooker! You're a little early," Howard called out to Jack and then said to Rachel, "Don't worry about it. I'll pull something on. Go take a shower. Relax. Love you."

Jack checked his cell phone for the time. *Five minutes* early? I know what they were doing…Right up to the last minute.

He opened the paper and read while he waited.

"Hey." Howard Goldman appeared at the door wearing a blue terrycloth bathrobe and moccasins. He opened it. Espresso?

"Sure."

Jack followed Goldman into the kitchen. Goldman flipped on the espresso machine, opened a cupboard, and took down a jar of coffee. Jack stood by the counter, spread out the newspaper, and read.

"I am five minutes early. I didn't mean to interrupt anything important," said Jack.

"What do you mean?" Howard asked.

"I know what you guys are doing."

"Ok. So what," Howard said.

"Cutting it pretty close," Jack said.

Howard shrugged.

Howard prepared two espressos. They moved to the living room to talk.

Hieronymus Bosch and Salvador Dali posters dressed the walls like cave drawings. An eternal clutter of CDs, tapes, and seventy-eight vinyl records supplied his stereo with Beethoven, Nirvana, and Jazz. Carelessly placed bookshelves blocked picture window views of the backyard.

Howard began camping here five years ago, sleeping in a down sleeping bag in the living room in a tent with fires burning in the fireplace. Rachel had changed a lot of things after moving in two years ago, turning Goldman's cave into a home with laundry detergent, toothpaste, and toilet paper. They were engaged.

"So, what's new with you? Howard asked.

"Nothing much, saw my dad, went out with Amy, had another fight."

Just then Rachel appeared. "Hi, Jack. Howard, I am going to the office. I have to see that new patient again."

"New one what?" Jack asked.

"You know, the one who cut herself yesterday. I'll tell you later."

"Okay, Luv…so when will I be seeing you?" Howard asked.

"Early afternoon, twoish."

"Okay, see you," Howard said to Rachel as she left the house. He then turned to Jack and said "She has a new patient. Yeah, a difficult case."

Rachel had finished her degrees and worked as a student therapist. Howard continued, "This one has lots of ups and downs. She was kidnapped last summer in Europe. Raped, beaten. Somehow she escaped. She has scars on her face and body. How would you like a few scars like that?"

"Oh, a little plastic surgery would help that."

"Not burn marks."

"Burn marks? Like on her skin?" Jack asked. Howard nodded. "That's sick. What a deranged perverted atrocity." The gravity of rape and torture offended Jack's shallow sense of chivalry. He squinted at Goldman. "I would kill those fuckers."

"These guys were pros. Sex slavery is bad, but at least they didn't make a lamp shade out of her… She's been cutting herself."

Jack growled and repeated, "I would kill those fuckers." In another era, Jack probably would have 'killed those fuckers' while perhaps living in a small village in northern Europe.

This was as close as either of them had come to trauma and their minds exited the un-experienced, but often discussed, world of violence and returned to their leisure in the comfort of Goldman's Lascaux cave.

"How's the Ph.D. process going?" Jack asked.

"Okay. Thesis is still being reviewed."

In spite of this, Russia fascinated Howard with its deep alluvial deposits of history and pre-history which hid mysterious secrets, like fifteen thousand-year-old dwellings made of mammoth bones. Howard loved Russian geniuses, like Tolstoy, Tchaikovsky, and the more recent Mathematician, Grigori Perlman, who had won the Field's Medal in Mathematics, but refused to accept the one million dollar award because he felt the money subverted the truth of Mathematics. Most of all, he loved the heroism the Russian people demonstrated in World War two.

Goldman had contacted many lost Russian relatives, including a cousin who fought corruption in Russia with an internet blog, Grigori Navalny. His blog had tens of thousands readers, including Howard, who avidly participated.

His irreverent wit easily pierced all sacred stereotypes, including Jewish ones, often causing Jack to laugh uncontrollably. They seemed unlikely friends. Goldman, the counter-culture intellectual, and Jack Hooker, the conforming fratboy, but they had much in common like their mutual disdain of self-important mediocrity and the tiresome shallowness of the people in general

Goldman handed Jack a pipe stuffed with pot. “How about a little of this?”

“Gracias.” Jack took a hit.

Chapter 24 – Amy's Breakdown

Amy threw open the door to her apartment, which hit the wall with a bang. Shards of panic ripped her insides. She collapsed on the living room couch, held her head in her hands, and growled in a low voice, "I hate you. I hate you."

She tumbled into the kitchen, took vodka from the freezer, and poured it into a tall glass. The chilly liquor felt like a cold compress on a bruise. She returned to the couch, flipped on the TV, and surfed channels, stopping on, "*Project Runway*, hmmmmm."

She sought comfort with the fatherly Tim Gunn, the glamour of Heidi Klum, and the drama of fashion design, but couldn't. She continued to surf channels, finding a classic movie she had once watched with her mother on a cold stormy night, huddled together in bed. A movie with a happy, comforting ending. It was a black and white classic, *To Have and Have Not*, but even with the warm, fuzzy memories the movie brought, it could not hold her attention.

Like a ball on a roulette wheel, her mind bounced from image to image, eventually settling on her mother and an event that occurred when Amy was fourteen. It was her mother's birthday and Amy had made a three layer cake with each layer separated by tart gooseberry preserves. She filled the empty cylindrical center of the cake with jelly bellies and painted it with white frosting. The uneven cake tilted to one side and a sloppy message on the top of the cake read, 'I Love My

Mom'. Dabs of frosting and jam spangled the kitchen counter and floor. A happy smear of chocolate colored her cheeks. Her enthusiasm bubbled over. She proudly surprised her mother with the cake.

Her mother was stoned, depressed, and not receptive. She began to ridicule Amy, "Look at this mess. You don't expect me to eat this. It's horrible. You'll never amount to anything." Mother threw the cake in the garbage. "Now clean up this mess. Estrella, show Amy how to clean."

Amy gulped vodka and banged her head with a fist as she spoke, "I tried…I tried."

She went to the bathroom seeking refuge in her plastic menagerie of pill boxes: Xanax, Valium, Ativan, and Klonopin. She took two Valium and then looked in the mirror at her dilated pupils, throbbing temples, and veneer of perspiration reflecting from her pale face. Her hands and arms tingled. She staggered to her bed, laid down, and listened to the thud, thud, thud, of each heartbeat.

She tried meditation. Placing her arms at her sides, she uncrossed her legs, closed her eyes, and regulated her breathing. She focused on her fingers, relaxing each one, then each toe, her hands and feet and so on, becoming aware of each muscle, consciously unclenching it, and then moving on to the next. Slowly, her pulse fell, the throbbing in her head eased, the prickling tingle left her hands and arms. She took a long slow deep breath and thought she might relax until she saw her father in her mind's eye: his weak chin, his insecure eyes. "What rock did you crawl out from under? YOU'RE A FAILURE, SPONGING OFF MOTHER. I HATE YOU!" She sat up and threw her empty glass across the room.

Panic returned and she rocked back and forth. She began speaking out loud to an absent Jack Hooker, “You don’t care about me, you just want my money. You’re just like him, like Daddy, a leech. You’re with me because I’m rich and you want my money. That’s all. I see right through you, Jack Hooker.”

Chapter 25 – Stoned Again

Goldman took a second hit. "More?" he offered Jack.

Jack looked lost in space. "Dude." He waved his hand, indicating no.

"Jack, I have some weird music. Wanna hear it?"

A slow grin spread across Jack's face as he slurred, "Uhhhhh, yeaaaaaah."

Goldman connected his iPod to the stereo, pushed a button, turned a dial, and then gradually eerie strains of violins and cellos rose from the speakers like mist of ghosts rising from tombs. "Have you heard this?"

Jack hung his head and listened to the ghosts. "Never. Pretty weirrrrrd."

"It's Bartok. *Music for Strings, Percussion and Celesta*...... The first movement is a fugue..."

"Fuuuuuuuuuuuuuugue, like musical fudge," Jack oozed.

"Yeah, a musical statement followed by a response. Each statement rises from the Key of A by a fifth while the responses start at A and drop a fifth...let me show you." Goldman sketched out the chord progression from memory on a pad of paper. "See?" He pointed to the paper. "It uses all twelve tones."

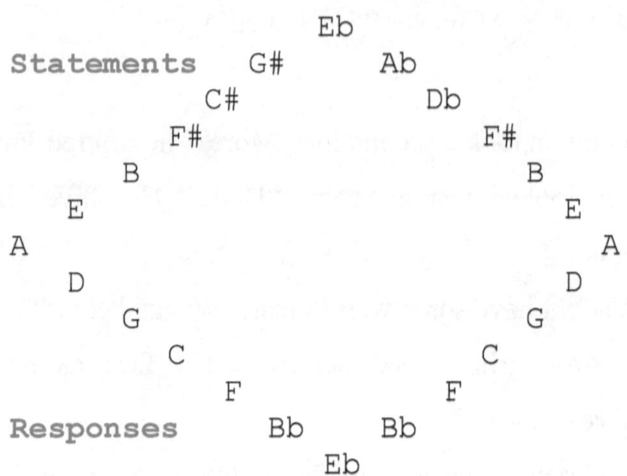

"It loooooks liiiike a parallelogram."

"It's weird."

"Agreed, How-Weird. But who cares about a chord progression except cone-heads?" The musical ghosts danced macabre across the backs of Jack's eyelids, like a movie while Jack mumbled lyrical nonsense, "Each ghost has its OWN CONE HEAD. It's Barble Talk. I mean Simon and Bartokle. I mean Barrrrrtok."

"*Music for Strings, Percussion and Celesta*."

"Music for Cone Heads." Jack changed subjects. "What about Amy and Kittridge? You never told me."

"What do you mean?"

"She dated him. Why didn't you tell me?"

"Oh, that." Howard's face became pale. "Would it have made a difference?"

"Hmmm, would it have made a difference? You know that party you and Rachel had, your engagement party? Amy and I came and he was there. That asshole came over and chatted with us for some time, like nothing had ever happened."

"Okay. So, what did you three chat about?"

"The French Literature class she took from him."

"And that's it?"

"Well, other irrelevant stuff. He leered at her. You know, undressing her with his eyes. She blushed. It pissed me off—this lecherous old guy hitting on my girl."

"He's not that old. Early thirties. Sorry, dude. I thought you knew. But answer my question, would it have mattered?"

"Early thirties! He's a FUCKING OLD MAN! Would it have mattered? Yeah, maybe I would have had a few words with that OLD FUCKER."

"Let it lay. It doesn't matter. Forget about it."

"You know what she said?" Howard shook his head 'no'. "She said that he TRAINED HER!" His voice inflected upwards to emphasize his outrage. "You know, LIKE AN ANIMAL!"

Jack's self-absorbed outrage, the dramatic voice inflections, and the words, 'TRAINED HER LIKE AN ANIMAL', struck Goldman as ridiculous and he chuckled.

Jack growled beneath his breath, hissing with disgust, "He trained her like an animal. To use for his own pleasure."

Howard's chuckle became a guffaw.

Jack repeated with the same rising voice, "TRAINED HER

LIKE AN ANIMAL." And Goldman fell over, beside himself with hilarity.

Jack started laughing and soon joined Goldman on the floor, out of control. "He trained her, he TRAINED HER! Like an ANIMAL," Jack blubbered.

Their hilarity climaxed and then waned.

"Ha, uh, huh." Jack tried one last time, but the humor had evaporated. "Yeah, I guess you're right. But that was funny while it lasted."

Stuporous silence followed until Jack said, "I'm kind of stressed."

"About what?"

"Amy. We had a huge fight. I left her by the side of the road."

"Another huge fight. Seems like a bad habit. What happened?"

"I'm still trying to figure that out. She just dove off the deep end."

"Let's run. We can talk about it," Howard said.

Part II

Chapter 26 - Risk Management in Financial Markets

Jack spent the first morning of the new semester in a class on Marketing after which he had lunch with a friend, and then he went to Financial Risk Management, a graduate level course on how to use mathematics to reduce financial risk. It was his first graduate level course and he approached it with care, arriving early and settling in the back with his face tucked beneath the brim of his cap. He peered out and watched students arriving as though lying in wait.

A couple of students in the front row arguing about energy policy caught his attention. One said with a drawl, “Big oil should drill off the coast of California and Alaska!”

The comment lit Jack’s fuse. He studied the man who was older, had grey hair, and wore a jacket and tie. “What an old geek!” Jack growled from beneath his cap brim.

The second big mouth responded with sarcasm, “Yeah, so we can become a brown-field state like Texas.”

Jack noticed the second guy wore slacks, a fitted shirt, and leather shoes. Everyone except Jack was dressed in business attire. Suddenly, he felt painfully out of place in his red polo shirt, designer jeans, and stupid cap.

Maybe I should drop the class, Jack thought.

The professor appeared on the hour and wrote his name on the board. "My name is Doctor Richard Greene and this is a class on Risk Management in Financial Markets. If you were expecting something else, you are in the wrong class."

One of the big-mouths in the front row quietly slinked toward the door, stumbling over a chair on his way out.

What a fool, Jack thought and curled his lips into a sneer.

The Professor jumped right into his lecture. "This is a very important field for the finance industry: banking, insurance, mortgage holders, international businesses, investing. It is a very mathematical field. We will construct a number of simple models of financial markets which help identify and analyze risk. Have any of you worked in Risk Management before?"

A woman in the front row raised her hand.

"What is your name and what do you do?"

"My name is Leena Kiraskaya. I am Senior Director at NovoRisk Bank in Russia. I am running Risk Management department", she said in broken English.

"NovoRisk Bank? In Russia?" Leena nodded. "How do you use Risk Management?" the professor asked.

"Oh, well." She waved a hand in the air. "We have many clients with business in Iran, Lebanon, Syria, and other countries with unstable currency and they deposit currency in local branch. We manage risk of currency exchange. This is one area."

"Has your bank ever taken a big loss because of exchange rate fluctuations?" he asked.

"We have big loss a few times. Mostly, we keep our money in basket of currencies to lower risk of fluctuations. Some fluctuations can be very large."

"Any examples?"

"Of currency fluctuations? When United States invading Iraq, there were large fluctuations."

"Did your bank lose?" he asked.

"I was not there, I do not know," she said.

"Interesting, I would like to see what your bank did to manage this."

Leena's brow knitted into supercilious half circles. "I can share some exotic techniques."

Doctor Greene said, "Exotic techniques? Yes, I'm sure you can. Perhaps we can talk after class."

Doctor Greene paused to clear his voice and then continued, "So, this is one example of how Risk Management is vital to the financial health of banks. Let's consider the financial meltdown in 2009, the so-called 'mortgage crisis'. There were actually negative interest rates. By that, I mean that people bought bonds for more than their face value. Why did that happen?" The class sat quietly.

Leena raised her hand again and began to speak, "It is simple, Professor. Everyone panicked and everyone wanting safety, so they overpaid for US Bonds, and over paying them, the rate is negative. It is simple, Doctor Greene."

She winked at Doctor Greene, who hesitated over his next

few words. "Uhhhh, right. Uhhhhh. May I asked about the impact on your bank, fall of 2009.Did you flee rubles for dollars?"

"No Doctor Greene. We sold dollars and bought rubles and made nice profit when saner heads returned to market."

The professor stopped and stared at the blonde. "You're kidding me."

"What it means, 'kidding me'?"

"Forget it. Let's talk later. Please, come by my office."

The lecture continued at a hectic pace as Doctor Greene outlined the subject matter. Competitive feelings towards the big mouth in the front who sat closer to the blonde with the cool accent robbed him of focus.

What geeks these old men are. I will prey upon them, Jack promised himself and imagined taking away their seats, sitting by the blonde and then lording it over them. He growled from beneath the cap brim like a wolf. *I am Beowulf. I will destroy them.*

After the first hour, the class broke for ten minutes. Jack sought refuge outside. He surveyed the older faces until he saw his reflection in a window. In comparison to the rougher, older looking men, he looked like a Ken doll with a stupid hat. He hid the hat.

Back in the classroom, Leena Kiraskaya began talking with the professor. "As you know, Professor Greene, specific events cause fluctuations, like U.S. invading Iraq."

"Or the Greek Bankruptcy."

"Or U.S. Bankruptcy, like U.S. mortgage crisis," Leena said.

“You made money then?” he asked.

“I am not allowed to say you this, but here is point I am making. Mortgage crisis shows weakness of western markets. No one saw this problem coming.”

“Not true, one guy did, uh, what was his name,” he said.

“Michael Burry. His name is Michael Burry,” she said.

“Yes, Burry. He’s blind in one eye. You might say Doctor Burry’s insight was anything but blurry.”

“What it is, ‘blurry’?”

“Oh. Not clear. Something that is blurry is not clear.”

Leena paused to acknowledge his pun while thinking, *That is stupid*, but then said instead, “It is not funny, Doctor Greene. He made fortune and U.S. almost went into bankruptcy. Is this good economic policy?”

“Come by my office. We can talk more. I have to run to the little boy’s room.” He smirked.

Little boy’s room? Disgusting! Leena thought

She walked outside to smoke. After lighting up and taking a drag she spotted Jack, his shiny brown hair, and baby face. *He is in class?* She made eye contact with him and smiled. He smiled back, looking insecure and worried. She liked that. *Like a puppy.*

Jack looked at the smoking blonde. She didn’t have the tough, jaded look of the others. She dressed more like a student: sneakers, jeans, and carrying a backpack.

She approached him. “Hello,” she said.

“Hi. You seem to have a pretty good handle on the class.”

“What? What is, ‘handle’?”

“I mean, you seem to know a lot about Risk Management.”

“Ah, yes.” She waved a hand in the air dismissively. She exclaimed with a flourish, “Oh, Well. I work in this area for long time. I like it.”

“It is new to me.”

“New? Don’t worry about it. It is not hard. Do you know Mathematics?”

“A little.”

“I have Masters in Mathematics from University of Moscow. Finance is like nothing.” She exhaled confidence with the cigarette smoke. “What is your name?”

“I’m Jack. Jack Hooker.”

“Jack Hooker. It is good name. Sounds like American Name?”

“I like. Yeah, I’m American.”

“Okay. I am Leena Kiraskaya. Pleasing to meet you.”

“Nice to meet you, too.”

“We can have a coffee after class, yes? And getting to know each other?”

Her offer caught him off guard. “Uh, yeah. Okay. Sure, after class we can get coffee. We should go back in now.”

After class they strolled to a nearby coffee shop while Jack listened to Leena expound on currency markets, risk management, the politics of the Middle East and Russia, travelling in Europe, skiing in Switzerland—she went on and on and on. She captivated

Jack, frolicking with the sound of language, embellishing it with coos, chirps, and ooohs and awwws.

And then she paused, took another drag on her smoke, and exhaled while speaking in a low, gravelly voice, “So, what about you, kid?” She exhaled, enveloping him in smoke.

She called me kid? He thought, and then said, “Me? Yeah, well, I’m a senior and I’m studying Account and Finance and—”

“I think it’s boring.” She interrupted. She dropped her cigarette on the pavement and then stepped on it.

The words stung. “Well, I like it and besides, I can make a lot of money.”

“Please, don’t tell me you are liking this accounting.”

“Well, I sort of like it. You know, it’s a living.”

“I am not believing you.” She exhaled her last puff. “No one likes accounting, Jack Hooker. Accounting is boring. It is financial janitor work. There are other things you can do that are not boring.”

“Like what?”

“Like what? You are stupid, Jack. How about Risk Management?”

“Never thought about it.” Her remark flattened him. He wanted to flee but couldn’t gracefully exit.

Soon they reached the coffee shop, went inside, ordered espresso, and sat. Fortunately, the subject shifted back to Leena, so all he had to do is listen. She talked and talked and then suddenly said, “Well, I have to go. Thanks for the coffee. You know, we can study together, Mister Hooker."

Study together? Why would she be at all interested in me? Why ask questions? He wondered. "Sure," He replied and they parted.

Chapter 27 - After Coffee

Jack trudged back to Sigma Chi while his mind replayed Leena's musing, sing-song voice as it man-handled Doctor Green's questions in class. "Oh well, it is simple, Professor Green."

She had coffee with me *and wants to study with* me, he smugly thought and grinned, until he reheard her voice say, "I think it is boring, kid," and, "You are stupid, Jack."

He disappeared into circumspection. Compared to the petty intrigues with the Brotherhood of Evil and his careening-out-of-control relationship with Amy, Leena unsettled him deeply. He knew that fate and a modicum of talent propelled him towards the high-paying world of accounting. He would get his degree, join a firm, probably make partner, marry someone, have kids, perhaps divorce, perhaps remarry, and live a long tepid life, safe from extremes, devoid of tragedies, overly comfortable, and very ordinary.

Leena is extraordinary, he thought. The epiphany created a hole in his stomach that felt like an ulcer. *Goldman has a good plan, too. How did he know? Was he born with an interest in Russian Studies?*

He stumbled home to his frat, oblivious to his surroundings, and sometimes stopping and gazing off into space. His cell phone buzzed a call from Susan. He answered.

"Hi, Jack. Where's Amy?

"No idea."

"I haven't seen Amy in a few days. Do you think she's having one of her things?" she said.

"One of her things? It's possible," he said.

"Did you have a fight or something?" She asked.

"Not that I can recall," He lied.

"Okay, bye."

He looked up and found himself in the courtyard of Sigma Chi staring blindly at Kit, who shot baskets. "Think fast," Kit said. Jack saw the basketball speeding towards him and, thinking fast, stepped out of the way. "You prick." Kit ran after the ball. "Do you wanna play some hoops later?"

"Huh? Oh, no, I'm busy." He looked at Kit, the frat elder, the Med student, the guru. *Would Kit understand Leena?* He wondered. Older than Goldberg, Kit still lived in Frat World. He wouldn't get Leena at all.

He wandered inside, past a group playing video games and drinking beer. "DUUUUUUUUDE!" one player exploded over the video game.

"Hey look, it's the Hook. World of Warcraft. Wanna play?"

"No thanks." Jack veered out of the living room and climbed the stairs to his sanctuary on the second floor. On his way, he passed the rooms of his peers, some with open doors, like Tony's, who snuggled with Nancy on a sofa. And then there were the closed doors, like John's, from under which pot smoke seeped into the reeking hallway. *Monday night and John is stoned again.*

Jack thought in disapproval.

He reached his room, stepped inside, hung a Do Not Disturb sign on the door knob, and locked the door. Starring out the window he wondered, *How can I get what I want? What exactly do I want?*

A knock on the door broke the tranquility. "You wankin' it in there, Hooker?" Laughter followed.

*The Brotherhood of Evil strike*s, he thought and shouted, "Go get naked with a man." *Silence. What cowards.*

He returned to his thoughts. *What do I want? I want Leena, to be a friend. That's what I want.* The mere thought settled him down, so he said it out loud, "I want Leena." He felt even better.

*How to get what I want? H*e wondered. Step one appeared in his mind. They would study Risk Management together on Saturday. *Start as study buddies. Risk Management.*

He pulled the Risk Management book from his backpack, plopped down onto his bean bag chair, and began to read. No, he began to memorize Risk Management.

Chapter 28 - Meeting Doctor Greene

Leena arrived at Professor Greene's office late, fully expecting him to wait. He had.

Leena's relationships with men were always warm. In her position at the bank, she dealt with an onslaught of them. Often they were men who expressed an interest in her and she had to be able to manage them. She thought of them as admirers. Many of the admirers became good friends, with friendships lasting years. Nearly zero became romantic relationships.

Leena understood Professor Green's interest in her. She would be kind to him. She felt a little sorry for male professors as a group because she saw them as having failed in the real world. Failures with women bruised their egos, fed a mild misogyny, and prevented them from accepting women as equals.

Once, she had been with a professor at Moscow University. After a short infatuation, his narcissism returned and he began picking at her flaws, grinning, while stinging her with sarcasm. After a few rounds of this she dumped him.

Greene was fairly typical: a little more naïve. A little less brash. He had mousy brown hair, a trimmed goatee, and stood a little less than six feet tall. He wore slacks, a jacket, and no tie. Greene's pale flab betrayed low testosterone and other missing hormones Leena required in a man. She was not attracted to him at all.

She stood at the doorway. “Doctor Greene. I am so sorry I am late. The day is too disorganizing for me.”

Greene looked up from his desk and smiled. “Leena.” He rose to greet her, bowing unconsciously. “Please, sit here.” He waved his hand towards a chair.

“Well, it’s been such a busy day,” she began, “rushing here and there. I am still not getting used to things in America yet. Driving and parking is so complicated.”

“You have a car here?”

“Yes, the bank has given me with everything, car, apartment, spending money, I will be quite comfortable. But I am still, how you say, ‘adjusting’.”

She looked around his office. Books and papers overflowed the desk and bookshelves poured onto the floor in stacks. Greene had plastered his walls with diplomas, academic honors, and photographs.

She compulsively ingratiated herself, “So, Doctor Greene, I love your class so far. Risk Management is such a fascinating area. Tell me, how long you are professor at Stanford?”

Greene seized the opportunity to talk about this favorite subject, which was himself, and launched a minutes-long soliloquy. She sat patiently, smiling, feigning interest, punctuating his comments with affirmations while her eyes roamed his office. One of the pictures showed Greene with a five- or six-year-old boy. *A son. There are no photos of woman.* From the dates on diplomas, she deduced he was forty-five.

"Do you mind if I smoke?" she asked.

"Huh?" Surprised at her request, he paused and then relented. "Uh, sure. I don't have any ash trays."

"That's okay. I will use trash can. Please, continue. It is so interesting."

He continued for a few more minutes. Finally, he stopped, satisfied. "Now, tell me about Leena Kiraskaya," he said, smiling smugly.

"Well, Doctor Greene, I do not think I can top that! I am Director at NovoRisk Bank in Russia. I am responsible for foreign currency exchange, risk management, bond portfolio management. I manage staff of sixty people."

"Sounds challenging."

She rolled her eyes and lifted a hand. "You have no idea, Doctor Greene. Billions are at stack."

"I think you mean, 'at stake'," He corrected her.

"Yes, that's what I mean."

"It sounds very stressful."

"Oh well, I am not stressful about it. We have computers and my staff is the best for it." She exhaled smoke out of the corner of her mouth.

"College?"

"Yes, I have Masters in Mathematics from Moscow University, with emphasis on Statistics and Probabilities. Financial equations are nothing. Easy." She waved her hand and then continued to rattle on about finance.

He tried to suppress a yawn and found himself interrupting her. "Very interesting. So, tell me about Miss Leena, the person."

His question crossed a line that Leena had anticipated. She decided to use it to her advantage. "What you mean, Doctor Greene?" She gave a demure look, but knew exactly what he meant.

"Well, what do you like to do for fun?" he asked with a sheepish grin.

She knew exactly how to respond. She froze and stared him in the eyes for a few moments, as though caught off guard. After waiting through a short, awkward silence and she slowly said, "Doctor Greene, I have told you about my career and academic background. Why you want to know what Leena wants for fun? It is not a right question, Doctor Greene."

His forehead moistened. "I'm just being friendly. You know, you are new to America, I don't know if you know anyone here."

"The bank has provided me with guide for my American trip," she said.

"Oh." Another silence followed. She let him stew a little. She decided to lead him on a bit.

"What do you like to 'do for fun', Doctor Greene?" She cocked her head to one side.

He took a deep breath. "Many things, many things. I am very active. I like skiing, scuba diving, I have a motorcycle, fine dining, theatre. Other things."

"You sound like a renaissance man, Doctor Greene. Are you suggesting me we have a date?" She raised an eyebrow.

"Well, no," he stammered. "Well, yes. Well, no, not a date. Just a friendly get-together."

"This is putting Leena in awkward position. You are professor and I am student."

"Well, yes, I understand, but I don't mean like a date. Just, you know, well, forget about it. I didn't mean to make you feel uncomfortable."

She didn't feel uncomfortable, but he did. She sat quietly and watched him squirm. "Well, if you like 'friendly get-together', perhaps. I will be thinking about it. I have to go now."

As Leena drove back to her apartment, she assessed Doctor Greene and decided he bored her. He could become a professional friend. Perhaps they could meet for dinner. Once. He faded from her mind.

Jack Hooker emerged in his place. *This American, Jack Hooker. Mister Jack Hooker. He is a tomcat,* she thought and rocked her shoulders back and forth, mimicking Jacks saunter. He exuded a mist of masculinity that Leena's pores had absorbed. Now infected, she obsessed over him.

She recalled the shocked, hurt face that followed her comment, 'It think it's boring, Jack.'

He is vulnerable, like a puppy dog. She wanted to cuddle Mister Jack Hooker. "I should not say him this, that he is boring."

She promised herself she would be nicer.

Chapter 29 - The Field Site Radar

It was Friday afternoon. Jack sat in the long shadow of Amy's latest breakdown, sipping espresso in a campus cafe. They hadn't spoken since Sunday. Their fight had shaken him, made him queasy, worried, and insecure. He had flushed the remaining cocaine down the toilet that same day, as though it had somehow been complicit in his problems. He squinted into the fall sun which cast its own long shadows while he contemplated Amy.

Meltdowns were nothing new. Over the six or so months they'd been together there had been about five, including one overdose and trip to the hospital. After each event, she disappeared, emerging days later as if nothing had happened. The only detectable change in her was that she completely ignored some of the people who had been involved in the event, as though they had been moved to her frenemies list. Her behavior was strange around them. If one were to speak to Amy, she would act as though she hadn't heard them by not even glancing at them.

Five days should be enough to cool down. Maybe I should call her. Maybe we should meet for dinner and a movie on Saturday.

Amy's charms still held sway over Jack and their pull outweighed the cost of her dysfunctional outbursts. He felt committed.

His mind turned towards Leena. She fascinated him. He

couldn't get his head around her at all. After ripping him to shreds during coffee, she morphed into a flirtatious coquette and asked him to meet and study that Saturday.

Each day Professor Greene made it clear that she was his favorite student. In class, Professor Greene discussed the financial policies of third world countries, the International Monetary Fund, historic financial crises, and numerous other topics. He directed many of his questions towards Leena, who confidently answered. He would often corner her after class to talk, joke, flirt, and interest her in him. It was embarrassing to watch.

A grin spread across Jack's face. *She's mine, at least this week*, Doctor *Greene.*

His phone rang. It was Amy. "Hi, Love. What's up?"

"'Hi, Love, what's up?'" She mimicked him. "Nothing much is up, except I have plans this Saturday night. We're not going out."

"Okay. Why?"

"I am having dinner with Doctor Kittridge," Amy said.

"WHAT?" He exploded. "When did this happen?"

"I saw him on campus and he asked whether I wanted to meet for dinner."

"Are you kidding me?" Jack asked.

"No, I am not kidding you."

"I hate that guy."

"Too bad," she said.

"You're my girlfriend. You're not supposed to be seeing

other people."

"Relax, Jack. It's just an innocent meeting for dinner at his place," Amy said.

"At his place? Relax? Are you kidding me? Nothing about that pervert is innocent. Isn't he the sex professor who—"

"Turned me into a jaded slut? Trained me like an animal to be his sex toy? Isn't that what you mean? Well, yes."

"I don't feel good about this," Jack said.

"Well, Jack, as you know, we are just dating. You don't own me. It's not as though we are engaged or anything. Why do you care?"

"Very funny. Why do I care? That's bullshit. We're together. That guy can't wait to get into your pants. I hate him," He hissed.

"What makes you think he wants to get into my pants? And besides, what makes you think I don't want to get into his pants? Bye." She hung up.

He texted her, "Just don't let him take any nude pictures of you."

He received a text from her, "If he does, I'll send you one. Love, your slut."

Jealousy engulfed him, setting him ablaze. Her naked picture appeared in his mind. He knew Kittridge took it. What could he do? He had to let her go on the date with that asshole. He needed a little pot and a run to calm him down. He fled the café for Goldman's.

When Jack arrived at Howard's, he heard Rock N Roll playing. He recognized the oldie: Cream's *Tales of Brave Ulysses*. He knocked. "Howard, Howard, Howard!" He sounded frantic.

"What, what, what?" Howard opened the door. "Oh, it's you."

"You were expecting someone else?"

"I was expecting you, but in fifteen minutes. Come in anyway."

"Oh my God, oh my God. I'm a wreck. I am just a wreck," Jack moaned.

"So, as one leper said to the other, 'what's eating you?'"

"I am totally losing it."

"Really? Quite a week eh? So tell me about the slings and arrows, your triumphs and failures. Was there another struggle with the Brotherhood of Evil?"

"The Brotherhood of Evil? Slings and Arrows? How about hydrogen bombs? Why do you make everything sound like a heroic odyssey?"

"I don't know, maybe it's the song." Goldman grinned. "With a little imagination I could see you as Ulysses. Maybe a third rate Ulysses, a bumbling, hapless, incompetent Ulysses."

"Thanks How-weird. Can you please listen to me, I'm losing my mind. I'm in serious psychic-pain here."

"Losing your mind, again?" He said incredulously. "I didn't know you'd found it in the first place."

"Very funny. Listen, Amy is going out with Kittridge

tomorrow."

"Ah, the sirens are not so sweetly singing anymore." Howard chuckled.

"I hate that jaded old man. Who the hell does he think he is, anyway?"

"So, what are you so mad about?"

"I don't want him to sleep with Amy," Jack said.

"It's a little late for that," Howard said.

"I mean again. Besides, that was years ago. You don't think they've been going out on me behind my back?"

"Hmmm, probably not," Howard said.

"God damn it!" Jack cursed.

"Hey! Let's not violate any commandants here," Howard said.

"What are you talking about? My woman is going to sleep with that motherfucker and you're telling me not to swear?"

"You don't know she's going to sleep with him. They may just be going out to dinner," Howard said.

"She will. She will, just to piss me off. And that smug prick and his smug look he gave me at your party. I HAAATE HIM," Jack hissed.

"So is it his smug look or the fact that she might cheat on you that bothers you?" Howard asked.

Jack said, "I'm not sure."

Goldman then said, "You don't own Amy."

"That's what she said. So what does that have to do with

it?"

"Look, I'm just pointing out a few facts. It's her body. She can do what she wants with it. Also, you have no idea what they are going to do. She could even be lying to you."

"Lying? No way. She's not lying. She's going out with that prick."

"Okay, okay, okay. Try and relax. It's not as though you never cheated on her," Howard said.

"That's different."

Howard looked at him and nodded. "Indeed. Please explain."

"Okay, it's not different, but I am entitled to my jealousy."

"Right, you're entitled to your jealousy." Howard handed him a pipe. "Take a hit. We'll run ten miles and then go get some sushi. You'll feel better."

"Yeah." Jack took a hit. "Oh yeah. Guess what else."

"Amy's pregnant and you think Kittridge is the father?"

"Wrong. I met this really exotic, brilliant woman from Russia."

"Really? She must be Jewish."

"Why do you think everyone that's brilliant is Jewish?" Jack replied. Goldman shrugged. "I doubt she's Jewish. She doesn't look Jewish."

"And how do Jews look?"

Howard gave Jack and opportunity to needle him about being Jewish. It was mean, but both thought it funny. "Like you,

you know, like Arabs except with bigger noses." Jack laughed.

"Asshole! I don't know why I'm your friend." Howard passed him back the pipe. Jack took another hit.

"Woa, I am getting really stoned. That's enough."

"So tell me about her."

"She's here for a semester."

"Let me guess. She is studying Computer Science. They all come here for computers."

"Nope, Finance. She is in my Risk Management Class."

"Finance? She's in banking? Tell me more."

"Gorgeous body, five feet, eight inches tall, big boobs. Blonde. Brown eyes and so smart. She speaks four languages or something like that. She has a Masters in Mathematics and manages a group of around sixty people at NovoRisk Bank."

"Mathematics? Are you sure she's not Jewish?"

"The Greeks invented Mathematics, not the Jews. Have you heard of NovoRisk?"

"NovoRisk Bank? Never heard of it."

"I think she said it is in the top one hundred banks in Russia."

"So, she's in finance at a bank. Does her voice sound like rubles?"

"No, it doesn't. And she's tough, no shrinking Daisy Faye," Jack said.

"Business in Russia is very corrupt," Howard said.

"What do you mean?" Jack asked naively.

“Corruption in business is the rule in Russia, government officials, school teachers, doctors, even the janitors are on the take. Janitors get bigger bribes than doctors,” Howard said.

“That’s bullshit.”

“Well, I’m not sure about the janitors, but I am sure that to get ahead, you don’t need talent, you need connections and to pay people off.”

Jack shrugged.“She has talent.”

“Yeah, I’ll bet she has talent.”

“Dude, that was uncalled for.”

“Okay, sorry.”

“I am studying with her tomorrow,” Jack said.

“Really. Interesting. Maybe she likes you.”

“Maybe. You should meet her. You could practice your Russian,” Jack said.

“She sounds a lot more interesting than Amy,” Howard said.

“Yeah, and less complicated. But I am sure she is out of my league.”

“Four languages, Masters in Mathematics? Oh, I’d say she’s out of your league,” Howard said.

“Why is it always about brains and education to you? Even Woody Allen thinks the cerebrum is the most over-rated organ. And he’s Jewish.”

Then they sat in stuperous silence, until Jack spoke, “By the way, the professor has the hots for her.”

"The who?"

"Professor. The guy teaching the class," Jack said.

"That's competition. What's his name?" Howard asked.

"Dick Greene."

"Dick Greene?" Howard repeated slowly. "Doctor Dick Greene? Hmmm, Sounds like a venereal disease. Is his dick green? Just asking. Never heard of him."

Jack laughed.

"Tell me more," Howard said.

"He's forty-ish. I think he's divorced. He's overweight. She's twenty-something. He's making a fool of himself."

"Okay, so this isn't competition. Why are you so pissed about Amy if you're scoping this new babe?"

"I don't like sharing my woman, and I don't like looking at that smug Kittridge bastard. He has that knowing, arrogant look. I can't stand the guy."

"Do you ever see Kittridge around campus?"

"No."

"So, if you never see his 'smug look' why do you care?"

"I can imagine it. I can see his smug face in my mind's eye."

"That's ridiculous," Goldman said. Jack was silent. "So this is really about your ego, isn't it?"

"So? You're acting like jealousy is not normal or something," Jack whined.

"Well, it is pretty silly. If Leena wants to fall into bed with you, would you?"

"Of course, so would you."

"Well, perhaps, but my point is, what's good for the gander is good for the goose, isn't it?"

Jack frowned. "So? I am entitled to my feelings."

"Agreed, you're entitled. Let's go run ten miles to get them under control. Then Sushi and Sake."

"Let's go," Jack said.

"Wait, listen to this." Howard flipped his iPod and put on the effete revelry of Mozart's *Prague Symphony*.

Mozart played on in Jack's mind as he sprinted towards the Dish, a huge radar at the summit of a small mountain near the Stanford Campus. His father called it the Field Site Radar. Hundreds jogged to it daily. Jack's sprint up the hill burned up the cortisol and other toxins in his blood, calming him. Upon reaching the top, he slowed to a walk, panting and with his red face slick with sweat. Howard followed minutes behind.

His dad knew all about Radar. He helped the military use them to spy on the Russians during the cold war. His dad would point at the Field Site Radar and say, "That Dish is one hundred fifty feet in diameter." It was as tall as a ten story building and could been seen from the 280 freeway.

He had forgotten about Amy. His focus turned to Leena and Mozart, the Prague. He thought about how he might approach Leena on the study-date. *Spend a lot of time observing and little time flirting. Look for an opportunity, an opening. Make a comment and then observe. Be patient, listen, sample the air for pheromones.*

Professor Greene had assigned *Big Short*, a book about the US Mortgage Crisis in 2008 and 2009. The book made it clear that these 'great financial geniuses' made some incredibly stupid mistakes. Jack wondered how the next financial crisis might occur and whether market regulators could foresee it.

"Dude," Goldman called to him. Usually Goldman beat him by a couple of minutes, but not today. "Dude, what happened? You flew up that hill."

"I feel so much better," Jack said calmly, having burned six hundred calories.

"So Leena is a Russian. Oh boy. Watch out. Russian women are like sexual predators."

"If that's true, then we have something in common," Jack said.

"Yeah, you can talk about sexual predation," Howard said.

"We can prey on each other."

"Yes, the couple who preys together, stays together." Howard added.

"Touché. She's amazing. You will have to meet her."

"Amazing huh? What about Amy?"

"Don't get me on that again. I had just forgotten about her."

"How old?" Howard panted.

"Twenty-five or -six. I don't know."

"Uh-huh, an older woman. Twenty-six and she's already a

director?"

"I'm telling you, she is gifted and talented."

"Yeah, everything you're not," Howard taunted.

"Thanks, asshole. So tell me about corruption in Russia?"

"Right. How do you think she got to where she is?"

"Where? Director? She's got talent."

"Yeah, I bet she has talent."

"What are you implying, schmuck?"

"Nothing, nothing. Just watch out."

"She manages Currency Exchanges and a bunch of other things for the bank. She has to know what she's doing. She deals in billions of dollars a year."

"I think you mean rubles."

"Right, rubles, billions of them. Let's go get some sushi and sake."

Chapter 30 - Studying Risk Management

In spite of massive doses of Saki and ninety minutes of running, Jack's fitful sleep broke into shards of disturbing dream fragments. He dreamt of failure, not with common failure themes, like being naked in public or forgetting to take a final exam. Instead, he dreamt about the Field Site Radar. He had to assemble it.

In the dream, he sat on the ground and studied the massive pieces of the radar. They were like Lego pieces that fit together with girders and bolts, a ladder, metal steps, and the half shell of the 'dish' shaped antenna. He had no idea how he could move things that huge. He tried to lift a bolt the size of his forearm, but couldn't because his hands had become deformed.

Suddenly, Leena appeared. She called to him, waved, and approached. He hid his deformed hands behind his back. "How are you, Mister Hooker?"

He tried to speak, but couldn't. Instead, he responded with grunts, pointing his deformed fingers at things.

She said, "You are stupid, Jack," and then gasped when she noticed his deformed hands. "Jack! What has happened?"

Jack froze; unable to move, unable to speak.

She looked at the radar pieces and said, "It is simple, Jack. The Field Site Radar is one hundred-fifty feet in diameter." She assembled the radar. Once assembled, it spewed forth computer printouts, which Leena read out loud in Russian. Jack couldn't understand a word and wondered whether Howard could translate.

He awoke, relieved it was only a dream. It was around five in the morning. *She's a goddess. A Risk Management goddess. Let's face it, being with her is a fantasy.* Nonetheless, Jack planned to slide a finger into each of her locks, trying to pick them and with luck open one.

He relaxed and tried to sleep again, but couldn't because the image of Amy's naked picture floated to the surface of his mind. Each time he saw it, his heart began to pound. He stared at the ceiling, listening to his throbbing heart which shook the entire bed with each beat. He gave up trying to sleep, rose, drank a quart of water, and then went for a run.

While he ran he plotted his next moves. He knew Leena liked to talk, so he would mostly listen, punctuating her monologue with insights and humor. If she turned the subject to him, he would say only a few words and then wait for her to take over again.

In class, he watched her deflect the advances ofDoctor Greene with agility and grace. She was clearly an expert at managing older men's flirtation. Jack was younger, inexperienced, powerless, and inconsequential. She probably viewed him as someone she could dominate, push around, and discard if he became a pain in the neck.

Jack practiced flirting, considering lines such as, *You're such a brilliant, blah blah blah. No, too intellectual. How about,*

'How do you like being surrounded by men?' And then I could say, 'I bet you love it.' He chuckled. *No, insulting.* Then he came up with, *I love your accent, the way you talk, the way you bend English into your own language. A unique voice all your own. I love watching your face as you speak, it's like a sea of smiles and winks, but far more complex. No, that sounds really stupid.*

He had prepared to study the Big Short about the U.S. Mortgage crisis. How else could he prepare? *My car, make sure it's clean. Dress nicely. Look impeccable. What else? Music. I'll play Mozart in the car. Show her some class.*

As his hunting strategy came together, he began to relax. He passed the rest of the morning at a café with the *Wall Street Journal*, a bottle of cold water, and double espressos.

That morning Leena lingered in bed with her thoughts on this curious, young American man, 'Mister Jack Hooker'. She liked him. She recalled how his face flowed between machismo self-confidence and vulnerable panic; effete sarcasm to outright confusion. His unseasoned youth needed nurturing. *Like a little puppy.* She conjured his muscular physique and imagined touching it. Then she looked at the clock. It was after nine o'clock. She got up and prepared for her study-date with Mister Jack Hooker. She made herself a coffee, curled up onto the sofa in the living room with her laptop, logged in, and found over one hundred emails. Most were from underlings at the bank which she ignored.

The rumble of the Corvette engine soothed Jack, giving him false confidence as he rode down Leena's street. He parked, revved the engine, and then texted Leena, “I’m here.”

She texted back, “I come now.”

In a moment, she appeared, waved, and sashayed towards his Corvette. She wore tight fitting jeans and a tight shirt that showed cleavage.

“Hel-lo, Luv,” he said in mock cockney and opened the car door. “How do you like it?” He asked, referring to his car.

Leena had never been this close to the fabled American Corvette. *A Corvette. I am expecting no less from him.*

“Is it a fast car?” she asked.

“A hundred and fifty miles per hour. Zero to sixty in around four seconds.”

“What is that in kilometers?”

“Don’t know.”

“You can approximate by dividing miles by point six. That is two hundred fifty kilometers per hour,” Leena computed.

“Okay, if you say so. Two hundred fifty kilometers per hour.”He shrugged.

“That is fast, Jack.” She nodded.

“Let’s go. I have a conference room in the library we can study in.” He revved the engine and pulled away slowly.

“I would like to go one hundred fifty miles per hour in your car.” She looked at him like a child asking for candy.

“I had it up to one-twenty on 280.”

“What does it mean, ‘one-twenty on 280’?”

“The 280 freeway. I went a hundred twenty miles per hour

on the 280 freeway. It was early in the morning when there were no cars. We can try it sometime if you like."

"I would like." She nodded her head.

Leena settled into the Corvette. She heard the Mozart. "You like Mozart?"

"I do." Jack hoped to impress.

"I think Mozart is boring." She said. His heart sank.

"Boring? What do you like?"

"I am liking Mick Jagger." She lit a smoke. "Do you have Rolling Stones, Mister Hooker?'And now presenting The Rolling Stones'," she said with feigned English accent.

"I do." He chose his *Hot Rocks* CD. "How about, 'Can't you hear me knocking'?"

Jack turned up the volume and waited until Keith Richard's steaming guitar riffs warmed the Corvette. They drove to the library.

Leena and Jack reviewed *The Big Short* in about two hours and then went for lunch, chatting as they drove. "So you see, Jack, if these Wall Street people at Lehman Brothers, Goldman Sacks, and AIG had been thorough, they would have seen that these, how you say, 'Collateralized Debt Obligations', were worthless long before crisis happened."

"What do you think leads to a situation like that?" Jack asked.

"Incompetence, easy money, greed, arrogance," Leena said.

"But these people are hugely paid."

“How much they make?” Leena asked.

“Many make over ten million dollars a year. Some make billions.”

Leena was astonished. NovoRisk paid her three million Rubles, around ninety thousand dollars. “Ten million dollars?” That was around three hundred million Rubles.

“Yep. I can make one million dollars as a Partner at Deloitte.” He boasted.

“In accounting?”

“You got it. You know, boring old accounting.”

“I would die of boring in accounting.”

“I think you mean boredom. You can make more as an investment banker. But it is very hard work. Very long hours.”

“I never knew you could make this money as banker. How much you think a Risk Manager for big bank makes?”

“Not sure. I’ll bet it’s a lot. Greene would know.”

“Yes. Professor Greene would be knowing this. I wonder why he is not working on Wall Street,” Leena said.

“I’m sure he makes plenty. He probably consults and money isn’t everything.”

Leena stopped talking. She would never see that kind of money in Russia. Russia had a salary cap of around one hundred twenty thousand dollars for any industry that does business with the government, which is practically everyone. She was quiet for the rest of the short trip to the Bistro.

Once seated at the Bistro, Leena and Jack both ordered

espressos. Leena lit up a cigarette.

"Uh, there's no smoking in the restaurant," Jack said.

"What is this problem Americans have with smoking? I think it is rude."

"Well, I guess it comes from smoking causing cancer and second-hand smoke."

"So, if I smoke here everyone will have cancer. Don't be stupid, Jack."

"Well," Jack began to reply just as a waiter approached them.

"Sorry, Miss, you can't smoke in the Bistro. You can sit outside and smoke. May I move you outside?"

"Yes, please," Leena replied. They moved outside.

"It is such an inconvenience," She complained. Jack shrugged his shoulders.

Just after they moved outside, Jack's phone went off. It was Amy. He looked exasperated and ran his fingers through his hair as his face reddened. He ignored the call. Then the phone beeped loudly. Amy had sent him a high priority text that said, "Where's my diaphragm? I can't find it."

He felt like screaming. He slumped in his chair. *That's great. She's really going for it with Kittridge. And she really wants me to know it, too. I can't stand it.*

He texted back, "No idea." She didn't respond. *She's on the pill. Why does she need a diaphragm anyway?*

His face betrayed a lot. "What is the matter with you,

Jack?" Leena asked.

"Nothing." He looked up at Leena.

"Is it your girlfriend?" She taunted.

"I don't know." He paused. "Are you married?"

"No."

"Seeing anyone?" he asked.

"No," She said.

"How come?"

"Well, I have lots of men in my life, but romantically, I am not having one."

"Yeah, I'll bet they are always hitting on you."

"Hitting on you? What this means?" she asked.

"You know, coming on to you. You're so pretty and everything," Jack said.

She had heard the compliment, "so pretty", so many times it had become a nuisance, but hearing it from Jack affected her differently and she was gripped by a demure, girlish feeling. She rocked her head to one side. "You have no idea how hard it is to be taken seriously when you are pretty," She said solemnly and pouted.

"But you are so brilliant. I am sure they are all respectful," Jack flattered and ingratiated.

She looked into his eyes. He blushed and then she blushed back and broke eye contact.

"Being smart makes it worse. They want me more." She sighed over-playing the forlorn, pitiful waif.

"Poor Leena," He consoled. "It must be horrible being desired by everyone."

"It is horrible, Jack" She said dramatically, teary-eyed by the sad burden she bore. She continued, "And they are all old and mostly ugly, but some have power and I have to get along with them. But you know what, Jack? I have learned how to use it." She became the usual confident coquette again.

"Use it?"

"Men's interest in me, to get what I want without compromising my integrity as a lady."

Jack smirked at the expression, 'integrity as a lady'. He mimicked her, "What it means, 'integrity as a lady'?"

She smiled at him and took a long drag on her cigarette. "Oh, you know what I mean, Jack. I mean I do not go sleeping with them."

"Well, I am glad to hear that."

"I am not a whore and besides, sleeping with people you don't care about is like scratching from the inside."

Jack was confused."'Scratching from the inside'? What does that mean?"

She made a silly face and looked at him. "I'm being naughty."

"Oh, I get it. I know what you mean."

"Do you really know what I mean, my dear Mister Jack Hooker?" She gave him a sidelong glance and raised an eyebrow.

"Listen, what are you doing tonight?" he asked.

"Tonight? I am alone and boring tonight."

"Should we do something? Have some fun?"

"I would love to have some fun. It is so boring being away from my friends. What should we do?"

"Let me look into it. I will call you later to make plans. I have some ideas."

Chapter 31 – The Ying and the Yank

"Oh my god!" Jack crooned into his phone grinning as he drove.

"Uh, who is this?" Howard answered his phone with sarcastic bewilderment.

"Unbelievable. We're going out tonight."

"Oh, it's you. I feel boredom starting to set in. So, tell me about the Russian Princess."

"Leena burns with desire."

"Shut up." Howard inflected his incredulity.

"She burns. I could taste her pheromones in the air. They settled on my face, like a mist, like a dew, condensing into small fragrant beads. I drank deeply the dew," Jack waxed.

"Don't you mean dog dew, Shakespeare?" Howard said

"Hey, I resemble that remark."

"There is a striking resemblance. So how'd you do it?"

"Let's face it, I'm a natural," Jack said.

"Right, you're a regular sex god with herpes," Howard said.

"LIAR!" he shouted. "Never say that. Someone might believe you."

"You're right, your only diseases are psychological and probably not contagious anyway. So, what are your plans?"

"Dinner and Jazz. Want to come? A double-date?"

"If she's Russian, she's probably anti-Semitic."

"So, why is that important?" Jack taunted. "And besides, according to you, everyone is anyway."

"Including yourself," Howard said.

"Especially me," he joked.

"Let me check. Rachel?" Howard spoke with Rachel as Jack listened in. "Do we have plans? Nothing? How about dinner and music with Jack and Leena? Who's Leena? A friend of Jack's. What? Jack, she wants to know about Amy."

"Tell her that Amy is going out with The Sex Professor and called asking me where her diaphragm was," Jack answered.

"I can't tell Rachel that."

"Think fast."

Goldman called out to Rachel, "Jack said that Amy is sick and can't join us. Okay." He closed the door to Rachel's room. The conversation became private. "Sounds like we're on for eight. By the way, neither of us will miss Amy. Rachel doesn't like her at all.

On the diaphragm issue, tell me about it."

"She sent me a text asking where her diaphragm is."

"That was Chutzpa," Howard said.

"Chutzpa? It's emotional terrorism. And it was while I was having lunch with Leena," Jack said.

"Wow, what timing. She really knows how to yank a man's chain," Howard said.

"Yank it right off, you mean. I feel completely

emasculated. She's more interested in castrating me than fondling Kittridge," Jack said.

"Well, if she's really looking for birth control, she has plans."

"What's weird about the diaphragm is that she is on the pill," Jack commented.

"Pill?"

"Yeah, you know, the BIRTH CONTROL PILL."

"I know what the pill is, stupid, but why would she want a diaphragm?"

"What do you mean?"

"If she's on the pill, she doesn't need a diaphragm."

"Yeah, I guess that's right. So?"

"So, I swear you have a hole in your head. She's totally bullshitting you. She doesn't need a diaphragm."

"You think she's bullshitting?" Jack asked.

"I'd say."

"Noooooo waaay," Jack purred. His eyes became two slits. "That bitch."

"She's psycho," Howard said.

"You know, in some ways I am relieved, but in other ways I'm disturbed," Jack said.

"She is disturbing," Howard agreed.

"I feel like calling and screaming at her," Jack said.

"I'd stay away. Don't ruin the evening," Goldman advised. "How about Italian Food and then Pasquali's for Jazz."

“We’ll meet you at eight.”

Jack hung up the phone as he pulled into the fraternity. He jumped out of his car and bounded up the steps.

“You’re pretty light on your feet.” It was Bob, the Voice of the Brotherhood of Evil.

“Hi, Bob,” Jack said.

“Check out the bulletin board, Jack. There is something for you there.” Bob smiled, showing his teeth.

A snicker echoed in the hallway. “What do you mean?” Jack asked.

“The bulletin board. Check it out.” Bob smiled mysteriously.

Jack ambled up the stairs to the bulletin board on the second floor and found a printout of Amy’s Facebook page with a new picture of Amy in a bikini. She had also changed her status to ‘available’.

“Gee, Jack, you must feel terrible.” Bob dealt in the abstract currency of social image and loved it when his social enemies suffered.

In spite of the twin shocks of birth control and Facebook, Jack still cared about Amy. He didn’t know why, but he did. Amy’s new breakdown shed light on her problem and the many episodes flashed before Jack. He tried to forget, but couldn’t.

Why injure the one who allegedly matters most?

“Why did you post this?” Jack attacked Bob.

“I didn’t post it,” Bob said.

Jack paused and stared Bob in the eye.

Bob blinked and looked away. "No idea who did? But Amy was here today. Maybe it was her," Bob chirped gleefully.

Jack knew he had to walk away from this emotional battery. He removed the posting, loped to his room, curled up in his bean bag chair and stared out at the dorm across the road. He blinked at the orderly rows and columns of dorm windows spread out against the sky like a waffle iron.

What is wrong with her?

He had no answer. All he knew was that Amy was having her nineteenth nervous breakdown and he wanted nothing to do with it or her.

Chapter 32 - The Dinner

In the early evening, Jack, Leena, Howard, and Rachel met at an Italian restaurant in San Mateo. They sat in a booth listening to Rachel speak while Howard blushed.

"So, it was Howard's first experience teaching at the University and the come-on from all the young girls inflated his head to the size of a house."

"He is pretty arrogant to begin with. No idea why," Jack added.

"Well, he is a pretty nerdy, geeky guy, and this was the first time he had ever had a lot of attention from women. He came home with an implacable smug grin. He bragged about it." Rachel swatted his shoulder. "Such a bad boy. So I suggested that maybe he wanted to date some of them, maybe we should see other people and if he wanted that, he could move out. That shut him up," Rachel said.

"Nice. Putting Howard in his place is beyond my ability. What happened next?" Jack asked.

"He gave me a diamond ring." She leaned over putting her head on his shoulder. "I thought, 'what a nice gift. Maybe I should let him stay for a while.' I took it, thanked him, but didn't say anything more. I let him stew in it for a few days."

"I saw it as a peace offering," Howard quipped.

"Yes, a peace offering, nothing more than that. A nice stone, two carats. An heirloom. His grandmother's or something."

"It was my grandmother's," Howard said.

"That's right. I accepted it and added the ring to my collection and said nothing. The next thing I knew, his mother called. She was so happy that Howard was finally engaged."

Howard offered meekly, "I always intended to marry you."

"Well, I didn't intend to marry you." She kissed him. "As far as I was concerned, we were just living together," Rachel teased. "I don't need a man. I earn a living on my own. I can have a child without a husband and I could keep his family heirloom. What purpose does a man really serve? What do you think, Leena?"

"Oh well, I need a man."

Jack smiled. "At least, we know we're still good for something."

"So, Jack told us you're a big banking executive from Russia. NovoRisk Bank?" Goldman said.

"Yes, I am Director in Bank."

"How many people?"

"I have around sixty." Leena nodded. "It is stressing, but I like it."

"Pay good?" Goldman asked.

Leena hesitated. "It's okay." Leena looked away.

"She reports to the CEO of NovoRisk," Jack added.

"Yes. I am Director and I report to CEO. I work in currency

exchanges and overall Risk Management. He is famous CEO. Dmitri Chesnakov."

"Sounds interesting," Howard said.

"I love it," Leena said.

A waiter interrupted, delivering menus. "Would you like something to drink?"

The waiter looked at Rachel first.

"I'll have a chardonnay."

The waiter scribbled on a pad and then looked at Leena.

"What kind of Russian Vodka are you having here?" Leena asked.

"Russian Vodka? Ah, a girl after my own heart." Goldman commented.

"I can have a vodka, too," Rachel chirped.

"Let's go for it. Four shots. Do you have Moskovkaya?" Jack asked.

"We do."

Howard ordered, "Four shots, chilled." The waiter bowed and disappeared.

"Jack says you met in class," Rachel said.

"Yes, we met in class. Risk Management class."

"They must think a lot of you to send you to Stanford for a semester," Goldman commented.

"Oh, well." Leena waved a hand in the air. "I am being trained as senior executive."

"Groomed," Jack refined her statement. He disliked

‘trained’ for personal reasons.

“Yes, I am grooming for that. It is a big reward to come to America and study.”

“Very impressive,” Rachel complimented. “Reporting to the CEO must be a challenge.”

“Dmitri is okay. You have to know how to handle a big boss like that. I know how.”

“So now you’re free in the USA and you’ve hooked up with Jack Hooker,” Goldman said, smiling.

Her voice became low and gravelly, “Well, I like this young American man, Mister Jack Hooker.” She smiled and put her head on his shoulder. “All the men I know are older, much older. I am tired of these older men,” She purred warmly.

“Like Doctor Green Dick, I mean Dick Green.” Jack chuckled. Rachel cringed at Jack’s crude pun which went right passed Leena.

Leena’s voice returned to its sing-song. “Yes, like Doctor Green, who is flirting to me whenever I am coming in his class,” She emoted. “I don’t like it, Howard.”

“I’ll bet it helps your grade.” Howard grinned.

“Howard!” Rachel batted his shoulder.

“That’s okay, Rachel. So many people think I use my charm to get what I want.” Leena paused and looked into Rachel’s eyes. “And the truth is that I do, all the time. Why not? Everybody does. And I am good at it. Doctor Green is no different. I am actually feeling sorry for him.”

The waiter arrived with the vodka. “A toast.” Goldman raised his glass, as did the others. “*Nostrovia*.”

“*Nostrovia*,” Leena and Rachel followed.

“What it means, *Nostrovia*?” Jack asked, mimicking Leena.

“*L'Chaim*, cheers, bottoms up, *skoal,*” Goldman answered

“Bottoms up. My favorite,” Jack commented and downed his shot.

“*L'Chaim*,” Leena toasted Rachel and Goldman.

“So what about you, Rachael? I know you are living with arrogant genius, Mister Goldman. What you do?” Leena asked.

“I am a therapist. I have a Masters in Psychology and I am doing my clinical training now.”

“You are seeing patients?”

“Yes,” Rachel nodded. “I have for a few years.”

“It is not my area of interest. I like finance, computer models, and mathematics. For me it would be hard to hear people's problems all day long. It would be sad for me.”

“It can be sad. It can be devastating, but I usually help, and that is satisfying. I have a patient now who had a severe trauma. I am helping her recover, ”Rachel explained.

“What was the trauma?” Jack asked.

“She was drugged, kidnapped, raped, and beaten last summer in Europe. She escaped.”

“Oh, that one. Howard mentioned her,” Jack commented.

“American girl?” Leena asked.

“Yes. She provided descriptions of the criminals. Interpol is looking for them."

"That's horrible," Leena said.

"Well, that really improved my appetite," Goldman added. "Everyone ready to order?" They all nodded. "Waiter," he waved to the waiter, who approached the table.

In spite of the somber anecdote, the evening continued with humor. Leena flowed with stories and anecdotes expressed with the mellifluous misuse of English, painting her ideas with gestures, using the ambience of the evening like a canvas.

Goldman feigned the curmudgeon, seasoning the air with peppercorns of black humor. Jack just kicked back and took in the scene of his friends frolicking with their wits and words, which occasionally erupted into hysterical, heartfelt guffaws bringing them all to tears. Personal bonds began taking root.

Leena could not keep her hands away from Jack. She touched his arms, then his legs, and then thighs. She rubbed up against him whenever possible, pressing her braless breasts against him, leaving her scent upon him, like an animal marking terrain. She encouraged him to play, reeling him all the way in and then pushing him away and then reeling him in again. On and off, up and down, over and over.

After dinner, they agreed to meet at Coyote Point before going to the Jazz Club.

Chapter 33 - After Dinner

Jack and Leena drove through the traffic and streets of Palo Alto to the 101 freeway, headed toward San Francisco, and then exited at Coyote Point by San Francisco Bay where the fog muffled the white noise of the Bay Shore freeway. They listened to Jazz and the purr of Jack's Corvette as they drove. Jack parked by a sandy beach, turned off the engine, and opened the windows. The breath of the damp night left wet kisses on their faces. The lights of scattered boats moved quietly through the darkness of the Bay. They could hear a fog horn punctuate the gentle hiss of ripples breaking on the beach. A full moon appeared, disappeared, and reappeared behind islands of clouds floating in the night sky. Leena held Jack's arm. They were slightly drunk and very happy.

Howard and Rachel arrived in Rachel's old diesel Mercedes. Jack jumped out, circumscribed the Corvette and opened Leena's door. As she arose from the car she brushed up against him, wrapped her arms around him, kissed him, broke away, and pranced over to the Mercedes. He followed. They disappeared into the back seat.

"Sooooo, before we go to the Jazz Club, Leena, we thought you may want to smoke a little of this," Goldman held up a pipe.

"It's a tradition. A little pot then a lot of music," Jack added.

“I have never done pot smoking before,” Leena said.

“It’s harmless. You’ll like it,” Goldman assured her.

“Do you smoke too?” Leena asked Rachel.

“Now and then. It’s okay. You don’t have to if you don’t want to.” Goldman handed Rachel the pipe and she took a hit. Then Goldman took a hit. Rachel lowered her window and exhaled outside.

“I only take one hit,” Rachel grinned.

“I can take one hit, too. May I?” Leena asked boldly. Goldman passed her the pipe. She and Jack both took hits. “How long does it take before I am feeling it?”

“A couple of minutes.”

Leena looked at her cell phone. “Okay. It isnine-oh-five.”

They sat in silence waiting for the drug to take hold.

“Feel anything?” Rachel asked.

“Nothing. Do you?”

“Oh yes. It’s starting to sink in. I’m starting to sink in. I’m sinking.” Rachel giggled.

Goldman turned on Miles Davis. “We can groove on this.” He took a second hit. So did Jack.

“I think I need a second hit too.” Leena reached for the pipe.

“Here you are, my dear.” Jack passed her the pipe and lowered his windows.

“How long has it been?” Leena looked at her watch. “Nine-oh-six. What is this music?”

“Miles Davis.”

“He is a famous black trumpet player. There are so many black jazz players in America. I wonder why that is.” Leena checked the time, “Nine-oh-six.”

“I love jazz,” Rachel said wistfully. “Isn’t it nice here? Quiet, cool, deserted.”

“Did we come here on our first date?” Goldman asked.

“We did. It was so long ago.” Rachel trailed off.

Leena looked at her watch. “It is still nine-oh-six.” A faint blinking spot on her phone, counting seconds, captured her attention and she said, “Oh, well. Look at that. I want to see your watch, Jack.”

Jack’s watch came from Spain and had the shape of a Salvador Dali soft clock. Roman Numerals marked the hours on its curved face. She followed the roman numbers and noticed that the four was not IV, but instead IIII. “Oh, Jack look at that. That is wrong.”

“What’s wrong?” Jack asked.

“Your watch. The four is wrong for Roman Numerals. Look.” She showed it to Jack.

Jack looked. “Yeah. I never noticed it before. Do you think it’s a mistake?”

“Let me see,” Howard interrupted. Jack took off his watch and passed it to Howard. “That’s not a mistake at all. Watch makers use IIII instead of IV to make it more readable. Think about four, five, and six in a row, they would be IV V VI. IIII is less confusing."

"Look at the colors of your watch," Leena whispered like a transfixed child.

"I think she is stoned."

"I am stoned?" Leena queried. "I am stoned." She checked her pulse."My heart is beating hard, Jack." She turned white. "I am stoned. Am I going to die?"

"No, you are not going to die."

"I am going to die now." Leena said dramatically.

"Oh, oh. I'll open the windows." Goldman opened Leena's window.

"Hold me, Jack. I am going to die." She leaned against him.

"It's the vodka and the pot together. Do you feel nauseous? You know, I've passed out before after pot."

"Hold onto me Jack. I am afraid." The brave, worldly risk manager melted into his arms.

"I think she's out," Jack said.

"Oh shit. Is she still breathing?" Howard asked.

"Yeah, I think she just fainted." Jack cradled her. He looked at her unconscious face. She no longer looked like an infallible titan of the financial world, but like a young, vulnerable woman who needed his help. He adjusted her body to make her more comfortable and brushed her blonde hair away from her face. He could feel the warmth of her body and the twin rhythms of her heart and breathing.

Goldman turned off the music and opened more windows.

Rachel was terrified. "I'll call nine-one-one."

"No, don't. She'll come to in a minute or so." They waited. Leena's eye lids parted. "Here she is. How are you feeling, Leena?"

"I am still alive? What has happened?" She said in a small, child's voice.

"You passed out for a minute. You're okay now, though. Did you ever pass out before?"

"Well, a little bit, now and then. Sometimes when there is a bad thing or accident." She snuggled into Jack's body. "Hold me, Jack. I am still afraid," she said with her small voice.

"You'll feel better in a while. Then I'll take you home. Okay?"

"Okay," She said feebly. "I still am feeling dizzy. Will I be all right?"

"Shhhhhh." Jack held her and rocked her slightly. "You're going to be fine. We'll go home soon."

"It is not fun to faint, Jack." Leena said tearfully.

"Sorry about that, Leena. I didn't think the pot was going to have that effect on you," Jack said.

"Howard, you always push these things on people," Rachel scolded. "Poor Leena. You'll feel better tomorrow."

"You know what, Rachel? I feel pretty good now," Leena said.

"We should go home anyway," Rachel suggested.

Jack opened the door and jumped out of Howard's car.

"Are you okay to drive?" Rachel asked.

"Yeah, I'm okay. See you guys later."

"See you." Howard started the Mercedes and slowly drove away.

Leena said, "I do not want to go home and being bored at home, Jack. Let's stay here a little bit. It is beautiful, Jack. See the boat lights on the water?"

They stood silently in the cool moisture of the bay air until Leena purred and pulled his lapel toward her. She stared at his lips while she said, "Sooo, Jack, is this place where you are bringing your girlfriends?"

"Well, not really," Jack lied.

"'Well, not really'," She mimicked him. "You are lying to me." Her cat voice dryly expressed skepticism with a touch of humor. She pretended to lose her balance and tipped towards him, pressing up against him. "I don't think pot is good, Jack." She brought her face right up to his. Her lips brushed against his cheek as she turned her head. She rolled to the left out of his arms and looked out at the bay, and then she rolled back, laying her body fully against his, moving her face to within millimeters, looking directly into his eyes, speaking a few sentences, and then rolling away like a yo-yo. She eventually said, "Please take me home now"

He held Leena's hand while leading her to the car. "Come here, beautiful. Let me help you."

"Thank you, Mister Hooker." She wobbled as he held her

hand. “I don’t like this pot,” She repeated. They drove back to her place.

Jack and Leena embraced and kissed at the entrance of her condo complex. She broke the embrace to open her door. “Do you want to come in?” She winked.

“Sure.” Jack didn’t know what to expect. Here was a woman who, about a week ago, treated him like a child and now she was asking him into her place.

The condo was large and well furnished. “Nice place.”

“It is bank’s place. It has three bedrooms and full kitchen, two bathrooms.” Jack compared it to his meager room at Sigma Chi with its peeling wooden floors, worn carpets, and group bathroom. “Go sit.” she pointed to the couch. “Would you like a coffee?”

“No, thanks. How about some water?” Jack asked.

“Good. I am having, too,” Leena replied.

“I’m really sorry about the scare with the marijuana,” Jack apologized.

“Hah, that’s okay. I feel fine now. I had to try it. Thanks for taking care of me.”

“It can be fun. I think it was the drinking and the pot together,” Jack said.

“I think you have satisfied my curiosity. I do not want to try this marijuana again.”

“Okay.”

“Here” She handed him a glass and curled up next to him

on the couch.

"So, why doesn't a girl like you have a man in her life?" he asked.

"That is forward question, Jack." She gasped quietly and raised her eyebrows. "It is none of your business." She leaned over and snuggled, laying her head on his shoulder. "What about you?"

"Why should I tell you? It is also none of your business, either."

"Well, I am sure a tomcat like you, Jack, probably roams from woman to woman like a stray tomcat." She looked at him and then kissed his cheek.

"No, nothing like that."

"I think you are lying to me," She said with a wry crackle and kissed his face again.

"I don't," he began, but she interrupted.

"Stop lying to me." She then gave him a deep kiss on the mouth. "Oh my Gods." She looked startled. "This is my first time to be kissing younger man."

He gently toppled her, pushing her down onto the sofa. He continued to kiss her, becoming passionate. He reached for her breasts, but she pushed his hands away and then sat up, breaking their intimacy. "I am not as easy as your other stray cat women, Mister Jack Hooker Tomcat."

"Okay," he said.

"I mean, Jack, what you think of Leena if you seduced me on first date?"

He shrugged. “I don’t know. Nothing probably.”

“You are lying again.” She looked into his eyes, pouting, almost smirking, moving her head slowly from one side to the other as she spoke, studying his face. She curled up into his arms and laid her head on his chest. They fell asleep.

Jack awoke to the sound of a car idling outside in the street. He checked the clock. It was after three in the morning. The light of the moon painted the room grey and cast a shadow through the French window panes onto the floor. He gently untangled himself from Leena and went into the kitchen for a glass of water. On his way back to Leena, he stopped at the window and looked out at his car below.

All’s well, he thought, but then something moved. Someone dressed in black near his car moved. They held something in their hands and raised it to their face. He opened the windows and yelled, “Hey, what are you doing?” The shape ran down the street and disappeared.

“Jack? You are still here. I have been sleeping.” Leena saw him by the window.

“There is someone down there in the street.”

Leena yawned and rubbed her eyes. “So, it is free country, is it not, Mister Hooker?”

“Yeah, but they were looking at my car.”

“It is a nice car. People like to look at it.”

“Yeah, but it’s after three o’clock in the morning. What are they doing?” They heard a car start and pull away. It was out of view. "I think I should go."

As Jack drove back to Sigma Chi, the images of the evening replayed in his mind and he smiled reflexively. In spite of Leena's overdose, the evening had been a success. Leena had morphed from critical, hard-boiled business woman into a fun loving, affectionate pussy cat.

It was around four o'clock when he turned down the last stretch of road in front of his fraternity. The street lights cast shadows on the sleeping neighborhood as he idled quietly down the street, looking for a parking spot when he saw Amy's car near the fraternity. *Oh shit. What is she doing here?* He could see her in the driver's seat. *She's asleep.*

He turned off the lights of the Corvette as he putted past her car and the parked. He exited his car and quietly shut the door. *Was she the one looking at my car at Leena's apartment?*

He tip-toed up the steps of the frat house when suddenly the lights of her car flashed on and shined on him. *Caught!* Amy glared at him from her car. She started the engine and sped away.

Chapter 34 – Beer Party

The big social event of the next weekend was the Sigma Chi Heidelberg party, whose Teutonic theme focused on beers, sausages, and sauerkraut. It had quaint rituals designed to humiliate the new pledges. One of which required they wear Lederhosen and Bavarian hats. They looked ridiculous.

The fraternity brothers transformed the Main Hall into a *Hofbrau* by covering the walls with faux dark wood paneling and posters depicting meaty beer meisters with crew cuts, burley beards, and rubber aprons toiling away in the shadows of the brewery, loyally tending to their craft. To some, they were sacred, but to Jack the burley, red-faced beer meisters with their thick lips and stubbly scalps looked disgusting.

The music was mostly rock 'n roll, but now and then someone tossed in a Bavarian drinking song like *Ein Prosit* or *The Ketchup Song*, whose lumbering oom-pah-pah perfectly accompanied the beer and greasy German sausage. The Heidelberg party aligned with Oktoberfest, which made sense, but the rest of the idea struck Jack as queer and he felt really uncomfortable around Lederhosen. He wanted to avoid the gawking crowd, but Leena's relentless curiosity required they go.

Before the party, Jack and Leena met Goldman and Rachel for dinner at a small café on University Avenue in Palo Alto. They arrived to find Rachel and Goldman studying menus. After Jack and Goldman greeted each other with the usual friendly innuendoes, Howard returned to the wine menu.

"You should see the wine list. You know, wine is my real drug of choice. It's nirvana in a bottle. Listen to this, *Pinot Noir:* 'Notes of black cherry and worn leather explodes on the nose.' I guess that's better than exploding in the nose."

"Worn leather?" Jack said.

"Yeah, I know. Sounds sort of kinky. Anyway, here's more, 'This is followed by hints of parsley, sage, rosemary, and thyme'."

"That's Simon and Garfunkel. I don't believe you," Rachel said.

"Okay, I made that up, but it goes on to say, 'The wine teases you at the finish with a burst of fruit and distinctive flavors of earth.' Ummmm, flavors of the earth?"

"Sounds like drinking dirt," Rachel said.

"I think I am preferring vodka, Howard," Leena said.

"Me too. A round?" Jack added. The four friends ordered drinks and food and then settled into the comfortable rhythm of friendly conversation. They discussed the events of the week, Leena's impression of America, and the tragic lore of Goldman's family in the chaotic and violent Great Bear, Russia.

"These are not the only tragedies in Russia, Howard. My mother was orphan because of World War Two. The Battle of Stalingrad." Leena solemnly nodded as she spoke, then sighed and changed the subject. "How is your patient? This raped woman?"

"Oh, good. On to merrier topics," Goldman cracked.

"I want to know more. It is such a horrible experience. How it happened?" Leena asked.

"It is quite a story," Rachael began. "She said she was partying at a club on the Greek Island of Mykonos with her friend and someone they met that day. She thinks he slipped something into her drink. The last thing she remembers is the club and then coming to, naked and shackled in a dark cell on a boat. Shortly after that the assaults began."

"That makes my blood boil. I would love to kill those deranged perverts," Jack spat.

"I don't think you would have much of a chance. There were five or six of them. She told the story to Interpol. Most wore masks, but she saw two of them. The guy who raped her and another guy. They spoke Russian. The police have made composite sketches of them."

"We have the sketches at home," Goldman said.

"So, she was on this boat, naked and shackled, beaten and raped, but now she is here? How did she get away?" Jack asked.

"Eventually, the boat made landfall. She and the other girls were given tunics and hoods. The women were handcuffed, except my patient, whose hands they tied because they were short one set of cuffs.

"They herded the women into the back of a panel truck. A guard sat with them in the back. The truck bounced and swayed, throwing them into the air. After a while, the guard couldn't take it anymore and banged on the cab of the truck. The driver stopped and he left the back.

"After he left, she worked on the ropes that bound her wrists, freed her hands and pulled off the hood. She removed the hoods of the others so they could breathe more easily and worked on their handcuffs, to no avail. When the truck hit a particularly large set of bumps, she used the rattling truck to cover the sound of her escape by kicking open the panel truck back door and jumping out.

The waiter arrived with the food, interrupting the story. "Vegetable Lasagna?"

Leena nodded.

"Pumpkin Ravioli?"

"Mine." Rachel reached for the dish.

The waiter served Jack and Howard, and then asked, "More bread? Anything else to drink?"

"No, thanks," Howard said. The waiter nodded and disappeared.

"So, then what?" Leena asked.

"She found herself in a barren desert on a dirt road in the pink light of dawn. She hid behind rocks until the truck disappeared in the distance. She walked along the road for hours, passing no one until she came to a small village with a Mosque. The town was called Lmoussaten. The clerics and people of the Mosque came to her aid. She said the people were good and that she was now safe in this small, remote village in Morocco.

"When the villagers heard about the kidnappings, rape, and torture they were horrified. One of the men swore he would find the criminals and kill them. Several of the town elders accompanied her all the way to the US Embassy in Rabat, hundreds of miles to the east. From there, she found her way home. Her recovery will take years. The other women were never found."

"Good God!" Jack exclaimed. "That was harrowing just to hear about."

Goldman said, "How about something a little lighter? Jack tells me you want to observe the rituals of the American Fat People, I mean Frat People. I didn't know you had an interest in cultural anthropology."

"I am curious, Howard," Leena said with her low, gravelly voice.

"It's a jungle. Be prepared," Goldman warned.

"I have Jack to protect me. I am not afraid." She snuggled up against him.

"The party started an hour ago. Maybe we should go," Jack said. Leena nodded and Jack flagged down the waiter.

Howard raised a glass. "One final toast, From Here to Fraternity."

Jack made a sour face. "That's just stupid, Howard."

"Punnus envy strikes again," Howard said.

"What it is, 'punnus envy'?" Leena asked.

"A form of Turret's Syndrome that makes him say stupid

puns. There is no cure."

Chapter 35 - Frat Party

Jack and Leena found themselves standing at the foot of the Sigma Chi steps which led from the street up to the landing by the front door. Leena looked at the brightly lit frat house and felt a twinge of pathos as she noticed its peeling paint, chipped slate roof, chimneys missing bricks, and gutters stuffed with dead leaves. A soggy,wet banner with a beer stein and Bavarian hat hung limply from a third floor window advertising the party. A group of people gathered on the landing to take in the night air. Jack's friend, Greg, and his blonde Swedish girlfriend, Anya, were among them.

"Captain Hook." Greg saluted with his left hand.

Jack ambled up the steps, hands in pockets. "Hi, Anya, Greg. This is Leena."

The four exchanged pleasantries and chatted until Greg led them into the Frat. He gave Jack a side-long look as they walked through the front door. "This place is buzzing with news about you and Amy."

They cruised through the living room towards the bar when Jack saw Susan and Ben. He waved, but they glared at him and then turned their backs. *I know whose side they're on.*

Then Jack spotted Bob, the spokesperson for the Brotherhood of Evil, who wore a fedora tilted at an angle. He stood on the lip of the fireplace, pontificating to a small group of men who wore lederhosen. While Bob spoke his eyes followed Jack, Leena, Greg, and Anya. *Who is that with Jack?*

Jack glanced at Bob, whose shiny face sparkled in the dim light of the living room. *Is he really wearing glitter and makeup? Ugh!*

The four entered the main hall, got drinks, and huddled together while Leena studied the beer posters on the walls and the men dressed in Lederhosen.

Bob approached with a big friendly smile, as though he and Jack were good friends. "Hey Jack." He gave Jack a friendly slap on the back. An invisible cloud of after-shave lotion followed him, perfuming the air. "Where've you been? We've been rolling along here for hours." He gave Leena an incredulous look and asked, "Where's Amy?"

They all looked at Jack and waited for a reply.

"No idea. Uh, haven't seen her around lately."

"You haven't seen her tonight?" Bob sounded skeptical. He turned to Leena. "So who is this? I expected to see you and Amy."

Jack cleared his voice and said, "This is Leena. She's from Russia. Studying finance."

"Pleasing to meet you, Bob. Yes, I am here for one semester. I am executive at NovoRisk Bank in Russia." She noticed the glitter and a smudge of makeup that covered a blemish on Bob's face. "What is this on your face? You are wearing makeup, Bob. I have never been seeing this before. A man is wearing makeup. In Russian, men do not wear makeup. Why you wear this, Bob?"

Jack answered, "Bob has a vanity issue, I guess."

"Well, Bob, you are very pretty tonight. Do you have date here, Bob? I would like to meet if you have date."

Bob was stunned and could only shake his head no.

"No date?" Leena said.

"Bob never has a date. Not sure why." He grinned at Bob, "In fact, no one is quite sure why. Why is that, Bob?" Jack asked.

"Nice to meet you," Bob muttered and retreated.

"Touché. I really can't stand that guy," Greg said.

"He is a gay man," Leena said

"Nope, he's real homophobic. A real right wing Republican type," Greg said.

"What is homophobic?" Leena asked.

"Someone who hates gay people," Jack said.

"Oh, well," Leena opined, dismissing Greg's statement with a wave of her hand. "These are the, how you say, the hiding gay people."

"We say, 'closet gay'. It's possible, I guess," Jack said.

"It is simple, Jack. These closet gay people who are hating themselves." She paused, sipped her drink and then continued, "And they are saying these bad things about gays to hide, so that are seeming normal. You know what I mean? I do not like Bob."

"Well, Jack, my friend. I will leave you to fend for yourself with this gorgeous, witty woman. Somehow, I think you will survive the evening."

Greg and Anya moved on. When Greg and Anya were out of earshot, Leena turned to Jack. "Who is Amy?"

Jack blushed. "Uh, well she's—" Before he could finish someone tapped him on the shoulder. It was Ben, the ugly dwarf.

"Jack, what's all this about you and Amy? Is she really seeing other guys?"

"Other guys? No idea. I haven't seen her in over a week."

"She's seeing Kittridge. That's what's going on," Ben tried to provoke a response.

Jack didn't care what Amy did anymore. "Good for her. I wish her well."

It was obvious to Leena that her man was under attack from this short, ugly man and she impulsively came to his aid. "For a tall, good-looking man like Mister Hooker, there are many fish in the sea." Leena grabbed Jack's hand and looked downward at the shorter Ben, making Ben feel small. Leena continued, "I'm sure you don't know what I mean."

Ben lurched backwards and glared upwards at the tall, impudent beauty. He tried to formulate a comeback, but couldn't.

Leena continued, "I think you have this, how you say it, Napoleon problem. You need to insult taller, better looking man. I am feeling sorry for you."

He fled.

She watched Ben retreat and then gripped Jack's arm possessively. "Sooooooo, who is this Amy who you forgot to say to me?" She rubbed up against him and raised an eyebrow.

Jack's smile evaporated. "Amy, um, well, I don't know her that well, or maybe just a short time, uh, well, she has a horse, uh, she's in a sorority. She has some problems, I guess."

"You are lying to me. Why you are hiding this Amy woman from me, Mister Hooker?" she said and watched him squirm. "Maybe you think Leena is jealous. I am flattered you are thinking this Amy make me jealous." She rubbed up against him.

Her words melted him while his libido lurched upward. He turned toward her, stepped forward, put his arms around her and pulled her into him. He put his forehead up against hers and stared into her eyes. "There is no Amy. There is only Leena."

Suddenly, Amy was standing in front of them. "Who is this woman?" Amy demanded loudly. People standing nearby stopped talking and watched. "I said, WHO IS THIS WOMAN?" She shouted and stamped a foot on the linoleum floor.

Quiet spread across the Main Hall as people stopped chatting and turned towards Jack, Leena, and Amy. Soon the only sound was the ridiculous Om-Pah-Pah of a lumbering polka. Jack began to sweat. He scanned the room and saw Ben and Susan sneering from the safety of the gawking crowd. He saw Bob in his fedora baring his teeth with a smile.

While Jack cringed with humiliation, Leena recognized the absurdity of the melodrama and appeared relaxed and amused.

Without warning, Amy threw a pint beer at Jack who, frozen with embarrassment, lacked the wherewithal to step out of the way of the beer. The beer hit him with a splash, drenching him. Leena calmly stepped aside.

"I HATE YOU!" Amy yelled and then threw her beer stein at Jack, who ducked. She stomped out of the fraternity, head held high as though she had won, although what she had won or lost was unclear.

The crowd stared at Jack and Leena in shock. Leena lit a cigarette and exhaled at the crowd. Leena and Jack looked at each other and began to laugh.

Jack then summoned his wits, smacked his lips as though tasting something and said, "A Pilsner, one of my favorites." Some of the on-lookers sneered, but most applauded.

"That was Amy," Jack said to Leena.

"She is crazy," Leena said.

"You noticed."

"I am hoping she is not dangerous," Leena said.

"Not at all, and now she is gone."

Jack pulled the soaking wet shirt away from his chest. "I have to go upstairs."

"I am coming with you, Jack. You cannot leaving me here with these wild animals."

"I wouldn't think of it." He leaned towards her and gave her a long kiss, careful not to soil her with his beer-drenched shirt. When their kiss broke they realized that the crowd was still watching.

Embarrassed, Jack initially covered his face with his hands.

Think fast. He slid his hands from his face to his chest, looked at the crowd and then said, “The show is over.” He grabbed a beer and held it over his head. “Bottoms Up.” Members of the crowd toasted Jack and Leena, “*Skoal*, cheers, salute.” Jack took Leena by the hand and led her out away from the crowd.

Chapter 36 - Post Frat Party

Jack settled Leena into the bean bag chair on the floor of his room and then put *The Girl from Ipanema* on the stereo.

"I'll be back." he said and then left for the shower with a towel and bathrobe.

Leena relaxed for a few minutes, and then rose from the chair to explore his room. Jack's dark wood pedestal desk and office chair on casters faced the window with a view of a dormitory a block or two away.

Across from the window was his closet behind closed sliding doors with full length mirrors. His king size bed ran parallel to the window and between the desk and closet. His bean bag chair sat in the six feet of space between the foot of the bed and the bookcase that stood by the fourth wall.

She found a book of pictures on a bookshelf. She couldn't resist her impulse to find pictures of the crazy Amy woman, so she took it down, sat down in the bean bag chair, and opened it. There were several pictures of Jack, a couple with his Frat Brothers at various social events, a picture of Jack in a track & field uniform holding a trophy, pictures of Jack skiing with friends, one of him standing on a dock holding up a big, ugly fish, and several of Amy. A twinge of jealousy surprised her. *What the hell do I care if Jack keeps a picture of this Amy?* She left the chair and continued looking through his things, leaving the book on his desk. She began to sway and hum with the music on the stereo as she meandered around his room.

Jack returned in a white terry cloth robe. He opened the closet and threw his beer-drenched clothing into a hamper. “Like the music?” he asked. She nodded. He crossed the room, took her in his arms and moved his head to kiss her, but she turned her head.

“I am seeing this Amy woman in your pictures,” Leena said and nodded towards the book.

“It’s over. She is an old girlfriend. She’s having trouble letting go, that’s all.” He felt a twinge of pathos for Amy as he spoke. He let his arms drop.

They stared into each other’s eyes, studied each other’s faces for several minutes until she leaned forward and planted her lips on his for a long kiss. Soon, his desire for her made a tent out of his robe, prodding her abdomen. She stepped back, put her hands on her cheeks and pretended to be alarmed and confused. “Huh?” she inhaled with false alarm. “What is that?” She pointed at his waist. “You are injured! I have injured you!”

He gave her a sly look and said, “I am sure you know the appropriate therapy for a man with my condition.”

She blushed. He took her hand and led her to the bed.

Hours later while Jack dozed, Leena lay awake looking at the shiny face of his uncorrupted youth and puzzled over her attraction to him. In Russia, power was her aphrodisiac and like her mother, she felt no guilt about being with men who had power and could afford her favors, but in America, her instincts had changed. Jack really had nothing; no power, no wealth. Although making love to a virile twenty-two-year-old with taut young skin, firm muscles, and huge stamina was a revelation. Her feelings went beyond physical attraction.

What is it about him? He is like a dog, a stray dog. She could nurture Jack, like a pet, like a Borzoi. Her desire to cuddle, kiss, and coo little love messages in his ear possessed her. She wanted to rub her face on his, to drag her lips across his smooth cheek, press her forehead up against his, and blink into his eyes. She slowly drifted off to asleep.

A loud knock on Jack's door startled him out of his sleep. He checked the clock: three-fifty-two. He glanced at Leena, who was undisturbed. He assumed the knock was the usual childish bullshit and so rolled over to go back to sleep, but then he heard a nearly unnoticeable sound come from the door, like a mouse scampering across the floor. The disturbance made him angry.

What the fuck is that? He heard footsteps in the hallway. He sat up and saw that something had been slipped under the door. He slid out of the bed, careful not disturb Leena, and tipped-toed to the door. Then he heard the front door of the Sigma Chi gently shut. *Is that the same guy who knocked?*

He found an eight by eleven inch manila envelope. *The Brotherhood of Evil strikes? Something to embarrass me? A picture of Amy throwing beer on me or maybe something worse?*

Years ago, the Brotherhood had posted photos on the bulletin board of Jack drunken, out cold, and naked on a lounge chair at a pool at a Palms Springs hotel. Hotel security arrested him for being drunk and naked in public. He believed Bob had called the security. After he sobered up, he apologized and the Hotel let him go. *Could it be those photos?*

Whatever it was, he knew he needed to hide it. *In the bookcase, between books.*

He began to tip-toe across the creaking hardwood floors when he heard Leena's melodious voice say, "What you are doing, Jack?" She sat up in the bed, holding a bundle of blankets about her nude body. She knew she had caught him doing something. What he was doing mattered little. She would use it as an excuse to play with her tomcat.

"Oh, nothing," he said and hid the envelope behind his back.

"What is that you are hiding from Leena?" Her voice descended from high notes to a low gravel as she spoke.

"It's nothing, really."

"You are lying to me, Jack" she teased, inflecting her voice to scold. He stood in front of her, naked, exposed, looking guilty. "What are you hiding from Leena?"

"Nothing. Really, it's nothing at all."

"If it is nothing, then you will show Leena." she held out her hand.

His face changed from an embarrassed apple-faced, frat

boy to a man taking charge, or at least that of a man experimenting with the notion of taking charge of the situation. “It is none of your business.” He emphasized each word, as though offended that she would even ask. He continued his long journey across the creaking hardwood floor to put the envelope away.

Leena raised her eyebrows. His defiance made her proud. She threw away the blankets, exposed her luscious body and studied his growing arousal. “Does my Tomcat want to make love to Leena?” she asked coyly and wiggled.

Jack dove into bed burying himself in her. Afterwards they slept.

Leena started awake and checked Jack’s clock. It was after nine o’clock. She had a lot to do and had to leave. She slipped out of bed, dressed, called a cab, and then gently rocked him until he woke up. His blinking brown eyes looked upward. “Hi,” he said. He smiled and sat up.

Leena looked at him with a tight-lipped crooked grin and spoke using her low crackling voice, “I have to go, Mister Hooker. Thank you for a very nice evening.” Her prompt and formal goodbye trampled his budding feelings of love. His lips relaxed into a pout; his eyes became watery and wide.

His startled disappointment touched her and her crooked grin became a smile. “What an interesting world, this fraternity is. Do woman usually throw drinks at you?” Her eyes twinkled with mirth.

His feelings changed; perhaps Leena wasn’t brushing him

off. "Not usually." He rolled his eyes to one side as though hiding something.

She raised a knowing eyebrow and stared directly into his eyes. "You must have quite an effect on women, Mister Hooker."

Something took hold of his voice as he spoke, "Well, Leena, I suspect you know all about the effect I have on women." *Touché,* he thought

Her face broke into a radiant smile. "I will call you later, Mister Hooker. *Ciao*." She left.

A minute later, he heard the front door open and shut. He rose from the bed and watched her from the window as she waited by the curb for the cab. He continued to watch her until she disappeared into a cab and left. He wandered blindly back to his bed, falling into the vacuum she had left. The warmth of her body and mild scent lingered on his sheets, which he pulled taught around his body, closed his eyes, and brought her into his mind, seeing her, hearing her speak, feeling her warmth while conjuring the intangible aspects of Leena. She had captured his very soul, molded it in her hands like clay, and, to his desperation, didn't fully realize it, didn't seem to care, and couldn't possibly feel the same way. He felt like a plaything that could be discarded at anytime. She didn't even look back at the fraternity while she waited for the cab. He pulled the sheets over his head. "Oh my God, oh my God, oh my God."

A chatter of voices from the downstairs at Sigma Chi brought him out of his love sick coma. He recalled the envelope that had been slipped under his door, bounded over to the bookcase, took the envelope in his hands, and carefully opened it, dumping the contents onto his bed. There were several snapshots, a sequence of images of an abdomen and a brown pubic triangle he knew too well as Amy's.

The first showed her abdomen, pubic area and a razor blade, the second showed the blade opening a slit just above her triangle, and the last showed a completed cut, streams of blood running downward. The last had written on the back, "See what you made me do."

He felt ill. His mind fell into a torrent of thought fragments. *She's violent. She mutilated herself. What if she stalks me? What about Leena? Would she attack us? Should I call the police? Should I call her father? I need to talk with Rachel and Goldman. Yeah, Rachel's a therapist. I'll call them later. This is so gross I can't believe it.*

Chapter 37 - After Glow Spoiled

While she rode home in the cab, Leena pondered the newly opened niche in her emotional landscape that Jack filled so well. She immediately desired his company again; to snuggle and hug. He was so different from the other men she had known: closer in age, younger, inexperienced, and vulnerable like a pet. In Russia, she had been drawn to powerful men romantically, but these relationships were cold and sterile. Jack was touchy, warm, fuzzy, and mammalian. Her feelings for him enveloped her, dazing her.

She arrived home and hurried upstairs for a shower. Afterwards, she wrapped herself in a towel, made an espresso, and settled on the living room sofa with her laptop to check email. She ignored most of them, but there was one she couldn't ignore. It was from Dmitri.

The email erased her warm fuzzy mood, replacing it with resentment over Dmitri interrupting her life. She looked away from the email and stared blindly across the living room while Dmitri's image floated in her mind. The pockmark on his nose that never bothered her before bothered her now. She noticed his jowls, hanging slightly below the corners of his mouth, limp and moist. They jiggled when he laughed.

Her mouth turned into a curled frown and her lips moved as she mumbled to herself. Her mind slipped backwards in time towards the early days with Dmitri.

Their romance exploded with spasms of passion. They were swept away by a tsunami of meetings, conferences, lavish dining, yachting on the Black Sea, and skiing in Sochi. She joined his coterie of friends, executives, and their mistresses, with whom she partied regularly. Together, they conducted business with a frolic and fury. Life was a continuous thrill.

Dmitri escorted Leena through the madness and chaos on his arm, providing mentorship, opportunities to learn the hard numbers of banking, and how to navigate the world of senior executives. She was fascinated.

They had a huge passion that was expressed frequently, perhaps even too frequently. Often in inconvenient places like parking lots and closets in offices, as well as in the comfortable settings of luxury hotels or Dmitri's dacha on the Yauza river, northeast of Moscow.

She had fond memories of the two-story dacha. It was rustic, had no electricity, was lit by kerosene lanterns, and heated by a wood burning stove and fireplace. It had a sauna in a separate structure from the main house where they basked naked in the heat, occasionally dousing the hot stones with water, which hissed and became steam. Dmitri plucked slender birch branches in the forest, which he tied into small bundles. They dipped the birch into a bucket of water and then set them on the stones where they sizzled, adding their fragrance to the cedar of the sauna. Dmitri then gently whipped Leena's back, shoulders, buttocks, and thighs until they became pink and redolent with birch.

They drank beer and baked in the sauna until their bodies were slick with sweat that formed beads which streamed down their bodies. When they could no longer bear the heat, they would dash to a freezing pond and plunge in, shocking their burning skin. The cold water pulled the heat from their bodies, cooling them until they were ready to return.

Dmitri led her in the bedroom, directing her with non-verbal cues, like pushing downward on her naked shoulders until she sank to her knees and then guiding her head towards the object of his desire. His command over her excited her and she allowed it to develop into lurid speech and elaborate, almost ritualistic sexual acts.

She rose from the couch and ambled into the kitchen for a third espresso. “Oh shits, the machine is off.” She powered on the machine and waited while the water heated. As she waited, she leaned against the counter over the sink and stared out at the street below. Her first introduction to Dmitri began to replay in her mind.

Leena and Dmitri had met at the NovoRisk Executive Christmas Party nearly two years earlier. Dmitri rescued her from her foul, drunken date, Alexi Andreovich, the scrupulous, but repulsive head of finance. She spent the rest of the party by Dmitri’s side. At the end of the evening, he thanked her for her company and summoned a driver to take her home, but that wasn’t the last she would hear from Dmitri.

The following Monday as she sorted through email, she

found an invitation to the weekly executive briefing that took place Monday afternoons. It was Dmitri's meeting. His administrator sent the invite. Nearly all of the invitees were senior bank executives, most of whom she had never met.

Oh my God. I am not ready for this. Her immediate supervisor, Jacov, wasn't invited; neither was his boss. She worried that this would make them jealous. *What am I supposed to do in this meeting?* She began to panic.

She called her friend, Tatiana, who managed a group of programmers in the IT department. "Tatiana?"

"Hi, Leena. I was just thinking about you. How was being the CEO's escort at the Christmas party?"

"It was strange." Leena recalled the vaulted walls of the Ballroom at Mindovsky House and how the crowd parted before them as they walked.

"Everyone noticed you. I'm sure there are some very jealous women around the bank now."

"I am not worried about that, but he invited me to the weekly executive briefing. It's this afternoon!"

"Oh my God! He must want to take a closer look at you, Leena."

"What? Why?"

"He's interested in you," Tatiana said.

"I'm scared to death."

"I would be, too."

"What should I do?"

“Well, I think you should go,” Tatiana said.

“Of course, I’m going to go. That’s not what I mean. I mean at the meeting, what should I do at the meeting?” Leena asked.

“I don’t know. I’ve never been to a meeting like that. I know. Don’t speak unless you are spoken to,” Tatiana said.

“What if they ask me something and I don’t know the answer?” Leena fretted.

“What do you normally say?” Tatiana asked.

“I say that I will look into it and get back to them later,” Leena said.

“That sounds good. Say something like that,” Tatiana said.

“I am so scared,” Leena said.

“If the CEO invited you, I think he is responsible for making you feel comfortable,” Tatiana said.

“Well, I don’t feel comfortable. What about the other executives?” Leena said.

“They will all have their knives out. Be careful,” Tatiana said.

“Alexi will be there. I’m sure he hates me now,” Leena said.

“I’m sure he doesn’t hate you. If anything, he’s angry at Dmitri Chesnakov.”

“He can be rude to me or put me on the spot in the meeting,” Leena said.

“Oh, he wouldn’t dare, not with Dmitri there. You are

under his protection. You really have nothing to worry about. Just don't do anything stupid. Keep your mouth shut. If anything, it could be an opportunity," Tatiana said.

"Should I tell Jacov?" Leena asked.

"Who is Jacov?"

"My boss," Leena said.

"Oh, I wouldn't mention it. That would just complicate things. Let him find out later. How are you dressed?"

Leena looked at her short skirt, boots and red blouse. "Like I normally do."

"You better change. When is the meeting?"

"Three o'clock. And my hair is horrible."

"Go buy something appropriate, something conservative. Get your hair done. Don't be cute or sexy. Be dignified and strong. Be confident."

She slipped out of the office and went to the mall for more suitable attire.

At two-thirty she returned dressed in black slacks, a black jacket, and white blouse. Her hair was neatly coiffed. She visited Tatiana on the third floor, where she found her sitting with a programmer staring into a computer screen.

Tatiana said, "One second, Leena." She quickly finished with the programmer, who then left her cubicle.

Once alone, Leena said, "What do you think?" She faced Tatiana and posed, turned, posed again.

"Very nice. Professional, mature, cute, almost too perfect."

Tatiana stood up and adjusted Leena's collar. "When's the meeting?"

"In twenty minutes," Leena said breathlessly.

"I think you're ready. Now calm down. You're as white as a ghost."

"I'm going now. Ciao."

Leena arrived five minutes early. The meeting was on the fifteenth floor in a conference room overlooking the Moskva River in the Tagansky district of Moscow. It had a glass wall facing cubicles that filled the floor. In the center was a table that ran the length of the room, large enough to seat fifty.

A nicely dressed woman in her fifties greeted her warmly, "You must be Leena Kiraskaya. I am Dmitri's administrator. Welcome. You should sit here," she gestured towards a chair near the head of the table.

Soon the others began to arrive, mostly men in their fifties and sixties—grey, flabby, wearing suits, some in pairs chatting, others alone and silent. There was a young brunette woman in her mid-thirties with shoulder-length hair wearing a black skirt, white blouse, black jacket, a string of pearls, and an Erte pin of Venus. She cast a long look at Leena before sitting near the head of the table. Leena had never seen her before.

Alexi Andreovich arrived and froze when he saw Leena. His mouth gaped open, his lips shiny with drool. He took a seat at the far end of the room, away from Leena, ignored her, and spoke with another executive. Leena's pulse quickened, she began to perspire, and her hands were like ice.

One older gentleman sat next to Leena and introduced himself, “I am Vlady Roshenko. I am the Chief Risk Officer for the bank.” Vlady was a rolly-polly, jolly man in his early sixties. He projected warmth and friendship and she sensed he was a father and a grandfather. She relaxed a little.

“How do you do? I am Leena Kiraskaya. I am in Risk Management.”

He seemed to already know who she was. He then leaned towards her and quietly asked a curious question, “Has anyone said anything to you yet?”

Said something to me? She turned pale and felt dizzy, but managed to reply coherently, “No one has said a thing.” She was afraid to ask about what.

Dmitri Chesnakov arrived and sat near between Leena and the brunette at the head of the table. Dmitri was tall, handsome, older, but fit looking. He had brown hair with grey at his temples. He dressed immaculately in a blue pinstripe suit.

The brunette leaned towards him and whispered something underneath her breath while he watched the room with piercing brown eyes. Slowly, the murmur of conversations trailed off. He then leaned forward and opened the meeting. “Okay, let’s start with an update from Karina on the Kiev Data Center consolidation.”

“It is going well, everything on track and within budget,” she said. NovoRisk had acquired three Ukrainian banks and was in the process of consolidating them, operationally, financially, and eliminating personnel. The consolidation included building a local datacenter for all of the banks.

Katrina continued, "This weekend we are moving the online banking systems. The cutover to the new system is planned for one o'clock Saturday morning. The details of the plan can be reviewed online."

"Thanks, Karina. Vlady, what's new in world of Risk Management?"

"Syrian Refugees in Turkey."

"Okay, so?"

"Hundreds of thousands of Syrian refugees have fled the civil war there and they are destabilizing some key countries where we do business, like Turkey. We have currency and bond holdings in Turkish Lira. The Lira has dropped two percent relative to basket of currencies last week and things are getting worse."

"What do you intend to do about it?" Dmitri asked.

"We are still formulating a plan", Vlady said.

"How large are our holdings?" Dmitri asked.

"Around two billion Lira."

"I want a plan in the morning," Dmitri said. "Leena, work with Vlady on the Turkish Lira plan."

"All right, who's next? Alexi, what's new in Finance?"

While Alexi droned on expounding on the tedious, but important financial details of the bank, Leena's mind began to wander. Dmitri sat quietly, lips pursed, tapping a finger on the table as he listened to Alexi. She gave Dmitri a furtive, side-long glance. No one noticed, so she gave him a second glance which was followed by a long look. He was older, but his skin was taught, his body fit, and handsome.

As the meeting broke up, Dmitri asked Vlady and Leena to stay behind. The brunette woman sitting next to Dmitri also stayed. She glared at Leena until Dmitri said, "Georgia, please," and nodded towards the door.

She left in a huff, humiliated.

"Leena, you will now report directly to me. You will attend this meeting each week. You will work with Vlady in Risk Management. Do you understand?"

"Yes, Mister Chesnakov."

"Call me Dmitri."

"Yes, Dmitri."

Dmitri left Leena to work with Vlady.

Vlady smiled warmly at Leena and patted her on the shoulder. "Leena, I look forward to working with you. It will be fun."

Leena felt safe with the paternalistic grey-haired man. She looked into his face, to find him looking back with twinkling blue-grey eyes.

"We have a lot to do. We will start now. Follow me. We will meet with my staff."

Vlady popped out of his seat and led her towards the door.

It was after three in the morning. Leena stared out of the

office window at the stars finding the Big Dipper and North Star. She was wide awake, over stimulated by coffee and thoughts about Dmitri Chesnakov and his sudden interest in her career. She wondered about his relationship with Georgia. *Are they together? Is she his mistress?*

Vlady interrupted her thoughts. “I think we have the strategy.” Leena turned away from the window and faced Vlady and his two staff members, Ivan and Pavel, who studied the plan they had worked out on a white board.

Ivan spoke, “We have already begun executing the plan. We began buying Lira two days ago. The reason for buying is that this drives up the volume and helps stop the Lira from falling.”

“Then we leak to the financial press that several important financial people see the weak lira as an opportunity to buy. We can get people like billionaire Vadim Novinsky to say they are buying Lira. The markets see the rise in volume, hear the rumors, and buyers flood in. We sell some of the bonds and lira in this first wave.”

“Then we have some economist state that the Turkish Central bank plans to raise rates. This creates a second buying wave that lasts days. We sell the rest over the next two or three days. Then we are out.”

“Leena, did you get all this?” Vlady asked. Leena nodded yes. “Prepare slides and a report. You will present to Dmitri in the morning.”

“Yes, I will prepare the presentation. But Vlady, is this

legal?" Leena asked.

"It is entirely legal," Vlady said.

"But it seems like we are manipulating the currency market for Turkish Lira."

"Well, we are, aren't we? Welcome to the world of international finance."

Leena went to her cubicle and completed the slides for the presentation just as the dawn painted scattered clouds shades of pink. Exhausted, she fell asleep in her chair. She dreamt that she and Dmitri were at a ball. He led her across the ballroom while the crowd toasted them. Tatiana toasted them and said, "Bravo Leena." Alexi Andreovich stared jealously, mouth open, running his fingers through his hair. Georgia approached them, but Dmitri held up his hand, stopping her, and she retreated tearfully.

Dmitri turned to her and said, "Are you ready to present?"

She nodded and knelt. The crowd turned and faced her. She suddenly noticed that she was naked. She covered herself and then awoke. It was after nine o'clock. She checked her emails. The presentation was at nine-thirty, in twenty minutes.

She ran to the bathroom, washed her face, applied new makeup, brushed her hair, straightened her rumpled outfit, and looked at herself in the mirror.

"Good enough," she said to herself. At first, she was nervous, but then she realized that she was well prepared and ready to present the Turkish Lira plan. *And what really do I have to lose?* She began to relax.

She ran to her office, grabbed her laptop, and went to the glass conference room on the fifteenth floor.

Vlady and Pavel were there. Vlady possessed the calm demeanor of a seasoned executive, but Pavel looked nervous and asked, “Are you ready?”

“Yes, no problem,” She said with confidence as she plugged her laptop into the projector and displayed the title page of the presentation on a screen. “Let me show you.” She flipped through the slides describing the main point of each.

“Sounds like we’re ready,” Vlady said.

Dmitri arrived five minutes late, followed by Georgia. “Hello Vlady, Leena.” He ignored Pavel. “Georgia, you do not need to be here.” Georgia looked hurt and left. He checked his watch and then said, “Okay, let’s get going.”

Fifteen minutes later, Leena finished. Dmitri asked, “So, we will be mostly out of Lira in what? Three or four days?”

“Yes, the Lira will continue down for at least the next few months as banks from around the world unwind their holdings,” Vlady replied.

“Any idea whether there will be a buying opportunity?”

“No time soon. Maybe if there is a panic in the market, but I can’t predict that.”

Dmitri tapped his fingers on his lips. “So, any Lira the bank receives should be sold immediately.”

“Right.”

“Okay. Sounds like you have things under control, as

usual."

"Thank you, Dmitri," Vlady said.

"What are you doing for lunch today, Leena?" Dmitri asked.

"Nothing."

"You will be my guest. Please come to my office at one-thirty."

"Yes, Dmitri," Leena said.

Dmitri left and the meeting broke up.

Leena, drowsy but triumphant, ambled to the ladies room on the fifteenth floor. She set down her computer by the sink, washed her hands, and splashed her face with cold water as Georgia entered.

"So, you are Dmitri's new interest," she said.

"What do you mean?" Leena asked.

"Don't pretend, Leena. You and I both know his interest in you goes beyond work."

Leena shrugged.

"I guess you are next."

"Next?"

"Don't play dumb with me. I have been with him for nearly two years. Before that, there was another one that I replaced. I guess it is time for a change." Georgia looked a little hurt, but also resigned to the facts of executive life at the bank. "It has been a good ride and great for my career, but I am done here. I am leaving. I have a better offer elsewhere. Good luck, Leena."

Georgia disappeared.

Chapter 38 – Therapy

"Howard! Howard! Can you hear me?" Jack barked into his cell phone. "I'm only getting two bars here." He sat in a café in Palo Alto, sipping his fourth double espresso.

"Yeah. What the hell is it?" Goldman sounded annoyed.

"Is Rachel around, I have to speak to her. I can't believe what happened."

"She's around. What's on your pitiful excuse for a mind? More Frat Boy Drama?"

"Dude, you have no idea what the last twelve hours have been like. Can I come over? I need to speak with you and Rachel."

"Okay, okay. Come on over."

When he arrived at Howard's, Jack leapt from his car, charged to the front door, and frantically knocked. "Hold on, hold on, I'm coming." Howard opened the door. "Are you okay? Jesus, you don't look so good. Come on in. Rachel, he's here."

"In the kitchen," Rachel called to them.

Jack jogged into the kitchen and collapsed into a chair at the table next to her. "Oh my God, I can't believe it," He panted. "It's just unbelievable."

"Calm down, Jack. What happened?" she asked. Howard wandered in and stood in the background.

"It's Amy. She's gone off the deep end."

"I thought she had already 'gone off the deep end'," Rachel said.

"Oh no, this is way, way off the deep end. She came to the party last night and threw a pint of beer at me."

Howard chuckled. "Hey, isn't that a battery? I think you can collect damages for dry cleaning."

"Well, that's pretty extreme," Rachel said.

"She made a scene in front of everybody. It was unbelievable. She saw me with Leena and then threw the beer."

"What did Leena do?" Rachel asked.

"Ummm, I think she lit a cigarette. Yeah, that's what she did. She lit a cigarette and smoked."

Howard laughed out loud. "That's ridiculous! Amy throws a beer and Leena lights a cigarette?"

"Yeah, she was unfazed."

"Then what happened?"

"Well, Amy disappeared, thank God, and I went upstairs to change and Leena came with me."

"Un-huh." Rachel smirked. "Did she come with you to comfort you or to help you change?"

"She didn't feel safe by herself," Jack said.

Rachel raised a skeptical eyebrow. "And then what?"

"Well, one thing led to another and…"

"And?" Howard asked.

"Well…you know," Jack said.

"Yes I guess we can imagine. So what? That's it? You

came over to kiss and tell?" Rachel asked.

"No, no, no. After that, the really bad thing happened. At around four in the morning someone slipped this under my door." Jack opened the envelope and poured the photos out on the table.

"Ohhhhh mannnnnn. Look at the cut right above her cleaver. That's totally gross," Howard gasped.

"Oh my god," Rachel said.

"It's Amy," Jack said.

Rachel turned white. "She has really gone off the deep end."

"Yeah, she's totally disturbed," Jack said.

"Disturbed? She's a maniac. Do you think she'll have a scar?" Howard asked.

"Maybe, or maybe she got stitches and plastic surgery" Jack shrugged his shoulders.

"Plastic surgery? What are you talking about? This is a cry for help. Don't you even care?" Rachel asked.

"What am I supposed to do? She's clearly off her rocker. I'm totally blown away and I don't want anything to do with her. You know, looking back, I can see that something was wrong with her. She was always breaking down, disappearing for days and then resurfacing as though nothing had happened. At least, once a month, sometimes more, she would explode whenever she didn't get her way over trivia stuff. Maybe she's bi-polar or something. I need to get away and stay away. She's toxic."

"What if she stalks you?" Howard added.

"Yeah, it's possible. I've had a patient who stalked and cut. Taking photos and sending them to someone. That's not a new one for me."

"At least, she didn't send you her ear or some other body part."

"HOWARD! That's disgusting!" Rachel reprimanded.

"Sorry, that just came out wrong. But seriously, do you think she's capable of something that weird?" Howard asked.

"Body parts? No. Stalking? Perhaps." Rachel shook her head.

"So what should I do?" Jack asked.

"Do you want to be involved?" Rachel asked. Jack shook his head no. "Then stay away. Let it run its course. Don't let it drag you down. Her family has copious resources. Her mental illness is their problem, not yours," Rachel said.

Jack slumped in his chair, relieved. "Thanks, Rachel. I am just going to stay away from her."

"Want some breakfast or coffee?" Howard asked.

"Thanks, no. I feel a lot better actually. Do you have any juice?" Jack asked.

"Orange juice?" Howard offered.

"Thanks, maybe a glass and then I need to leave. Thanks for listening."

Chapter 39 – Resurrection

Jack returned to the sanctuary of his room mostly exorcised of his terror over Amy. The calm aftermath quickly filled with tidal wave of desire for Leena, putting him into a burning stupor. He lay on his bed and starred at the ceiling while images of Leena floated through his mind: her voluptuous body, her low, gravelly voice biting him gently with sarcasm, and her faint into his arms. His desire and self-doubt paralyzed him until his phone rang. It was her! He grabbed his phone with a tremulous hand. "Hi, Leena."

"Hello, Mister Hooker."

"So, how is my girl from Moscow doing this afternoon?"

"I didn't know I had been promoted to 'your girl'."

"Well, how should I refer to you?"

She calmly stated, "I am not your girl, Mister Hooker."

Her words hurt. "Okay, okay. At least, you can drop the formality and call me Jack."

"I know, but I like to say, 'Mister Jack Hooker'. It just falls out of the mouth."

"You mean, 'rolls off the tongue'. Well, it sounds kind of funny when we're intimate. 'Mister Hooker'. It's kind of weird."

"The reasoning for my call is that I am wondering if you like to have a dinner tonight, at my place?"

"Yes, yes, yes. How could I say no to Leena Kiraskaya,

who has enslaved my heart and possesses my very soul?"

She chuckled. "Do not exaggerate, kid. We do not know each other long enough for me to possess your soul."

"It's already too late."

Her voice squealed sarcastically, "Oh well, Mister Hooker, I do not want your soul."

He mock-whimpered into the phone, "You are rejecting my soul? I am wounded."

Leena quipped, "Let me warning you, Jack. When I capture your soul, I will show no mercy."

"Now I'm scared."

"Yes, I am sure you are. So, shall we meet for dinner?" Leena asked.

"I'm at you beck and call. Just us two?"

"Yes, Jack. Just Mister Jack Hooker and Miz Leena Kiraskaya. Do you trust me alone, Mister Hooker?" Leena asked.

"Yes, what about me? Aren't you a little afraid of what I might do with you, Leena?"

"It is my hope, 'what you might do to me', Mister Hooker."

"It sounds so kinky when you call me that."

She ignored him. "It won't be as exciting as Heidelman party."

"Heidelberg party."

"Yes, whatever." He could hear her exhale smoke through the phone and imagined her aloof expression. "No jealous women throwing beer. I hope you do not find it boring."

"That's a good thing. No dry cleaning bills."

"That, Mister Hooker, depends on what we spill tonight," she said suggestively.

He chuckled.

"How about seven? I will cook for you," She added.

"Seven-ish. I will bring a bottle of wine. Something red?"

"Yes, something red." She confirmed and then said, incorrectly, but with the tone of confident erudition, "So, Mister Hooker, shall we say, 'hello'?"

"No, we should say 'goodbye', because this is the end of a conversation."

"Yes, goodbye, Jack." She hung up.

Jack was elated and sprang out of bed. It was four-thirty and he decided to go for a jog. Maybe five quick miles.

Chapter 40 – Wine Bar

After jogging, Jack showered, shaved, and manscaped bits of fur from his body. He dressed in designer jeans, a black button-down shirt, loafers, and then left. He drove to the Village Wine Shop to buy something special. The proprietor steered him to an Italian wine, a *Borgogno Barolo Riserva* 1974. After making the two-hundred-dollar purchase he had forty minutes to kill, so he took a seat at the wine bar and ordered a flight of reds; Sonoma County wines. The bar tender (or was he a sommelier?)poured out six two ounce glasses, set them on napkins printed with the winery name, blend of grapes, and lugubrious description. A smile came to Jack as he recalled Howard's ridicule of the high-brow wine descriptions.

A now tipsy couple, perhaps in their fifties, sat a stool or two away from Jack. The man asked about his purchase. "What's in the bag?"

"A Barolo. Older than I am, 1974." He pulled the bottle from the bag.

"Wow! Now that's a wine," the women commented. "We couldn't talk you into opening and sharing a little."

"I don't think so," Jack said.

"Must be a special occasion," the man said.

Jack sipped his first taste from the flight and stared into

space dreamily. “The occasion? It is special. A woman.”

“An engagement?” the woman chirped. “A toast to your engagement.” She held up a glass.

“Hell, no. Thanks to God.”

“A disengagement?” the man queried.

“Now that’s something worth celebrating,” Jack held up his second taste, a Cabernet-Franc with earth tones, hints of berries and mint. He swished the taste around in the glass, inhaled the bouquet, and sipped. “My former girlfriend is having a nervous breakdown.”

“The poor thing,” The woman said.

“The poor, rich thing, you mean. She never has to work. Spoiled rotten,” Jack replied.

“Sounds like you passed up a good thing. Rich? I would have gone for her,” the man added. The woman batted his arm as though offended.

Jack grinned. “You wouldn’t be interested if you know what I know about her. She’s nuts. She needs professional help.” He shook his head.

“So, is that what you are celebrating? Your ex’s mental health problems?” The woman frowned. “Why not champagne?”

“No, no, no. I actually hope she’s okay. The big occasion is a new woman.”

“It sounds like the ink hasn’t dried on your breakup settlement. You’re changing women the way some men change ties. I think I hate you.” The woman pouted.

“Hey, wait a minute. You haven’t heard my side of this yet.”

“I have only heard your side,” she corrected him.

“Yeah, but listen to what she was like. We had a fight and the next thing I know she is dating a new guy. And then she called me to find her some birth control. So what do you think of that?”

“Did you believe her?”

“Of course. Then I find out later she was lying.”

“Pretty sneaky.” The woman smirked.

“Sneaky? How about psychopathic. She did some unbelievably destructive things. She’s toxic and now out of my life. I am having dinner with the new one, alone, at her place.” Jack raised an eyebrow and winked.

The couple rose to leave. “Well, don’t do anything I wouldn’t do. Maybe bring some champagne,” the man said as they left.

“Yeah. Maybe champagne and the red,” Jack said to himself.

“I think champagne is appropriate.” A man had settled down next to him. The man had grey hair and grey eyes. He wore glasses and black gloves. He had an accent.

“Hello, didn’t see you sit down. Champagne huh?” Jack asked.

“Yes, I think champagne is good,” The man said.

“You must have been listening in.”

“Forgive me,” the man apologized.

"No problem. This is a wine bar. People talk, mingle, etc, etc. Jack Hooker." Jack extended his hand. "Nice to meet you…"

"Roma," He introduced himself, holding out a hand.

They shook. "Are you from Russia? I noticed your accent."

"Russia? My accent is Romanian. I am American now."

"So your accent is Romanian, huh?"

"To American's ears I sound like Bella Lugosi, I am told."

"Yeah, now that you mention it, sounds sinister, like Count Dracula. Can you say, 'I vant to suck your blood'?"

"I would rather not. Tell me about the girl?"

"Amy? She's nuts, poor girl. I think she's bi-polar," Jack said.

"No, I mean your date tonight."

"My date? She's something really special. Not America. Russian."

"Russian? What is she doing here?"

"Studying Finance at Stanford. I met her in class. She's gorgeous. I think I'm in love. Well, at least, I am infatuated."

"Infatuation is good. Let's drink to that." They toasted. "Her name?"

"Leena. Leena Kiraskaya." Jack peered into the distance with a dazed look.

"Leena," Roma repeated. "I have to go. Enjoy the evening." Roma finished his drink and left.

Jack finished his flight, bought a bottle of champagne, and left.

Chapter 41 - Dining with Leena

Leena buzzed Jack into her building. He entered, took the elevator to the third floor, and he found his way to her apartment. The door was ajar so he knocked, poked his head inside, and said, "Hello."

"I am in the kitchen cooking Beef Bourguignon."

He entered and found himself in the living room. A sofa faced a flat screen television that broadcast Russian news. Her laptop sat open on the coffee table in front of the couch amid a scatter of homework and magazines. *Hey, she reads* Cosmopolitan, *in English, that's good.* A formal dinner table, large enough to seat eight, but set for two, with candles, china and silverware, stood by a picture window that overlooked a garden.

"I have some champagne. It's getting warm. Let's open it."

"Bring it in here."

He followed her voice to the kitchen. He found her standing over the stove fussing about with a wooden spoon. She wore an apron, white chiffon blouse, yellow shorts, and no shoes. *Pretty feet.*

"Hello, Miz Kiraskaya," he said.

"My dear Mister Hooker." She turned away from the cooking, walked to him, and gave him a hug. He gave her a quick kiss, then a second, then a third long, wet kiss. She broke away. "I will put this in the oven. Have you had Beef Bourguignon before?"

"Nope."

"You will like it. I am specialist on that." She went back to cooking.

"Yes, I'm sure." Jack wrestled with the champagne cork. *Pop!* "Where are the glasses?"

"Over there." She pointed.

He opened the cupboard, took out two glasses, poured, and handed her one. "*Skoal*," he toasted.

"*Nostrovia.*" They sipped while she cooked. "There are some crackers and cheese over there."

He prepared a cracker for her. "Here" She opened her mouth and he popped it in.

"Take them into the living room. I will be right there," she said. He took the crackers, champagne, and glasses to the living room placed them on the coffee table, settled onto the sofa, and began trying to make sense out of the Russian News program. It was impossible.

Leena appeared, sans apron, and gathered herself into the far corner of the couch, like a cat, pulling her legs up, and wrapping her arms around her knees. "How is your day so far, Jack?"

"Good. I mean great, well sort of a mixed bag. Really good and some really bad stuff."

Leena pouted. "Can you tell Leena what is wrong?"

He shrugged. "No. It has nothing do with you. Personal

stuff."

"That woman who threw beer?"

"Well, maybe."

"Well, I don't want to talk about her," She said curtly. "Let's talk about you. Who are you, Mister Hooker? We must talk all about you."

"Geez, there is a lot to tell. Where do I start?" He ran his fingers through his brown hair.

"How about where you from?"

"Where I am from? I'm from here. I grew up in Los Altos, just a few miles from here. We moved here from New York so my dad could do science research. He is a physicist. He doesn't care about money and stuff like that. Instead, he loves science, the mysteries of the Universe; black holes, string theory, neutrinos. It's all he talks about."

"Really?"

"Yeah. He's lucky. He found himself in life."

"He sounds artist, except he is a scientist."

Jack nodded. "He's consumed by it. It's his identity. Science is his career, his hobby, his leisure activity, and he finds it meaningful."

"You are telling me about your father, not yourself, Jack. Who are you? You are not your father."

"Well, one's father is a big part of a man's life."

"I wouldn't know. I did not know my father. I have no idea who he was, what he looks like, even his name."

"How do you feel about that?"

"Well, I am glad I don't have a complex about my father, like you do." She sipped her champagne.

"I don't have a complex."

"Tell me about Jack Hooker then."

"Okay, so, I am going to be an accountant. Probably at a large firm, like Deloitte, where I interned last summer. Probably make a lot of money. I am in a fraternity, as you know. I used to be a jock."

"What is jock?"

"An athlete."

"Oh." She nodded.

"Track and Field. I ran the four hundred meters. I could outrun everybody in High School but then I joined the track team at Stanford. I was totally out classed. It was pointless. I lost interest and eventually quit."

Leena said, "You don't like accounting, do you, Jack?"

"I am studying it to make a living. I don't hate it."

"And your father is an artist/scientist. I can see why it bothers you."

"Well, why do you do banking? Don't tell me you have a great passion for banking," Jack said.

"Well, I do, Jack. It is financial mathematics. I like it. Mathematics is music to me and in banking there is so much at stake, so much money. What I do is important, interesting, and gives me a varied and interesting life. My career is why I am in

USA to study."

"Okay. I guess it is sort of glamorous. All the travel."

"And important people I am meeting, like the heads of other big banks, finance ministers, the World Bank, politicians. Things like that."

"Wow! Why no man?"

"I never said there is no man, did I?" she gave him a supercilious look.

Jack blushed with jealousy. "Married or engaged?"

She laughed. "Neither, thank God. I don't want to be owned by a man. Besides, I am too young."

"How old?"

"Never ask lady her age, Mister Hooker."

"Okay, tell me more," Jack asked.

"You already know I am Director of Risk Management with NovoRisk."

"You don't have a father. Do you have a mother?"

Leena grew quiet. "I told you. My mother was orphan after World War Two."

"Oh, right. So what else?"

"She is retired now. She was a laborer. She breeds Borzoi, now."

"What's Borzoi?"

"It is a Russian wolfhound. It is very old breed, a very traditional Russian dog."

"So, now you are telling me about your mother. Sure you

don't have a slight complex of your own?"

"I do not, Jack," She said emphatically. "I love my mother. I have more money and can help her, so I do."

"Money has never been a problem in my family," Jack commented.

"How nice for you," Leena quipped.

"I didn't mean it that way, you know, like arrogance or something like that. It's a fact. We have been in the USA since the beginning, like since the Pilgrim Times and things have mostly been good for us."

"So you have all the material things you need and want. What do you do then?" Leena tipped her head.

"That's my big problem, Leena. It's easy to be affluent in the USA, if you're smart and work hard. But that's it. There's nothing new. My father, on the other hand, has a passion. He solved that problem."

"So, you are feeling that affluence is more common. You don't live in a country like mine. You have no idea. We did not have refrigerator when I was a kid. But you think you have problems. You are whining, Jack, like a baby."

"I am bored, uninspired," Jack said.

"And like a coward, Jack, you are playing safe. You could make a big change, take a big chance."

"And do what?" Jack asked.

"How about Peace Corp?"

"Get real. Sleep in a tent in Africa? Catch bizarre diseases?

I don't think so."

"And do something a little more meaningful," Leena said.

"No thanks, I want to live a long life. Any other ideas?"

"What do you like thinking about? For fun?"

"You."He sidled over to her on the couch.

"She pushed him away, annoyed. "Please be serious with me, Jack."

"Okay, I have a mild interest in archeology."

"So, why not be archeologist?"

"Yeah, live someplace without electricity, dig holes with a spade, and sift dirt to find stuff. No thanks. I like reading about it. That's good enough."

"Okay, Jack. If you could change things and choose anything, what would you choose?"

"Hmmm. Never really thought about it that way before. I guess I would be gifted at something, anything. Music, painting, even science. I wish I was able to create something new, novel, unique, and valued."

"Like your father. Did he do that?" Leena asked.

"To a small extent. He solved a few interesting problems. He had a couple of friends who won Nobel Prizes."

"So, what can you do about it, Jack?"

"Nothing really. I think this sort of talent is inborn. Don't you?"

She paused for another sip of champagne. "Yes, but it also requires development and a huge desire, an obsession. Maybe even a little bit of mental illness."

"Yeah. That's a problem. I am not mentally ill enough to do anything great." Leena smiled at Jack's sarcasm. "I'm smart, but I will never really scintillate."

"What it means, 'scintillate'?" Leena asked.

"It means sparkle."

"Well. I think I have seen Mister Hooker sparkling." She looked into the bubbling champagne. "Poor Mister Hooker. So lost. So sad."

"What if my greatest talent is Love?" Jack asked.

She placed her head on his shoulder. "Love. Well, it is a little early for me to know about love, but for love making, I think you are sparkling a little bit."

Then she stood. "It's time for dinner."

After eating they cleared the dining room, loaded the dishwasher, and washed the pots and pans. They hadn't opened the Barolo.

"We will save it for another dinner," Leena said. As she placed the last pot in the dish rack to dry, he wrapped his arms about her from behind, pressed his body up against hers and nuzzled her neck. He turned her towards him and they kissed.

She broke the kiss and pushed him away. "I am sweating and dirty from cooking and cleaning up dinner. I need bath." She turned her head to one side and gave him a side-long look. "You are coming with me to the bath, Mister Hooker." She took his hand and led him into the bathroom. She sat on the lip of the tub and turned on the water, waited while it heated up, adjusting the water, setting the right temperature. After what seemed like an eternity to Jack, she rose, walked to Jack and embraced him. They kissed and then he turned her so that she faced the mirror. He unbuttoned her blouse, opened her blouse, slid it off. Left arm first, and then her right arm. He then unhooked her bra and removed it to expose her breasts in the mirror.

"You are very beautiful, Leena."

She turned, unbuttoned, and removed his shirt and then pressed her bare torso against his.

He slid off her skirt and underwear and then dropped his pants. They stepped into the bath and sat facing each other, their legs mingling. Suddenly, she mounted him, closed her eyes, and began to slowly slide down him, twisting her head to one side with pleasure. Soon, she began to move rhythmically on him.

Jack suddenly blurted out, "Oh my God! I think I love you!"

Leena stopped moving, opened her eyes and looked down at Jack with languid pleasure, quoting him, repeating his words as though asking a question, "'I love you'?"

She said it a second time, "I love you." This time as a statement.

"I think I love you, Leena," Jack said.

"I think I am loving you, Jack. At least a little bit." She closed her eyes.

Leena awoke and looked at the clock. It was after one in

the morning. She switched on a night light and then nudged Jack. "Jack, Jack, wake up. You must leave now."

"Huh? Oh yeah. What's the time?"

"One twenty-two."

"Right, we have class tomorrow." Jack slowly rolled out of bed, yawned, scratched, and pulled on his trousers.

"I will not be in class tomorrow."

He looked disappointed. "Okay. Why is that?"

"Business."

"NovoRisk business?" Jack asked.

"Yes. The CEO is coming and there is some business. I am gone until Sunday night."

She rose from the bed, naked, and sashayed over to him and gave him an affectionate hug, pressing herself against his shirtless chest. "Oh, Jack. I am going to miss you," she purred, "but I will be back on Sunday. Can we meet Sunday?"

"Absolutely. What time do you think you will be back?"

"In the evening."

"I will miss you too, Leena." They held each other for minutes.

"You have to go," Leena finally said.

"Right." Jack finished dressing and left.

Jack stepped out of the foyer of Leena's building into the chilly darkness as tree leaves murmured in a breeze that swept down the street. Jack zipped up his jacket and headed to his car. He heard footfalls up the street and noticed movement out of the corner of his eye. He turned to look. *Nothing there*. Paranoia took over. *Is Amy stalking me?*

He jumped in his car, started the engine, and then putted up the street, high beams on. A grey cat sat on a cinder block wall. *It's a cat! I've got to get a grip on myself.* The cat jumped onto the grass below. Jack's eyes followed the cat's stroll across grass where he noticed footprints on the dew covered lawn. The footprints continued to the sidewalk, to the street, and then evaporated. He froze. The hair on the back of his neck stood up. *Fresh tracks, Amy's? God, I hope not.* Fear kept him from taking a closer look. *I'm getting out of here.* He revved his engine and fled.

Chapter 42 - Dmitri Arrives

At around three o'clock that same morning, Leena's phone rang, waking her. She answered, "Da, Dmitri."

"We are here. We will be at your apartment in about an hour or two."

"Okay, I will be waiting," she said mechanically.

Social norms required that Dmitri ask Leena, "How are you?"An unnecessary question in his mind.

"Fine, a little sleepy." Leena yawned.

"See you soon." He hung up. The cold call and abrupt end was their norm. Any desire she might have had for emotional intimacy with Dmitri had been supplanted by their lifestyle from the beginning. She simply never felt a need for it and neither did he. For both of them, it was all about living fast: an endless rush of thrills, challenges, social gatherings, trips, passionate love making, and gourmet eating.

For Leena, most days began at five in the morning with a race to the gym. This was followed by a shower, makeup, hair, and dressing. Then a dash to meet Yuri, or some other business associate for coffee at six-thirty.

Yuri had been a friend and peer in the Risk Management Department until Leena's elevation. They had become better friends since her rise. She liked Yuri and loved his wit. He entertained her by weaving together fragments of ordinary life into ridiculous anecdotes that made her laugh.

He was also her confident and would patiently listen to her concerns, helping her sort through challenges at the bank. She helped him too, inviting him to meetings, asking for his help on projects, and persuading Dmitri to promote him to manager of a department of fifteen.

The rest of the day was slammed. Often triple booked with meetings through lunch and into the evening. After work, she met Dmitri for a late dinner, after which he followed her home to her place for a tryst.

She understood that their relationship would be limited from the beginning. Their relationship would never progress past mistresshood. That didn't matter to her. She wanted the thrill of it.

There was little intimacy in the relationship. Leena never troubled Dmitri with her hopes, dreams, or feelings. He had no interest. She didn't know his either. They kept separate their inner-selves. Sex and business circumscribed their relationship.

As she lay in bed, she compared the two men. The powerful CEO with the insecure college student. The virile fifty-five-year-old with the indefatigable tom cat. The taught skin of Jack's apple face with the softer, flabby Dmitri. Power and experience versus chemistry, youth, and enthusiasm. She didn't want to be with Dmitri anymore, but the circumstances required she keep up appearances.

The air smelled of food, smoke, and sex. The bed smelled like Jack. His taste lingered in her mouth. She had to erase all traces of their liaison before Dmitri arrived. She sprang from the bed, stripped off the sheets and remade it. She had loaded the dishwasher, but had forgotten to turn it on, so she started it. She opened windows and sprayed air fresher.

After a hot shower, she removed makeup, brushed teeth, and donned a negligee and robe. She searched the rooms for incriminating footprints, stains and dirt, finding nothing. She began to relax. As a finishing touch, she put two high ball glasses into the freezer to chill, next to a bottle of chilled vodka. She turned on the TV, settled onto the couch, and watched the Russian channel until she fell asleep and dozed on the sofa. The doorbell rang, startling her. She went to the intercom. "Da, Dmitri."

"I am here with the driver. Let us in," he barked.

"Yes, Dmitri." She buzzed them in and opened the door. A minute later Dmitri appeared followed by a man carting luggage.

"How are you, Leena?" Dmitri took off his rain coat, opened his arms expecting Leena to approach. Leena stepped into his arms and hugged him rigidly. She gave him a peck on the lips and then stepped away.

"I am fine," Leena said.

The awkward embrace caught Dmitri off guard. He raised his eyebrows, pouted, and scratched his cheek. *Perhaps the driver is inhibiting her.*

"Where should I put the bags, Miss?" The man asked Leena.

"Put them in the bedroom, Petrov," Dmitri said. Petrov

knew his way to the bedroom.

"Yes, Dmitri." Petrov disappeared.

After a pause, Dmitri asked, "Tell me about Stanford, the students, the professors. What do you think of America?"

"Really great. It's all really great. I love it. And I am learning so much, but it is hard and I am very busy." She clipped out her words curtly as she settled onto the sofa.

"Hmmmmm, yes, I am sure you are studying too much. Well, I am here now and you can take a break, have a little fun." The driver appeared from the bedroom. "Plan to come by tomorrow at around eleven-thirty in the morning, Petrov." He turned back to Leena. "We can spend time site-seeing in San Francisco before the seminar."

Leena gave the driver a quick once-over. Petrov was tall, good looking and trim, unlike the typical fat, toad-like drivers.

"How about that drink?" Dmitri asked.

"Three?" She queried.

"No. He's leaving. Just us two." Dmitri leered at his possession.

"Anything else, Dmitri?" The driver bowed.

"No, Petrov. You may leave."

"Goodnight, Miss, Dmitri." He bowed and left.

Dmitri followed Leena into the kitchen. "It is four-thirty in the afternoon in Moscow and I slept on the plane, so I am wide awake."

"So for you it is cocktail hour, but for me it is very early in the morning," Leena complained. Dmitri grimaced. Leena retrieved the chilled glasses and poured ice-cold vodka.

Dmitri toasted, "*Nostrovia*! To your adventure in America."

"Da." They clinked glasses. Dmitri took a gulp while Leena sipped.

"Nice crystal. Isn't this a nice place? We use it to house our people when they come to Silicon Valley. We make it too comfortable, don't we?"

"Yes, Dmitri. It is very nice," she obliged.

Her flat demeanor contrasted with her usual mirth and enthusiasm. "You sound tired, Leena. I know. It's early. Maybe a little more Vodka will perk you up."

"All right," she complied, pouring them each another. She hoped more vodka would blunt his desire as well as her revulsion at being touched by him. She downed her drink. "Yes, maybe a little more vodka." She poured herself another and added more to his glass. He furled his eyebrows. Leena wasn't a heavy drinker.

"Three vodkas?" he asked.

"Let's celebrate our reunion," she lied and downed the third.

"Why is the dish washer running?"

She blushed and hesitated. "Oh, well," She emoted. "I cleaned things up before you came." She looked at him with a sheepish grin.

"Now? In the middle of the night?"

She sighed and shrugged. “I don’t know. Does it matter? Let’s go to the living room.” The drink numbed her senses. She carried the bottle and glass. “Please sit. I will be right back.” She retreated to the bathroom for one last check. She sprayed a puff of perfume and looked at her face in the mirror. Everything looked fine except a small purple mark on her neck left by Jack. She raised her negligee and checked her thighs and abdomen and saw a small nip on her inner thigh. Leena applied makeup to the mark on her neck and hoped Dmitri wouldn’t see the love bite below. After finishing her drink, she poured another. Now tipsy, she stumbled over the throw rug on her way back to the living room, spilling half the drink. After righting herself, she took a deep breath and tippled back to the sofa.

Dmitri frowned while he surfed TV channels. He planted himself in the middle of the sofa. She gradually settled onto the sofa, pulled her legs up beneath her, and touched his thigh.

In no time, he slid his hand onto her abdomen, and then downward, taking possession of her.

She squirmed at his touch and tried to suppress her arousal, speaking to him with drunken, slurring her words, “Oh, don’t, Dmitri. It is too fast. Can you be gentle?” She put her hand on his, but didn’t have the will to stop him. He directed her to stand in front of the couch, and then he removed her panties so he might touch her more directly. She surrendered to a flood of passion.

After a quick, furious round of sex, Dmitri put on his pants and shirt, leaving it un-tucked. She reached for her negligee, but he stopped her. "No, I want to caress my lover while we chat."

She lay uncomfortably exposed as he spoke. "Back in Moscow, it is business as usual. Nothing really new. Tell me more about America." He probed giving her an indifferent look.

"Oh, Dmitri. I don't know where to start. Well, I am taking Risk Management in Financial markets and it is very interesting."

"Professor's Name?" Dmitri interrupted.

"Doctor Richard Greene. It is very interesting course. There are many things we might apply at NovoRisk."

"Richard Greene." he sounded suspicious. "What's he like?"

"Typical professor. Bookish, glasses, flabby, boring," she said.

"Boring? How so?"

"Well, I really don't know him. He just strikes me as boring."

"Uh huh, well, what else?" He appeared satisfied. "Have you seen the sights? Any good restaurants?"

"No, not really. No restaurants, no friends. I've only been here three weeks. It is still a strange place to me."

"Yes." He seemed satisfied. "Come to me." He opened his arms.

Her drunkenness allowed her to hide her true self. She put on her kitten face and sidled over to him. "Oh, Dmitri. If you only knew how lonely and bored I am." She buried herself in his arms.

After a second round of love making with a second lover in

the same evening, Leena fell fast asleep, leaving Dmitri wide-awake and bored. He went to the kitchen in search of food and found the Beef Bourguignon. *Looks like she's been cooking.* He served himself and sauntered back to the sofa in the living room, switched on the TV, and began eating. *Pretty good.* He surfed channels noting the panorama of American media: Oprah Winfrey sharing secrets, an aged Regis Philbin interviewing a beauty queen, and the pudgy and pious Hannity of Fox News spinning outrageous conspiracies. Dmitri yawned and returned to Russian News. After a few minutes he sighed. "Nothing new." He left the sofa and tiptoed back into the bedroom for his laptop.

The sound of the TV disturbed Leena's sleep. She rolled over and mumbled, "Yes, Mister Jack Hooker." Dmitri stopped and waited to see if she would say more, but she was quiet. He closed the door, disturbing her further. Leena rolled over, opened her eyes. "Oh, it's you, Dmitri." Leena pulled the pillow over her head and went back to sleep.

Dmitri crept out of the room and back to the sofa. He opened his computer. While it booted he grabbed his plate and went to the kitchen, placing it the sink. He paused. *Dishwasher.* He opened the dishwasher and peered in. *Two wine glasses, one with a faint stain of lipstick. Leena's lipstick. Two plates. A dinner party for two?*

He slipped back into the bedroom and quietly closed the door. He scanned the room and found nothing. He went to the bathroom. Humidity from a recent shower dampened the air. The hamper held a wet towel and soiled sheets with wet spots, one with a crusty white border. Repulsed, he dropped the sheets and washed his hands.

He thought with cool mannerisms, *Things are amiss. Is she lying to me? Doctor Greene? Mister Jack Hooker? Who?*

Chapter 43 - Morning After

The sound of the doorbell awakened Leena. She opened her eyes and heard Dmitri's voice, "Mikhail?"

"Uh, no. It's Petrov." She heard Petrov's voice through the intercom.

"Oh, right. Come in." Dmitri buzzed open the security door. Leena sat up in bed.

Petrov is here? She looked around her room. Dmitri's open suitcase sat on one chair and his coat draped across another. The faint leathery odor of shoes invaded her nostrils, marking his territory and she felt intruded upon.

The front door opened. "Hi, Petrov. Sit on the sofa. Coffee?" Dmitri asked.

"Yes, please. I bought a newspaper. The Wall Street Journal."

Leena listened to the men's voices.

"Thanks. Here's the TV control." She heard a Russian talk show host interviewing a guest. "Cream?" Dmitri's voice echoed from the Kitchen.

"Black, please," Petrov answered.

"Here" Dmitri's voice returned to the living room. "Is there any news from Sheraz?"

Sheraz. I have heard that name. He is Persian, from Iran.

What was his last name? She couldn't remember.

"Everything is fine. The money has been wired to Switzerland".

"Did you check with Klaus?"

"Everything is in order. No trace of anything," Petrov said.

"Good. Ummm. Have you checked up on…" He lowered his voice and didn't finish the sentence.

Leena noticed the sudden drop in his voice, and knew they were talking about her. She tiptoed to the bedroom door, peeked out, and listened in. *Why discuss money transfers with a driver?*"

Petrov shook his head no. "I have surveillance. There is nothing."

She returned to the bathroom to shower and found that Dmitri's razor, tooth brush, and other toiletries had taken up residence on her sink. She picked up his razor with disdain. A bottle of Viagra poked out of his dopp kit. *Viagra! Yuck!*

Dmitri's face appeared in the mirror startling her. "Oh!" she exclaimed and turned to face him. She covered her pubic area with her hands.

"Good morning, Leena. I hope you feel rested." Dmitri eyed the naked Leena. His eyebrows furled. "What is this mark?" He reached down to the Jack's love-bite on her inner thigh, pushing her thigh outward. She surrendered, dropping her hands. She once liked standing naked in front of him, being examined, being touched. In a way, controlled, her being the vulnerable, nude sex object, and he the hungry man-beast examining his prey. Now she felt violated, humiliated, and nervous and worried he would recognize the mark as a love-bite.

“What’s what?” She played dumb.

“Here, on your thigh.” Dmitri fingers pressed into the soft flesh of her inner-thigh twisting it so she might see. Her skin reddened beneath his fingers.

“I don’t see anything.”

“Here” Dmitri pulled a small mirror from his dopp kit, lifted her leg, and placed her foot on the toilet. He held the mirror down below, exposing herself to both of them while rolling the flesh near the mark between his thumb and index fingers. “Do you see it?” He looked into her eyes. His pupils dilated.

She looked at the purplish circular mark. “I don’t know, Dmitri. I must have bumped into something.” His skeptical look frightened her. He pinched her inner thigh, making her blush. Dmitri stepped back and studied her face and body savoring his power over the naked young woman. She turned away from him, mortified and frightened.

“Okay. Well, hurry up. We have a long day.” He slapped the white flesh of her rump, leaving a mark of his own, andleft.

A hot jet of steaming water shot from the shower head and massaged Leena’s neck and shoulders. She began to relax, to meditate, to feel relief, until images of Dmitri’s flabby stomach, wrinkled leer, and prickly grey chest hair jolted her back, filling her with a vague feeling of revulsion. She felt soiled. She soaped and scrubbed each square inch of skin, obliterating any remnant of him.

Dmitri appeared in the bathroom again, startling her. "Still showering? Pick it up."

"I am hurrying, Dmitri," she said.

"I can't see a thing in here." He waved his hands in the steam.

"Can you turn on the fan to clear the steam?" she asked. He turned on the fan and disappeared.

She left the shower, dried herself, and went into the bedroom. Dmitri sat on the unmade bed. "Is Petrov still here?" she asked.

"Yes. He is waiting in the living room."

"May I have some privacy?"

"Why?"

"Please, Dmitri. I want to dress with a little privacy. Is there some reason why you want to watch me dress?" He relented and slipped out of the room.

She painted her eyes, applied lip stick, and threw on a white blouse and black skirt that came to just below her knee. She put on black pumps, a necklace of black and white pearls, grabbed a light coat, and left her bedroom.

"I'm ready. Where's Petrov?"

"Getting the car." Dmitri put down his coffee and switched off the television. "At the seminar, I want you to work the room. Try and find potential clients who are interested in investing. I also have reservations at a spa in Napa for the weekend. Does that sound fun?"

No, Leena thought but said, "Yes, Dmitri. Sounds exciting."

"I've never been to the California Wine country."

"Neither have I, Dmitri." She tried to sound excited

Dmitri put on a coat and offered her his arm. "Let's go."

Petrov double-parked a limousine in front of the complex. He stood holding the door open, waiting. Dmitri led Leena to the limo. "Please get in, Miss." Petrov's servile behavior contradicted his impressive physical appearance.

"Oh my God. Look how big this car is. Wait, Dmitri. I want a picture," Leena emoted. Dmitri looked annoyed, but nodded in agreement. "Here, Petrov, we can use my phone. Close the door." She leaned against the limo and smiled. Petrov snapped a shot and then held out the phone, returning it. "Take a few more, Petrov."

Petrov complied, taking a few more shots. An impatient Dmitri touched her shoulder. "We must go now."

"Here is your phone, Miss." He helped her inside the spacious limo. Petrov shut the door. Dmitri sat in the front with Petrov. They left for San Francisco.

Chapter 44 – Seminar

Jack's phone pinged, announcing the arrival of a text message. It was from Leena. *Hello, Mister Hooker*, it read and had an attached photo of her posing by a limousine.

He texted her back, "Kisses, beautiful," and sighed. *Stuporously smitten.* He looked again at the shimmering picture of his girl. She smiled with mirth and happiness. *I'm in love.* He looked again and noticed a hand touching her shoulder. A man's hand. A hand touching her shoulder with familiarity. *Hey, wait a minute. Who is that guy?* Adrenaline surged, setting him ablaze. *Relax, relax, relax. She wouldn't send this if there was anything to it.* He could see the cuff, with cuff links and a monogram of a fitted shirt. He fumed. *Who the hell is touching her?* He couldn't relax and decided to go for a run to burn away the bad feelings.

After running he still felt bad. He stripped, wrapped himself in a towel, and headed to the bathroom for a shower and shave. On his way he passed Skippy Brown, a member of the Brotherhood who taunted Jack as he passed, "Hey, Hooker, had a beer with Amy lately?"

Jack ignored Skippy, passing in silence. *Skippy Brown! Reminds me of gay peanut butter.*

He showered, dried, walked to the sink, and painted his face with shaving cream. Bob, the 'Voice' of the Brotherhood, entered the bathroom. "Jack, Jack, Jack. If it isn't my favorite Hooker. Ever wonder where you got a name like that? Like you had whore in your ancestry?" Jack barely noticed the 'Voice'.

"No comeback? You're getting slow in your old age. Dating older women too, right?" Bob asked.

"A more mature, more sophisticated woman, you mean," Jack said.

"Gosh, Jack, you're so grown up. I can't wait until I'm a grown-up like you."

Bob exited the bathroom, giving Jack a hard slap on the back as he passed. Jack's razor slipped disfiguring his face just above his lips. *Damn it. That fucker.* Blood trickled down his philtrum, across his lips, and splattered onto the white porcelain sink. He dabbed at the wound with a damp face cloth and applied an oversized bandage onto which a red clot appeared. He looked at himself in the mirror, *Holy shit that's repulsive. I can't stand being ugly.*

He fled to his room where he settled into his beanbag chair to heal the wounds to his psyche and flesh. The darkness soothed like an ice pack on a throbbing bruise. Strangely, the familiar sounds of Sigma Chi comforted him. A cheer from the gamers in the living room below. A voice calling out 'duuuuuuuuude'. Insipid, but carefree music playing down the hallway.

He switched on his phone and stared blankly at Leena's pic. *The monogram, the initials ДЧ. What the hell's that? Egyptian? Goldman would know.* He sent the photo to Howard's phone and texted. *See the cuff in the pic. What are those things? Hieroglyphics?*

Goldman's phone pinged the arrival of Jack's message as he navigated the heavy traffic on his way to the Mark Hopkins Hotel in San Francisco. Darkness, fog, and buckets of rain obscured the city and intimidated the Californian drivers who bunched the traffic into stops and starts. Their incompetence irritated the New Yorker in Howard Goldman who felt inconvenienced. He couldn't pick up the phone, not in this traffic. *I'll get it later.*

Goldman exited on 4thStreet, South of Market (SOMA) and drove towards the Mark Hopkins Hotel, dodging cabs and pedestrians who haunted the streets in billowing rain gear. He waited for a bum who stopped in the middle of the street to rant at the sky.

Once he arrived at the Mark Hopkins, a valet greeted him with a smile and umbrella. Howard hustled inside, took an elevator to the California Room on the twentieth floor,and found his client, Sigmund Bettelheim, nicknamed Siggy. Siggy, a gifted engineer who made his first fortune designing computers, now dabbled in venture capital and sometimes relied on Howard's advice on matters of Russian culture and commerce.

"Howard. Good." Siggy waved and then he returned to his conversation with a tall blonde woman. It was Leena.

Goldman approached. "Hi, Siggy." He shook hands. "Leena, this is a surprise." He bowed.

"Howard!" Leena emoted and held out a hand.

"I would introduce you to Leena Kiraskaya from NovoRisk Bank, but you have met, yes?"

"We have," Goldman confirmed. Leena's reddening face undermined her characteristic confident look. "What brings you here?"

Her low voice sounded like dry gravel. "My bank is here. And why you are here, Mister Goldman?"

"Siggy is my client. I help him with Russian things in business, now and then. Not that often."

"She is recruiting me to become a client," Siggy said.

"I am sure Leena can show you around the Russian world of Finance better than anyone."

A grey-haired man tapped Leena on the shoulder. He had been sent to summon her, like an assistant. He spoke to Leena in Russian. "It is time to sit." Howard noticed his unusual accent. Leena pardoned herself and followed the man to some seats where they joined a tall, frowning man. They sat.

"Who's that guy over there?" Howard asked.

"Dmitri Chesnakov, CEO of NovoRisk Bank."

Dmitri turned to Leena. "Who are they?"

"The men? Well, a very wealthy man, a Mister Sigmund Bettelheim. A silicon valley millionaire."

"What did he want?" he snapped.

"He is an investor. That's all."

"And the Jew?" Dmitri's audible contempt made Leena

cringe.

"I don't know," she lied and turned pink.

"He seemed familiar with you, like he knew you."

"I never saw him before," she lied. Dmitri studied her face.

The conference began with a presentation about an investment opportunity in Mongolia. Goldman listened with one ear while he watched Leena and Dmitri. Dmitri regularly leaned toward her and whispered. Sometimes she would raise a hand to her mouth to suppress a giggle. Once she batted his shoulder, feigning displeasure. He draped his arm around her shoulder, leaned towards her, and pulled. She fell into his arms, pulled away, and then furtively glanced at Goldman to see if he had noticed. Goldman looked away.

The assistant stood by the exit. Goldman caught him staring at him. Goldman shifted so that he could watch the assistant's reflection in a window without him knowing. The assistant took out a camera and pointed it at Goldman. Goldman suddenly turned, faced him directly. The assistant's camera disappeared and he looked away.

The conference broke. Dmitri held Leena's arm and led her towards Siggy and Goldman. The assistant trailed. "My associate says you are an investor and thinking about Russia or perhaps Mongolia." Siggy nodded. "I am Dmitri Chesnakov, CEO of NovoRisk. Perhaps we can help you."

"Sigmund Bettelheim. Entrepreneur. Pleased to meet you. Yes, your charming associate has enticed me. Perhaps we can speak later. I am sorry, but I must leave. Here is my card."

"Here is mine." Dmitri offered his card. Siggy thanked him and left. Dmitri turned his gaze to Goldman. "Who are you?"

"Me?" Goldman chuckled sheepishly. "A mere consultant, an advisor, at your service." Goldman bowed subserviently.

"Do you have a card?"

"No, I'm afraid I don't," Howard cowed.

"Then how can you be of service?"

"Good Point! Please excuse me. I have to run as well." Howard retreated.

"Did you catch his name, Leena?"

"I am afraid I did not, Dmitri."

The three watched Howard leave. Dmitri turned to the assistant who nodded a reply.

Chapter 45 - Jack Alone

After the razor blade gash to his upper lip, Jack composed himself in his room. He had nothing to do. He had no homework, no upcoming exams, and no girlfriend to hang out with, so he went to the web for entertainment. He read the news, checked the stock market, looked at YouTube, and considered watching a movie. He wandered down stairs. Some of the guys were watching *The Social Network* on the TV in the living room for the hundredth time. Kit was there. "Hey. Jack, how the hell are yah? What happened to your face?"

"Cut myself shaving. Bob hit me and the razor slipped."

"Nice guy, isn't he?"

"He's an asshole."

"Poor Jack. What troubles you have seen this week. First with Amy/Beer incident, and now this. And who is this woman Leena from Russia? Quite a week, eh?" Kit said.

"It's been heaven and it's been hell. Things are still careening out of control. I have no peace," Jack said.

"So, tell me about it."

"Tell you about it? Where do I start?" Jack knew that anything he told Kit would find its way into the gossip mill, so he didn't tell all. "Well, not much to say. I think Amy and I are through. I met this Russian girl in class, Leena, so I'm sort of dating her. Amy is hell, Leena is heaven." He didn't mention the pictures of Amy, and Leena's world class life. "That's about it."

"The cut looks gross," Kit said.

"Thanks. I'll change the bandage once it stops gushing blood. I'm going back upstairs. Adios."

Jack started back to his room, but before climbing the stairs, he stopped to check mail to see if he had any magazines. Jack had adopted Howard's habit of reading the *New Yorker*, *The New York Review of Books* and anything with the word New York in it. Being a Northern Californian, he never looked at the vapid *Los Angeles Magazine. No magazines. A letter? Shit, not another Amy thing.* He grabbed the letter and raced back to his room.

Once inside, he tore it open. *More photographs, of me and Leena, in Leena's bed? What the fuck!* He turned white. *How did Amy do it?*

Chapter 46 – Dinner

Leena and Dmitri waited in uncomfortable silence in front of the Mark Hopkins while Petrov fetched the limousine. “Three weeks and we are already strangers,” Dmitri said. Leena looked up meekly. “And you’re keeping secrets. You know the Jew, don’t you?” She nodded and looked away. “Why lie? You think I’m a bigot?”

“No, but I know you don’t like Jews. Listen to the way you talk. I don’t even know if he is Jewish.”

“He looks Jewish.”

“So, what does that mean? And besides, people don’t talk like that here. Calling someone a Jew is vulgar.”

“So I am a vulgar bigot now?” He grimaced downward at her.

“America is different,” Leena said.

“What does he do?” Dmitri asked.

“A student. I think his field is Russian Studies. Getting a Ph.D.”

“Interesting. Where did you meet him?”

“Oh, at a coffee shop. We debated politics,” Leena said. Dmitri frowned at her. “He is engaged and lives with his fiancé. That’s all I know.”

Petrov pulled up and they climbed into the back. “Petrov,

take us to Alfred's Steak House. It is on Merchant Street."

"Yes, Dmitri," Petrov replied.

"Alfred's Steak House? Alfred sounds like a butler. Let's see what I can find out about it." Leena picked up her phone and Googled Alfred's Steak House. "Here is a review, '*Alfred's Steakhouse is a classic steakhouse serving massive cuts of beef in a plush dining environment.*' Oh, here's the menu. Oh my God. There is a diagram of a cow showing where each cut of meat comes from. That's appetizing. And they serve oysters, of course." Her lips formed a cute pout. She looked Dmitri in the eye and winked.

"Here it says, 'Classic Décor'. It looks like a bordello, Dmitri. You are taking me to a bordello?" She batted her eyes. "This is a place for fat old men who need to eat oysters because they have ED." Then she leaned over on Dmitri and put her head on his chest. "But my Dmitri does not have ED. He should take his mistress elsewhere."

Dmitri couldn't resist Leena's antics. He smiled. "Okay, where then?"

"Oh, well," Her voice swooped up an octave with enthusiasm and then became low and gravelly, almost a gurgle. "I will tell you the place to go, Dmitri. It is called the Slanted Door."

"Am I permitted to know the style of food?"

"Yes, of course, Dmitri. Vietnamese, Asian Fusion."

"Vietnamese, Asian Fusion, like rodents with lemon grass," Dmitri said.

"Do not be ridiculous, Dmitri."

"Okay, where is the Slanted Door?"

Leena looked at her phone. "The Embarcadero."

"To the Embarcadero, Petrov," Dmitri commanded. "We are going to Slanted Door for dinner."

"Yes, Slanted Door," Petrov said.

Petrov pulled up in front of the arched windows and clock tower of the Ferry Plaza on Embarcadero, near Market. Dmitri and Leena jumped out and disappeared inside. They wandered through the maze of shops and booths, some selling fresh produce, one specializing in pork, another gourmet coffee. They passed a book store where a crowd drank coffee and listened to live poetry. Dmitri and Leena exited the back of the Ferry Plaza onto the wharf on the water of the bay.

"Oh, look, Dmitri." They paused to view the sparkling Bay Bridge arching across the dark waters, connecting San Francisco to Yerba Buena Island. The outlines of cargo ships mutely drifted across the black waters in the distance. They strolled down the wharf to the Slanted Door, passing a melee of dinners slurping shellfish, gulping beer, and belching at *Hog Island Oysters*.

The Slanted Door seethed with diners. The air smelled of grilled meats and spices. A slender forty-ish man with dyed-blonde hair and a dangling earring greeted them. His name tag read, 'Fernando'. Dmitri visibly cringed at the host. "Two for dinner." He frowned.

The gay host returned Dmitri's frown and exercised his

power as host. "The wait is forty-five minutes." He stared Dmitri in the eye, smiled, and waited for a reaction.

Dmitri gave Leena a doubtful look. "Forty-five minutes?" He tapped his lips with his index finger.

"Oh, Dmitri. We must wait. This is such a special restaurant." Leena turned to Fernando and lit up, radiating charm from every pore. "Fernando, can we please sit at the bar? My friend is here from Moscow and we have heard so much about Slanted Door. He must try it before he leaves San Francisco."

The host warmed to her. His earring swayed as he turned his head towards the bar and nodded at Leena."Yes, one moment." He walked to the bar and persuaded a man to move over a seat, then waved to them. They approached and settled onto stools at the bar.

"This is lively and noisy," Dmitri complained.

Leena smiled as she absorbed the ambience. "This is much better than that boring meat house for old pimps. Look at the people here." Leena scanned the room. "Ha." She inhaled with surprise. "Look at those two." Two gay men cuddled and kissed in a corner of the restaurant.

"Yuck." Dmitri looked away.

"Dmitri! What do you care? They look happy."

"I don't care if they're happy. They could kill my appetite. Look at those two." Dmitri nodded towards an old bald man dressed in leather whose arms were covered with tattoos. His young female date also wore leather, as well as a studded collar and a spike that pierced the membrane in her nose between her nostrils.

"Is that more your style, Dmitri?" She asked.

"They probably have hepatitis. I wonder if her nose ever gets infected," Dmitri said.

"We're really in San Francisco. Don't worry, you can't get HIV from eating food."

"Yes, but you can get food poisoning."

"No you *won't*." She squeezed his hand.

A Bar tender approached. "What would you like to drink?"

"What is your best vodka?" Dmitri asked.

"Oh, we have many handcrafted vodkas."

"Anything from Russia?"

"You are so predictable, Dmitri." Leena interrupted. "Always Russian vodka. He isn't having vodka." She told the bar tender. "I will order for him. Do you have a martini menu?"

"We do." He provided two.

"We only need one." Leena handed him back one of the menus.

"Oh boy." Dmitri ran his fingers through his hair and looked exasperated.

Leena smirked. "Let me see. Which brew should I use to poison Mister Chesnakov tonight?" She used her rye, crackling voice as she spoke. "Hmmmmmmm. How about a Singapore Sling?" She looked at Dmitri and waited.

"Singapore is not Vietnamese. What's in it?"

"Gin and many other secret ingredients, my poor Dmitri."

"I hate Gin."

"No problem, Dmitri. I will ask him to use vodka instead of gin. A Russian Vodka. Consider it a compromise." She waved down the bartender. "Bartender. My friend would like Singapore sling with your best Russian vodka instead of gin and I want 'Agricole Rhum Punch'. May I please have a menu? We are going to have dinner at the bar."

"You are going to order my dinner too?" Dmitri asked.

"You are at my mercy, my dear Dmitri." She chuckled.

"Please, no dog, reptiles, insects, and nothing that is still alive."

"You are such a child. There is nothing like that here, anyway." The bartender returned with their drinks. "We are ready. We would like spareribs and Hawaiian tombo for starters and shaking beef and caramelized shrimp."

"Why does the beef shake? Is it still alive?" Dmitri asked.

The bartender replied, "Oh no, it's quite dead."

Leena laughed. "Dead meat, Dmitri. Just the way you like it."

They sipped their cocktails and studied the patrons for a minute. Leena broke the silence. "Petrov's kind of strange. Very quiet. So formal and polite. He always calls me Miss. He does not seem like a normal driver. Does he work for the bank?"

"Yes, he works for the bank. He works for security and reports directly to me. You are right. He is a very quiet man. I do not know much about his personal life."

"How long have you known him?" Leena asked. "Since the army?" He nodded. "Chechnya?" She asked. Dmitri nodded yes again.

Chapter 47 - Howard at Home

Howard started the drive home in the rain. A worn out wiper scrapped the windshield, smearing the vista of red tail lights into a blur. He picked his way through street traffic on his way to the 101 freeway while his mind wandered back to the seminar. *That CEO is way too hands-on with Leena. No need to tell Hooker. It'll just piss him off. The assistant was weird. More like a body guard.*

When he arrived home, he parked, traipsed to the porch where he left his wet shoes, and entered the dark house. "I'm home. Rachael?" A lone light came from the living room where he found Rachel stretched out on the sofa. A crackling fire cast orange shadows on the floor and walls. "So, how goes, honey?"

"Ohhhhhhhhhhhhhh." She yawned, stretched, and put down her book. "I had a long day. I saw three patients including the rape victim."

"Sounds like a long, horrible day. What's the latest on her?"

"I'd say she is clinically depressed. She can't sleep, won't eat, she doesn't get out of bed. I don't know how to help."

"How about medical marijuana?" Howard quipped.

"Only a quack would prescribe dope for depression, you dope."

"Yeah, I guess." Howard shrugged.

"How was the conference?" Rachel asked.

"It was a seminar. It was BO RING." He stood by the sofa and stretched. "The traffic was murder."

"I don't know why you do it"

"Money! Siggy paid me two grand just to show up," Howard said.

"Yeah. I'll bet he really gets his money's worth."

"Well, today I gave some advice."

"I'm sure it was worth two thousand dollars. What was it?" she asked.

"I told him to work with NovoRisk Bank," Howard made his Groucho Marx face and flicked the ashes from an invisible cigar.

"That's worth two grand?" Rachel asked. Howard replied with a shrug. "Hey, isn't that Leena's Bank?"

"Yep. Leena was there and I met the CEO, too," Howard gloated.

"Leena's boss?"

"Yep."

"What's he like?" She asked.

"Tall, handsome, aggressive, kind of a prick, a little scary, and in his mid-fifties."

"What did Leena have to say?"

"She said hello," he answered.

"And what else?"

"And, nothing else." Howard became quiet.

"Didn't you talk to her or anything? Did she introduce you to the CEO? Tell me what happened?"

"Did she introduce me? Well, not exactly," Howard said.

"Getting anything out of you is like pulling teeth, Howard. So you didn't talk to her?"Rachel asked.

"Well, actually, when I showed up, I found her talking to Siggy. I advised him to work with Leena. That's all."

"What about the CEO?"

"After the seminar he came over to Siggy. That's when I met him."

"That's strange. She didn't say, 'This is Howard, my friend' or something like that?"

"Nope," Howard said.

"That's weird. Not terribly friendly," she said.

Howard shrugged and changed the subject."Speaking of the rape victim, do you still have those sketches of the rapist?"

"Yeah, they're in her file."

"Can I see them?" Howard asked.

"Sure, how come?"

"I'm curious," he said.

Rachel rolled off the sofa, ambled out of the room, and returned with a file, leafing through it as she walked back to the sofa. "Here" She set it on the living room table.

Howard slid the file across the coffee table into the light, opened it and shuffled through the papers until he found the sketch.

"That's him. That's got to be him."

"Who? Don't tell me you recognize the rapist. Fat chance, bullshit artist." She swatted at him with a pillow.

"This is too weird. It can't be him." He looked perplexed.

"What? Really? I don't believe you. What bull puckey." She crossed her arms.

"I saw a guy who looks just like this guy." He set the sketch on the table.

She raised her browse superciliously. "The accomplice? I don't think so. It's elementary, Señor Goldman. It's a case of mistaken identity."

"The guy who looks almost exactly like this sketch," Howard said.

"Well, it's probably not the same man. How could it be?" Rachel asked.

"Yeah. Well, what's his name?"

"His name is" She thumbed through the file. "Mikhail Kazakhstan."

"Kazakhstan is a country not a name. So he wasn't the rapist. Why is he wanted?"

"He's an accessory. My patient told Interpol that he was picking up a payment or something like that," Rachel said.

"The resemblance is uncanny. But this guy's name was Petrov, not Mikhail."

"A coincidence," she concluded.

"Yeah, probably." He put down the sketches.

"I still can't get over how Leena behaved at the seminar," Rachel said.

"It was weird. I didn't feel comfortable. I left right after that. Is there anything to eat?"

"I don't know. Look in the fridge." Rachel went back to her book. "That's not very nice of her."

"Nice? Who knows, who cares? I'm going to eat." Howard aped as he sauntered into the kitchen scratching his ass.

Chapter 48 - Howard and Jack Speak

Howard carried a bowl of chili, a beer, and a newspaper into the living room. Rachel had gone to bed, leaving him alone in front of the fire. He put a few more logs on the fire and then nestled onto the couch, basking in the warmth. He put on Miles Davis' *Kind of Blue,* which sedated him like codeine cough syrup— warm and purple. He grooved on Jazz until around eleven o'clock when he awoke from his Jazz stupor and found himself amid a scatter of albums and discs strewn across the floor. He glanced at the picture of Mikhail Kazakhstan and recalled the mysterious faces of Dmitri and Petrov. *Mikhail Kazakhstan. Who is he?*

He picked up his phone. *Oh yeah, a message from Hooker, a picture.* He looked at the picture Jack sent earlier and read the message. *See the cuff in the pic. What are those things, hieroglyphics?*

No, they are Cyrillic, letters DC as in Dmitri Chesnakov, he texted back to Jack and then he called Jack.

"Hi, Howard," Jack answered his phone.

"What are you doing?"

"Studying the paint on my wall."

"That's profound. Learn anything new?" Howard asked.

"Yeah, there's a trickle of ants searching for crumbs. They're feeding a couple of hungry spiders," Jack said.

"Gee that's deep, Jack. The poor ants," Howard said.

"I'm siding with the spiders."

"Yeah, naturally. I just read your message. Those 'hieroglyphics' are the letters D and C in Cyrillic. Where'd you get the picture from?"

"Leena sent me the picture. This guy is touching her."

"Interesting coincidence. I went to a seminar on investing in Russia today and guess who I saw?"

"Nikita Khrushchev," Jack said.

"Right. How did you know?" Howard said.

"Shit, you're kidding me. I thought he was dead."

"He is dead, you dope. I met DC and Leena," Howard said.

"DC! Owner of the mystery hand? Oh nooooo. So who is DC?" Jack asked.

"Dmitri Chesnakov. The CEO of NovoRisk and Leena's boss. It's his hand in the photo," Howard said with sinister gravitas.

"Shit. Did you talk to the guy?" Jack asked.

"A little."

"So, what was he like?"

"Old, arrogant, sort of an asshole, probably a fraternity president in a former life or something similar."

"So how was Leena?"

"She looked fine. Nothing to report," Howard said.

Jack sighed relief. "Good."

"Hey, listen. Did Leena ever mention a guy named Mikhail

Kazakhstan?"

"Nope. No Mikhails at all. Why?"

"I am going to send you a picture, hang on." Howard used his phone to photograph the drawing of Mikhail Kazaki and then sent it to Jack. "Let me know when you get it."

"Okay. Got it. Hey, I saw a guy that kind of looked like this," Jack said.

"That sounds pretty unlikely. Tell me about it."

"At the wine bar, Sunday night. Yeah, I went to the wine bar to buy some wine for dinner and I had some time to kill, so I had a flight of reds and he was there at the bar. We spoke. He had brown hair though, not grey."

"Okay, I saw this guy at the seminar. The CEO's assistant," Howard said.

"Maybe it's a common look in Russia," Jack said.

"Yeah, Maybe."

"So, what else about it?"

"So, nothing else about it," Howard said.

"Okay. Amy did something else that was weird. She sent me photos of me and Leena in Leena's bedroom. What do you think of that?"

"I think she's insane and she broke the law. Can you prove they were from her?"

"They had to be from her. She must have hired someone to plant a camera."

"Call the police."

"No. She may be destructive and nuts, but I can manage this."

"How?"

"Get rid of the camera."

"What if she does it again?"

"Then I'll call the police. Don't mention it to Rachel. It will just upset her."

Their conversation veered onto other subjects, ending a few minutes later.

Howard switched off the lamp and peered into the orange embers of the fire until sleep took possession of him.

Chapter 49 - The Hyatt after Dinner

After dinner, Petrov dropped Dmitri and Leena at the Hyatt Regency near the strange V shaped intersection of California and Market. The rain began to pour as Dmitri led Leena into the cavernous inner space of the Hyatt and then to an elevator. The rode to their floor and went to the room.

Once inside, Leena dropped her bags and pulled back the curtains to take in the view of the Embarcadero and Bay Bridge, which sparkled with multi-colors in the mist and rain. “Oh, Dmitri, look.” She lit a cigarette and opened the window a crack to let the smoke out.

Dmitri sidled up from behind her and hugged her, aligning his body with hers, and nuzzling her neck. “I have missed you.” They took in the view together. Dmitri rested his chin on her shoulder and he melded his body to hers. She felt the contours of his body, which seemed soft and mushy.

She was not in the mood, but played along, coaxing herself along with each step. Press *backwards into him. Turn and kiss him.* His stubble scratched her cheek. His body odor revolted her and she felt a faint gag reflex. *I can’t do it. He has old man skin, he smells old. There are grey lines on his ghost face.*

Her body went taught in rejection of his advance. She wriggled away and walked awkwardly to the bed, where she sat cross armed, staring at the floor. Dmitri sat down beside her and turned towards her. He put a hand on her shoulder. Leena didn't move.

"What is the matter, Leena? You seem remote, pensive. What are you thinking?"

How to escape. "Nothing, Dmitri. I am just a little worried about school. It is a challenge to take a class taught in a foreign language."

He moved closer to her until their thighs touched. He put his arm around her. She turned her head away from him. He took hold of her chin and turned her head towards him, moving his face to hers; his lips to hers. She turned again. He removed his arm from her shoulder.

"Who is Richard Greene?" He asked.

"I already told you. One of the professors. Arrogant, paunchy, old. I do not know him well."

"Has he shown any interest in you?"

"All the time. He flirts all the time. I resent it, but I smile and tolerate it. He asked me for a date."

"What did you say?"

"Oh, I made him feel guilty. There was no date."

"What about Robert Hooker?"

"I don't know a Robert Hooker."

"No, I mean Jack Hooker. Yes, Jack Hooker."

The color left her face. "I don't know a Jack Hooker either. Why do you ask?"

"You said his name in your sleep."

She shrugged. "I don't know Jack Hooker."

"Leena. Are you sleeping with anyone here?"

Leena took offense. "What kind of woman do you think I am? Do you really think I would jump into bed with Doctor Greene? He's too old, wrinkled, and besides…" She stopped.

"Am I too old for you now?"

"No. You are Dmitri, he is nothing. A boring professor."

Dmitri put his arms around her, pushed her back onto the bed and began to kiss her. She turned her head to the side and tried to push him away. He held her fast.

"No, Dmitri. I am having my period."

As he held her, he stared coldly into her face. He then pulled up her skirt and put his hand between her legs.

"No, Dmitri. I don't want to." She pushed him away, but he didn't budge. He continued touching her. She rolled to one side. He pulled her back, tearing her blouse. "No." She struggled again and then smacked him on the cheek.

He bolted into a sitting position with his hand on his face, completely surprised. She sat up. He wacked her across the face and she fell back on the bed. He panted with anger and glared at her. He raised his hand again and she flinched. He then rose from the bed and walked into the bathroom. Leena began to cry.

She heard him say, "Mikhail. Come get her. She will be in front of the hotel. Also, get me a flight back to Moscow in the morning. I am going home."

He returned to the bedroom. "Leave now. Take your things. He knows where to take you." She sat tearful and stunned. "LEAVE NOW!" She hesitated. He glowered and punched his left hand with his right. "I said leave."He walked into the bathroom and shut the door.

She gathered her things and left.

She waited near the Hyatt doorway on Drum Street. She didn't know who Mikhail was and worried what he might be like. Soon the limousine appeared with Petrov driving. He waved. A bellboy opened the passenger door for Leena. She threw her suitcase into the limo and got in. To her confusion, Petrov was driving the limo. She said nothing to Petrov, but wondered why he was picking her up instead of Mikhail.

As Petrov drove down Market Street, Leena peered out at the faceless silhouettes pushing shopping baskets, huddling in doorways with dogs, or camping in soggy cardboard. The sights made her shiver in the warmth of the limo. Soon he turned left, heading South of Market, down a street bordered by windowless buildings made from corrugated steel siding. Merchants haunted the street peddling drugs and flesh. A slow procession of cars slithered down the street, their drivers negotiating with the underbelly of San Francisco. Petrov pulled up to a curb, left the car and opened the passenger door. "Please get out, Miss," he said politely.

"What? You are asking me to get out here?"

"Yes, Miss."

“I can’t. Look at this place.”

“Please get out, Miss. Dmitri wants you to be let out here.”

“But where am I, Petrov?”

“Dore Street.” Petrov reached in, grabbed her suitcase and placed it on the sidewalk. “Please get out, miss.”

“I will not. You take me back to Stanford right now,” she ordered.

“Please get out, Miss,” he said calmly and then reached into the limo, grabbed her wrist, and started to pull her out of the car.

“I WILL NOT! I WILL NOT!” Leena struggled.

Petrov pulled her from the car, slammed the door shut. “Good bye, Miss,” he said politely and left.

The fuzzy outlines of soggy human shapes turned towards her. She looked at her bag which Petrov had left next to a pile of human excrement.

Chapter 50 - Jack to the Rescue

At around half past eleven at night, Jack's phone rang. *A call from Leena.* He picked up. "Hi, beautiful. What's up?"

Her bruised voice sobbed, "Oh, Jack. I need you. I need your help."

"I thought you were gone until Sunday."

"I had a very bad time, a very bad time. I am at Market and Powell. Oh, Jack."

"In San Francisco?"

"Yes, Jack. Please hurry. I miss you so much."

"I'm on my way."

Jack arrived at the Bart Station at Market and Powell a little after midnight. The intersection was filled with street people, many of whom were buying and selling drugs. While Jack waited for a traffic light to change, he watched two gaunt men enter a public bathroom Kiosk on the corner together. *That's a good way to catch HIV. Maybe they both have it already. Oy, the stench, gag.*

Policemen monitored the crowd from a parked police car ensuring that the petty crimes didn't escalate into violence. Jack saw Leena waving. He made a u-turn across Market, swooping to a curbside stop. She galloped to the car and jumped into the safety of his Corvette.

Leena sobbed, breathless and tearful. "Oh, Jack." She

pressed her cold face against his.

"You're soaking wet." He switched on the light. "Your lips are turning blue, your blouse is ripped. What is this on your cheek?" He touched the mark. "What the hell happened?" He set the car heater to high and turned on the seat warmers. "Were you mugged or something?"

As she began to explain the bleep of a police siren interrupted her. A police car pulled in behind, lights blazing. "Oh, shit." Moments later, a flashlight shined through the passenger window.

"Lower the window," The policeman ordered.

Jack smiled sheepishly. "Evening, officer. A bit of rain tonight. Keeping dry?"

"May I see your license, registration, and proof of insurance?"

Jack handed it all over. "What's the matter?" The policeman ignored him and walked back to his car.

"This is just great. I can't believe this." He glared at the police in his rear view window, shook his head, and then looked at Leena. "So what happened to you? I thought you were gone 'til Sunday?" Jack asked.

"It was horrible, Jack. I do not want to talk about it."

"Poor Leena. It's okay. We'll be home soon. What went wrong?"

"I got into a fight with Dmitri and he left me on the street in the rain."

“You’re kidding me? He dumped you on the street? What a jerk.”

“Take me home, Jack. I want to go home.”

“Sure, after we finish with the cops.”

“You should tell that rude cop to be polite and not insulting you, ”Leena said.

“Yeah, sure. That would really help.” They waited, watching the street people. “These cops ignore the people selling drugs, but not traffic violations. Jeeze. Hey, hey, look at those two guys coming out of the bathroom.”

“Oh my Gods,” Leena said.

“Gross. They walk free, but I get a traffic ticket.”

A tap on the driver’s side window startled them. Jack rolled down the window. “That was an illegal u-turn.” The policeman handed him a ticket.

“It is not fair officer that you are giving Jack ticket when they are selling drugs here,” Leena blurted out.

The policeman shined his light in her face. “How do you know they’re selling drugs?”

“We don’t know anything, officer,” Jack said. The policeman towered over him like a bully. Jack continued, “Look. I’m sorry, but she’s just had a terrible ordeal. She doesn’t know what she’s saying.” The officer walked back to his car. Jack’s heart sank. “Great. Now what?”

The officer returned with a dog and ordered them out into the rain. “Excuse me, officer, do you have probable cause here or anything like that to search my car?" Jack said.

"Yes, your friend's statement. Please get out. Now." The policeman was firm. "Go stand on the sidewalk." They did.

In no time the dog began to point; it smelled something on Jack's seat. *Oh shit. I have a pipe in my pocket. I'm doomed.*

Chapter 51 - Dmitri and Petrov

Dmitri had little experience with rejection, particularly from women and his anger roared. He inhaled deeply, loosened his tie, and paced back and forth, coming to rest at his window. After pausing to look out at the rain and the city lights, he then paced back across the suite to the bathroom, looked at himself in the mirror, took a hard stare into his brown eyes, and measured the aging flesh of his face. *I should get my eyes fixed. Maybe a little Botox for those wrinkles.* He looked at his teeth. *They need whitening.*

He returned to the window. *That tramp. That bitch. I should never have sent her here.* He paced back to the mini-bar in his suite, stopped, grabbed a couple of vodkas, and dumped them into a glass. *Absolute vodka. What do the Swedes know about vodka? It will have to do.*

His feet pounded their way back to the window and he stared down at the bay bridge while pumping the vodka into his stomach, one gulp at a time. Instead of soothing his anger, the vodka kindled a desire for carnal companionship. He felt trapped in the room. *I'm suffocating. I have to get out of here.* He left the room and went to the hotel bar on the lobby floor in the spacious inner space of the Hyatt. "Vodka, neat. Do you have Moskovkaya?" The bar tender nodded. "A double."

He scanned the bar. There were a few thirty-year-old silicon valley types, excessively clean cut, over dressed, and fervently pitching their billion dollar fantasies, looking for that lottery ticket. *There's no action here. I hate this place.*

He called Petrov. "Mikhail," he said, which was Petrov's real name.

"Yes, Dmitri?"

"Is she gone?"

"Yes, just as you said. Everything is in order."

"Mikhail, I have to get out of here. Come get my things. I will check out and wait at the bar. I want to go to the Fairmont."

"Yes, Dmitri," Mikhail said.

While waiting, he dashed off an email to the head of personnel from his phone.

> Marta,
>
> I am terminating Leena Kiraskaya's position at NovoRisk. Please follow the normal termination procedures.
>
> Dmitri Chesnakov

That was easy enough.

Dmitri ordered another vodka. At six-foot-four and two hundred forty pounds, he barely felt the vodka he had inhaled over the last half an hour. He felt no contrition about Leena, only rage at being denied.

Mikhail appeared. “Your bags are in the car, Dmitri.”

“Let’s go.” They left for the Fairmont.

The rain stopped when Mikhail pulled up to the Fairmont. He gave their bags and car keys to the valet. “Here are your room keys, Dmitri. You have a corner suite on the tenth floor. Your bags will be there in a few minutes. I am in room 571. Good evening.” Mikhail bowed and left Dmitri alone.

Dmitri’s blood boiled with anger and desire for female companionship. *I can’t sleep. Maybe a walk.* He charged down California to Mason and then headed towards China Town. The bad weather had cleared the streets except for an occasional sleeping pile of a ragged homeless person or a sickly whore turning tricks to feed drug habits.

After a thirty-minute march in the cool, moist air, his anger diminished, but his desire for female flesh had not. As he approached the lobby of the Fairmont he noticed a beautiful brunette woman, dressed to the nines, almost shimmering, pulling the tie of her boyfriend with whom she flirted. *That’s what I need. In fact, I’ll take two.*

He passed them as he walked through the lobby and then he heard, “Where’s the party? Where’s the party?”

He felt a tap on the shoulder. He turned. *It’s her?*

“Or should we have our own party?” He looked into her green eyes. She returned a seductive, dreamy look.

“Uh, come in for a drink,” He offered.

“Sure, sailor.” She took his arm.

They sat in the bar. A waitress came for their order "Vodka. Neat. Moskovkaya," he said.

"I am sorry; we don't have Moskovkaya. Grey Goose?" Dmitri nodded. "And you, Miss?"

"*Fumé Blanc,* please." The waitress turned and left. The woman then turned to face Dmitri. "You are Russian. Nice accent. What brings you to San Francisco?"

"Business. What brings you to the Fairmont?" he asked.

"Pleasure." She tipped her head to one side. "Nirvana, Euphoria, Ecstasy. Interested?"

He drained his vodka. "Yes. Let's go to my suite." They left the bar.

The corner suite provided Dmitri and the prostitute with a spacious view of the lights below. She glimmered like a fertility goddess against the backdrop of city lights and clouds. She had exactly what he wanted, unfettered access, no complications, no resistance, and willing to provide him with exactly what he asked for.

"Do you want any of this?" She held a pipe to her lips, flicked on a lighter and inhaled.

"What is it?"

She exhaled. "Rock Cocaine. Ever had it?"

"No."

"Want a hit?"

"Sure," he said. She reached into her purse, took out a pill box and added a couple of rocks to the pipe bowl. He walked to her, took the pipe and inhaled. The cocaine rushed to his head, his pulse rose, and he collapsed into a chair. He held the arms of the chair while acclimating to the drug. He felt euphoric.

"How is it?" She asked.

"Good," he understated.

"Now, what do you want?"

"You to do as I tell you."

"Okay. A thousand bucks now," she said.

He opened his wallet and placed ten hundred dollar bills on a small table. The money disappeared into her purse.

"Stand by the window." She moved to the window. "Now strip, take it all off. I want to see you naked."

Chapter 52 – Close Call

Jack gingerly pulled the pipe from his pocket, dropped it to the sidewalk, and gave it a kick. It skipped into the gutter and then rolled a safe distance away.

"How you know if the dog is finding something?" Leena asked.

"Don't know. It looks pretty intense right now. Keep your fingers crossed."

The policeman brought the dog over to Leena and Jack. "The dog smells something," the policeman said. The dog began sniffing and then stopped and pointed at Jack. "So, what have you been up to? A little crack, hashish? What?"

"Nothing, Officer. I don't use drugs," Jack lied.

"Well, my dog thinks you have."

"Who do you believe, Mister Officer? A dog or a human being?" Leena argued.

"Dogs don't bullshit. Okay, buddy, empty your pockets," the policeman said.

"You're wasting your time, Officer," Jack said.

"None of your lip, kid." He shined his flashlight in Jack's face. Jack pulled his pockets inside out. They were empty. He took his wallet from his back pocket and held them with his keys over his head.

The officers frisked him and found nothing. The officer knew something was amiss. “Okay, what did you take?” He shined the light into Jack’s eyes and studied them, looking for signs of intoxication.

“Nothing,” Jack replied.

“Close your eyes and hold your arms out. Now touch your nose with your right hand. Now your left hand.” Jack performed the sobriety test perfectly. “Well, I know you’re on something. You can leave.”

“Thanks,” Jack said. Leena and Jack returned to the car, shaking with cold.

“Jesus Christ! That was sooooo close.” He started the car.

“He is a bully and he was bullying you. He is jealous, I think.”

“Jealous? Right, sure he is. Another fucking ticket. Shit!”

“What is this on your face, Jack?” Leena pointed to the bandage.

“It’s been a real good day. I mutilated myself shaving.”

“Mutilated?” she asked.

“Disfigured. Cut badly,” he said.

“How you did that, Jack?”

“Some idiot slapped me on the back while I shaved. I cut myself. Like I said, it’s been a really shitty day.”

“That is not a friendly thing to do. I am not sure the fraternity is healthy place. Girl throwing beer at you, someone else making you cut yourself. I do not like it, Jack.”

"Well, I'm stuck there for the time being."

The small hours of the early morning cleared the 101 Freeway of traffic and Jack sped home.

They parked in front of Leena's place, entered the building, and took the elevator to her floor. They entered the condo and then her room. Leena ran to the bathroom, started a bath, stripped and wrapped herself in a towel while Jack waited in the bedroom. She returned to the bedroom. "May I have some privacy, Mister Hooker?"

"Uh, sure. Wait a minute, though." He positioned a chair by the air vent, stood on the chair and peered into the vent. "There. I see it."

"What?"

"Do you have a screwdriver?"

"No."

"Can you get me a knife, then?" Leena disappeared, returning a few seconds later with a dinner knife. "Thanks." Jack used it to unscrew the vent grating. He reached in and pulled out a camera.

Leena paled. "A camera!"

"Someone emailed a picture. I figured there was a camera here." He climbed down and showed her the picture on his phone. "Look."

"Oh my God."

"Yeah, I know. I freaked out too. Well, the camera is gone. Amy must have planted it."

“Amy? You mean the girl who threw beer?”

“Yep.”

“Why she would do that?” Leena looked at the picture.

“She’s jealous and she’s nuts.”

“How could she do this? She doesn’t have a key.”

“I think she hired someone,” Jack explained.

She remembered overhearing Dmitri and Petrov discussing a camera while she dressed. “I don’t think it was Amy. I think it was Dmitri and Petrov.”

“Dmitri and Petrov? Who are they? Sounds like a Vegas Magic Show.”

“Dmitri is CEO and Petrov works for security at the bank.”

“A security guy? You think they planted it? That would be way, way bad.”

“I heard them talk about camera. Who else would do this? Amy cannot get into my apartment. Petrov can.”

“Then they would know about us. Do you think they know? Do you think that’s why he threw you out?” Jack asked.

“No, we were fighting. We are not getting along.”

“Well, if Petrov is in security and he sent me this photograph, wouldn’t he tell Dmitri?” Jack asked.

She nodded. “Yes.”

“Well, maybe it doesn’t matter anyway. Your boss isn’t interested in your private life, right? So why plant a camera? Amy on the other hand, well she’s jealous and out of her mind. She won’t be coming back though.” He left the camera on the bureau.

A guilty pang pierced Leena's heart and she confessed, "I was involved with Dmitri, so he would care."

Jack sat straight up, turning bright red. "You and Dmitri? Oooooooooooooooh noooooooooo." Jack emptied his lungs, slammed his fist into the bed and then collapsed burying his face in a pillow, becoming inert.

Leena looked lovingly at him. *Ooooouch. That really hurt.* She stroked his back. "I am sorry, Jack, but this is my life and I am not required to make excuse or feeling guilty about it." She stroked him again. "Shhhhhhhh. Jack, you are my love, Jack," She purred. She lay down and cuddled up next to him.

Jack's eyes popped open. She repeated "You are my love, Mister Jack Hooker, who I want to stroke and caress and tell about my love for him. Oh, Jack," she sobbed. "What has happened? Hold me, Jack." She snuggled up more. "Please hold me, Jack." Her whimper become a soft sob. Unable to resist, he turned towards her, wrapped his arms around her, and kissed her. They fell asleep.

Chapter 53 – Epiphany

Jack awoke the next morning to hear Leena rustling around in the kitchen. He smelled eggs, bacon, and coffee. He rolled out of bed, pulled on his pants, and walked to the kitchen. She had set the dinette, poured orange juice and coffee, and served plates with eggs and bacon. She wore a robe. Her mascara from the night before smeared her gaunt face. "Hi, Jack. I made a breakfast."

"Thanks. How are you feeling?" he asked.

"Hoh, Jack." She emoted tears and hugged him for comfort. "What has happened, Jack?" She put her head on his shoulder.

He rocked her slightly. "Shhhh… shhh… shhh. We'll get through this."

"What can I do? I am lost, Jack."

"Get another job, I guess, right? Let's talk about it later." He sat and began eating.

She sat, breathed a heavy sigh and said, "I cannot eat, Jack. I am nervous. My stomach is having pain."

He nodded sympathetically, but continued eating. "Best scrambled eggs I have ever had." He smiled.

She replied with her low gravelly voice. "You are lying to me. Scrambled eggs are always the same."

He finished eating. "I'll clean things up here."

She left for the bedroom.

Jack loaded the dishwasher and then phoned Goldman.

"Howard."

"Hey. Soooo, vat's up?" Goldman replied.

"I'm at Leena's. She had a big fight with Dmitri and he dumped her in the rain in the middle of some criminal-filled street in San Francisco," Jack said.

"You're kidding me? What a cad. Sheesh. With you the drama never stops, does it?" Howard asked.

"Well, I guess they were involved or something. But it's over now."

"'You guess they were involved or something'," Howard mimicked Jack. "So he was her sugar daddy, wasn't he? In hindsight, it's sort of obvious, isn't it?"

"What do you mean?"

"Well, how about her rapid rise at the bank. Her trip here. Stuff like that," Howard said.

"Hey, that's insulting. She's brilliant. She finished a Masters in math at age twenty-one. Look, she needs a little sympathy, not New York sarcasm. This schmuck even slapped her. She has a little bruise on her face. Her blouse was torn."

"He slapped her? Jesus, just like a real man. And this is a CEO of a big Russian bank. That sucks," Howard said.

"Yeah, it sucks big time. Well, she hit him first anyway. They were having a fight."

"Really? Well, good for her. I hope she really socked it to him."

"She feels horrible. What a creep that guy is," Jack said.

“Yeah, no doubt. Mind if I change the subject? You know that picture I sent you?” Howard asked.

“Yeah, what?”

“It looks a lot like a guy who was with Dmitri at the seminar. He was like an assistant or something. His name is Petrov,” Howard said.

“Really? How come you have a photo of him?”

“Remember Rachel’s patient? The one who was kidnapped and raped? The photo is a sketch of one of the guys involved.”

“What? Get out of town. You’re saying Dmitri’s assistant is a rapist? I don’t believe that,” Jack said.

“He wasn’t the rapist. He was sort of like a bag man. He picked up a payment. Something like a hundred killograms of gold, according to Rachel’s patient.”

“I don’t believe that either. So they look alike? It’s a coincidence,” Jack replied.

“Maybe. Listen, why don’t you two come by once she’s dressed and check this out?”

“Okay. Give us a little time.” Jack hung up.

Leena emerged from the bedroom dressed in black jeans and a crew-necked black sweater. “I want orange juice. You too, Jack?”

“Sure. Then we should go to Goldman’s.”

“Why we need to see Howard?” Leena took a bottle out of the refrigerator and poured. She handed Jack a glass.

“He thinks he has seen that security guy before. You know,

uh, Petrov? Is that his name?"

"Petrov? Ridiculous. How would Howard see Petrov before?"

"Yeah, seems way unlikely."

"I am feeling bad, Jack. I do not want to socialize with Howard and Rachel." He hugged Leena, who collapsed into his arms. "What am I going to do, Jack?"

"Yeah, sleeping with the boss and then having a big fight with him is a pretty career-limiting move."

"It is, Jack," she emoted tearfully. "You are not jealous, are you?"

"Hell, yes I am." He held her tight.

"Do you think I am a whore, Jack?" she asked demurely.

"No, not at all, but I am still pissed off."

"Are you mad at me, Jack?" she asked faintly.

"No, but I am pissed off at Dmitri. I hate it when guys mess around with my girlfriend. And he hit you and then he dumped you in the street. He's a piece of dirt."

She sounded vulnerable. "Am I your girlfriend, Jack?"

"Of course." He kissed her on the temple.

"My job at NovoRisk will come to an end."

"Well, do you really need Dmitri in your life? You're pretty damn smart and experienced. Why not try another bank?"

"In Russia, you need connections, and when I was with him I had connection I needed, but it is over now."

"So, this means your career is over? Get real."

"It is, Jack. It is not like here. In Russia, you need connections or you're nothing. Forget about doing good work."

"Let's go to Goldman's and figure this out. Come on." He finished his juice, took her by the hand and led her out of the condo.

Jack and Leena knocked on Howard's door. The peep hole opened and Howard's brown eye peered through. He opened the door. "Hey, guys. Come on in. Hang your coats." They hung their coats and followed Howard to the living room. Howard noticed the smallish bruise on Leena's face and Jack's bloody bandage. "Oye vey. What happened to you two?"

"I told you, that Dmitri guy hit her. Look at that mark on her cheek," Jack said. Leena looked away and blushed.

"What a bastard! Jesus! And what happened to you?" Howard asked Jack.

"I cut myself shaving," Jack said.

"Nice. I'll hide all the sharp objects. Just in case," Howard taunted.

Rachel sat on the couch. "Coffee?" she offered.

Leena pouted. "I will have a coffee, please."

"Sure." Rachel disappeared into the kitchen.

"What did you think of the seminar, Howard?" Leena asked.

"Well, it's not my thing. I go to assist Siggy."

"How you are knowing Siggy?" Leena asked.

"We met at a party. He asks me about Russian things. I

advise here and there. Interesting man. From Germany. His father made a humble living designing the gear-works for Cuckoo Clocks. Siggy designed high-speed computers and became very rich."

"Here you go, Leena." Rachel returned with coffee and settled onto the couch.

"Thank you, Rachel. What a funny name. Siggy." Leena giggled.

"Not as bad as Sigmund. His middle name is Ludwig." Howard smirked and then continued, "Soooo, I met Dmitri at the seminar."

"'Soooo, you met Dmitri at the seminar'," Leena mocked, looked down at her sweater and brushed away a piece of lint. She looked Howard straight in the eye. "So, you met him. So what?" She said nothing more.

"Right. So what? Who was his assistant? He was kind of strange."

"Petrov? He works for Dmitri. In security," Leena explained.

"Security?"

"Well, he has a number of jobs. He drove us around San Francisco. I think he is sort of a bodyguard."

"How long have you known him?" Howard asked.

"This is first time I have seen him. But he works for the bank. Dmitri has known him forever, since the Army."

"How's that?" Howard asked.

"Dmitri was captain in the Army. He served in Chechnya and Petrov was in his unit, years ago."

Howard laid the sketch on the table and pushed it towards Leena. "Is this him?"

She picked it up. "Yes, well, where you get this picture?"

"Police. This is a sketch that was made by the police in Morocco."

"Why they make this sketch?" Leena asked.

"He was involved in a crime. Do you know his last name?"

"No."

"This man's name is Mikhail Kazakhstan. Ever hear of him?"

"No, I never hear of him. Kazakhstan is not normal name, Howard. It is a country, not a person's name," Leena said.

"Strange that Petrov and Mikhail Kazakhstan look alike," Howard said.

"It is strange. Kazaki is Russian name. Kazaki is common name in Russia." Leena suddenly remembered the wire transaction she managed just before coming to Stanford. "There is a Mikhail Kazaki who works at the bank. There was financial transaction for him. I do not know who he is. What was crime?"

"Do you remember Rachel's patient? The rape victim who was kidnapped in Greece?"

Leena looked horrified and covered her mouth with her hands. "Did he rape her?"

"No, but he knew the rapist and the girl saw him. He picked

up payment for something, a lot of gold. A hundred kilograms according to Rachel's patient. What do you know about this guy?" Howard asked.

"Oh my Gods."Leena turned white. "It can't be same man as Petrov. There was financial transaction. It was from him. That is all I know. But next day there was transaction with gold, exactly same amount, one hundred kilograms. It cannot be same man." Leena raised a hand to her astonished face.

Jack picked up the sketch. "I met a guy at the wine bar who looks like this, too. He had a weird accent, like Bella Lugosi playing Dracula. He said his name was Roma, not Petrov or Mikhail. The same guy wouldn't be at a wine bar in Palo Alto."

"Petrov has Romanian accent," Leena said.

"Romanian, that's right. I noticed his accent. I couldn't place it, though. So it's Romanian," Howard said. "The question is whether Petrov and Mikhail are the same man."

"I know what I can do. I can look at personnel records at the bank," Leena said.

"When you get back to Moscow? Are you going back soon?" Jack asked.

"I can find out now. Can you connect your computer to the internet?" Leena asked.

"It's connected." Howard handed her the laptop.

Leena typed into the laptop. "I will see what there is. Here, there are three Mikhail Kazaki. It is common name. One is janitor, one in accounting, and one in security. Here is picture of Kazaki in security."

The four gathered around the laptop. "There he is. Grey hair. It matches the sketch, and looks just like this Petrov character. His birthplace is Bucharest, Romania. Petrov has got to be Mikhail Kazaki and he is a criminal," Howard said.

"And look, he was in army, in Chechnya, like Dmitri," Leena added. "Dmitri said Petrov was with him in Chechnya. I think they are same man," Leena said.

"What was the 'financial transaction'?" Howard asked.

"It was not, how you say, 'kosher' transaction," Leena said.

"Why do you say not kosher?" Howard asked.

Leena turned red and was quiet for a moment. "Okay, I will tell you, but it is secret. Can I trust you?"

"Of course, you can trust us," Jack said and took her hand.

"Well, it was a secret transaction and records of transaction were deleted. It was large amount. It came in from Swiss bank and I moved it to account for Kazaki, and the gold came next day. I moved gold from Monaco to vault at Swiss bank. Dmitri told me to, so I did."

"Secret, like laundered money or something?" Jack asked.

"What is laundered money? You mean illegal money? I do not know." Leena said.

"Why did you move it to Kazaki's account?" Howard asked.

"Dmitri told me, so I put it," Leena replied

"So, is that illegal by Russian banking standards?" Howard

asked.

"It is grey area, Howard. Dmitri takes care of things like this," Leena replied.

"Do you know where the money comes from?"

"No, I never asked. I was just doing as I was told," Leena said.

"Yeah 'just following orders'. Where have I heard that before? I hate to say this, Leena, but you were, are, an accomplice to a crime."

She looked worried. "What is 'accomplice'?"

"Someone who helps with a crime," Jack said.

"It means you are guilty. It means you could go to jail," Howard added.

Leena became agitated and raised her voice, "I did not know this money is part of rape crime! I did not know! Jack, you must believe me. I did not do any crime that I know."

"I believe you," Jack assured her.

"I believe you didn't know about the sex slaves and so on, but you did know this transaction was illegal," Howard said. Leena was silent. "Are there a lot of transactions like this?" Howard asked.

"A couple each year, not many. Dmitri knows all about these things and tells me to handle them. I am just doing what he tells me to do."

"Do you think Dmitri knows that this is dirty money? He must know. Dmitri launders money and this money was made from selling women as sex slaves. He must know," Jack said.

"I do not believe this thing. Dmitri is not a bad man. Not a criminal. He would not do these things," Leena said.

"Well, how do you explain the sketch and name matching the personnel records? And you know he is laundering money?"

Leena paled and crumbled into Jack's arms. "It is not true. It is not true," Leena mumbled. "You cannot prove it, Howard."

"Okay, so the evidence is circumstantial, but it looks pretty convincing. What was the date of the Kazaki transaction?" Howard asked.

"What was date? It was on a Wednesday, October second. Yes, it was October second and gold was next day," Leena said.

"October second and third. My patient was with the kidnappers on those dates," Rachel said. Leena became quiet.

"Still, it is hard to believe, Howard," Leena said.

"Petrov and Mikhail are the same guy. And Mikhail is Dmitri's close associate going back to the Army," Howard said.

"I know how to confirm this. Call Dmitri and ask him," Jack said.

Howard laughed." 'Hi, Dmitri, a question for you. Is Petrov's real name Mikhail Kazaki and is he a criminal? And, by the way, do you launder money from sex slavery'?"

"No, not like that. Something a little more subtle," Jack said.

"I am having idea. How about I call Dmitri and saying him that I am leaving bag in the limousine last night and want to know if Mikhail has bag. If he says, ‘I will ask Mikhail’, then we know whether Petrov is Mikhail,” Leena said.

“Good idea. Let’s go for it,” Jack said.

“They are leaving for Moscow this morning. I have to call now.” Leena retrieved her phone from her bag and dialed. “It is ringing.” she said and put it on speaker phone.

Dmitri answered in Russian, “What do you want?”

Leena answered in Russian. “Hi, Dmitri. When Mikhail dropped me off last night I left a bag in the car. Do you know if he has it?”

“I have no idea.”

“Is he with you? Can you ask Mikhail whether he has it?”

“He is not with me.”

“How can I contact him?”

“You cannot.”

“I thought he works for the bank. I can contact him when I get home. Mikhail Kazaki is his full name, correct? Kazaki is his last name?”

Dmitri was silent.

“Do you think Mikhail Kazaki has my bag?” Leena asked.

“Leena, you are fired. Goodbye.” Dmitri hung up.

Leena slumped on the sofa. “I am fired now and he is behaving like Mikhail is Petrov’s right name. He did not say anything like, ‘you mean Petrov’. I think Petrov is really Mikhail.”

“Okay, that’s enough evidence for me,” Howard said.

“He fired me. My life is over,” Leena said despondently.

"He fired you? Just now?" Rachel asked.

"What do mean, your life is over? It's just a job and besides, you don't want to be involved in something like this anyway," Jack said.

"It is everything Jack, and Dmitri will stop me from getting new job by saying bad things," Leena said.

"Look, Leena, now that you know all this, do you really want the job? You probably would have resigned anyway."

"I think a job is the least of your worries. You're lucky to get out before it's too late. If Dmitri thinks you know what's going on, well, you could become a target," Howard said.

"He would not dare," Leena hissed. "We were together for almost two years. He would not touch me."

"Maybe, but after two years, he dumped you pretty easily. Like he just turned off a light switch."

"Howard!" Rachel shot him an angry glance.

"Yeah, sorry, but logically, well, you know what I mean," Howard stumbled searching for words.

"I am knowing what you mean, Howard," Leena said and sighed. "What can I do now?"

"Well, there's something else, Goldman," Jack said. "We found a hidden camera in her apartment. Someone sent me a picture from it. It shows me and Leena together."

"That's too much. That's the weirdest thing I have ever heard. Do you think that's why Dmitri dumped you, Leena?" Howard asked.

"I don't think he knew. He was not acting jealous," Leena replied.

"So, who sent Jack the picture?" Howard asked.

"No idea. Could it have been Amy? If it was this security guy, Mikhail, it seems like Dmitri would've known," Jack said.

"Amy? Amy couldn't have done something like this alone. Do you think she hired an investigator or something like that?" Howard asked.

"Who knows? She's crazy enough," Jack said.

"Breaking and entering Leena's apartment is illegal. I guess it's possible, still…" Howard's voice trailed off.

"I heard Dmitri and Mikhail talking about camera. I think they put camera," Leena said.

"That seems more likely, but why wouldn't Dmitri have known? Look, either way, Leena has to get out of there. Where can she go?"

"She can move into the Frat with me until we figure this out. I can smuggle her in without being seen," Jack said.

Chapter 54 - The Call

Leena and Jack returned to her condo to pack up her things before fleeing. When they arrived, they gingerly opened the front door and scanned the living room. Her laptop still sat on the living room table, opened, and on. No one was there and nothing had been touched. Leena went to the bedroom to pack while Jack turned on the television and surfed channels.

"Jack! Jack! Come here!" Leena called out. "This place where camera was hiding. It is back on. The camera is gone."

Jack entered her room. "Holy shit!! Someone put the grating back on the air vent. We've got to go, like soon. Get your stuff and let's vamoose." He turned off the TV. She returned with a bag, packed her laptop, and they left.

Safely back in Sigma Chi, Jack called Howard. "Howard?"

"Hey."

"Someone went through her apartment. They took the camera. I stupidly left it on the bureau. They took it. "

"Really? This is starting to get really interesting. You guys have to disappear. Do you think they can find you at Sigma Chi?"

"They can't come in here without being seen. I think we're pretty safe," Jack said.

"Ask Leena to pull up the web page with Mikhail Kazaki. I just sent the URL to her phone."

"What web page?"

"It shows Mikhail on the Interpol Web site. Just a little more evidence."

"Leena, Howard sent a message with the Interpol Web Page that shows Mikhail. He sent it to your cell phone. Check it out."

Leena looked in her bag. "Oh shits, Jack, I left my phone in bedroom, on the bureau," Leena emoted.

"You're kidding? That's just great. Now what?" Jack asked.

"I am needing my phone, Jack. If they get my phone they will be seeing everything."

"Yeah, like this message about Kazaki. Howard, I got to go. Later."

Jack motored over to Leena's condo complex alone, parked around the corner and down a side street, hiding his car in the long shadows of the late autumn afternoon. Cutting the rumble and shake of his Corvette's engine felt emasculating. He felt vulnerable. His heart began to pound and his viscera tingled as he contemplated entering her condo. After a deep breath, he left the safety of his car and walked towards the condo complex, scrutinizing pedestrians and parked cars for signs of Mikhail, Petrov, Roma, or whoever this guy was.

After entering the foyer, he chose the stairs over the noisy elevator to ascend to the third floor. After climbing to her floor, he crept towards the door, stopped when he reached it and listened; nothing stirred inside. He unlocked the door, opened it a crack and peeked in. Nothing had changed. He stepped inside, stopped and listened again to hear only silence. After closing and locking the door, he tiptoed to the kitchen; no one was there. He moved quietly to the bedroom, then bathroom, checked the closets, looked under the bed and found no one.

He didn't see her phone on the bureau. His pulse raced and the hair on his neck and arms stood at attention. *Someone has been here. Mikhail?* He kept his terror in check as he searched the condo for her phone, without success. He decided to dial Leena's phone so he could follow its ring. The phone rang and rang and rang; he heard nothing in the apartment. Then it picked up, "YOUUUUUUUU ASSSSSHOOOOOLE! I HAAAAAAATE YOUUUUUU!" Amy shrieked into the phone.

Jesus Christ. How did Amy get Leena's phone?

Amy continued her rant, "I'M GOING TO KILLLLLLLL MYSELF. DO YOU HEAR ME? KILLLLLLL MYSELF. I HATE YOU!" This was followed by hysterical sobs. He stared out the kitchen window in shock scanning the blue sky for solace from Amy's howling breakdown. His eyes fell to the quiet street below, empty except for a woman pushing a stroller, a man dressed in black approaching the building, and two students chatting on the sidewalk. Amy's sobbing became a faint whisper. "I can't go on. I can't go on. Do you hear me, Jack? Don't make me do it, Jack. Don't make me kill myself."

Should I call 9-1-1?

"And don't you hang up. Please don't leave me alone. I need you, Jack," Amy begged.

I can't hang up. I'm trapped. He was paralyzed, until a car alarm went off outside startling him. Beneath the alarm's *honk, honk, honk*, he heard a blue jay shriek and felt the building elevator jolt into action. His attention returned to the call. Finally, he spoke, "Amy, we can't go on together. I'm sorry. We can't."

"I know," Amy's frail voice surrendered.

"But we had some times I will never forget," He said warmly.

"I know. You are soooo bad," she giggled. "But now I am alone, Jack." The vision of her cute, sad pouty face tugged at his heartstrings.

"How did you get Leena's phone?"

"WHO IS LEENA? IS SHE THAT RUSSIAN WHORE WOMAN YOU'RE SEEING.I DON'T HAVE HER FUCKING PHONE!"

Huh? He checked the number and found he had accidently dialed Amy.

Nice job, fool. He said, "Amy, calm down, but you have to accept that things between us are over. You know they are, but, you know, I will also have a special place in my heart for you."

She became calm again. “Yes, I know. And I for you, too.”

“That’s very generous of you, Amy. Thank you, sweetheart.”

Someone began fumbling at the lock of Leena’s door. *What?* Jack panicked.

“I just need someone to talk to,” Amy continued.

“I’ve got to go. We’ll talk more later.” Jack, in terror, ended the call, scampered into the bedroom, and hid under the bed.

Jack heard the door open and shut. The footfalls of a large person tread across the living room. A phone rang. A man answered, “Da.” A short conversation in Russian followed.

The ringing in Jack’s ears rose with his terror, deafening him. He prayed Mikhail wouldn’t hear him pant or his pounding heart which nudged his body with each throb. He saw black boots walk passed the bed and into the bathroom. The tinkle of peeing and a flushing toilet followed. The boots left the room. He heard the television switch on and assumed the man settled in the living room.

The condo buzzer sounded. Jack heard steps towards the door. “Hello,” Mikhail said.

"Is this Mister Roma?"

"Yes, is this José?"

That's the same voice and accent as that Roma guy at the wine bar. It's him!!

"It is."

"Come in. Apartment 311," Mikhail said and buzzed José in.

Jack heard a knock at the door and the door open, "Mister Roma?"

"Hi, how are you? Yes. I want a new lock on the front door," Roma said.

"No problem. Give me an hour or so."

"Okay. Do you mind if I lie down while you work? If you need anything let me know. I will be in the bedroom."

"No problem."

The boots reappeared in the bedroom and approached the bed. Mikhail sat on the bed, removed his boots, dropped them by the side of the bed and then flopped down. The immaculate boots smelled of leather and shoe polish.

Jack felt his breathing quicken, his pulse rise, and the

deafening tinnitus return. Jack could hear has heart pound in his open mouth, so he shut it and breathed through his nose, hopeful his deep breath wouldn't be heard.

Soon he heard the rhythmic breathing of Mikhail sleeping. The storm of his panic ebbed away. *I could be trapped here for hours, or found by this guy, and I have to pee. Should I leave? What if the locksmith sees me? That doesn't matter. Seize the moment.*

Jack reached for the boots, moved them a foot or so towards the head of the bed, stopped moving, and listened. Mikhail continued to sleep. Jack inched his way from under the bed, towards the bedroom door. Once he cleared the bed, he stopped and listened. No change. He crept on all fours towards the door. The locksmith suddenly made a loud noise and Jack froze. The noise caused Mikhail to change the cadence of his breathing, smack his lips a few times, and then return to undisturbed sleep. Jack waited while the locksmith fiddled and fooled until the noise stopped. He then slowly turned the door knob, opened the door, and crawled out. He took a look back at Mikhail. *It's him!! Holy shit.* He slowly shut the door.

"Hi, who are you?" José asked.

"No one. No body, just on my way out, adíos," Jack said.

"Adíos."

Jack fled, taking the stairs and running to his car. *Mikhail must have Leena's phone.*

Chapter 55 – Fear

Jack bounded up the stairs to his room at Sigma Chi, fumbled at the lock, and popped inside to find Leena reading a book on Risk Management. She looked up and asked, "Did you find the phone, Jack?"

"Nope. But I did see Mikhail Kazaki."

"WHAT? Oh shits, Jack." Leena's eyes opened wide and she turned pale.

"Yeah, I was totally freaked. I barely got away. He came back to your place when I was still there. I hid under the bed."

"Oh my Gods. He almost caught you?"

"You got it," he said.

"Thanks to God he didn't. So he is still here. He did not go back with Dmitri. Do you think he has my phone?"

Jack said, "It is very likely he has your phone. It's an iPhone isn't it?" Leena nodded. "So, he can dump all the messages and emails to a file and then look at them."

"Oh no, Jack. How he does that?"

"There is software for that," Jack said.

"So he will find out everything," Leena said.

"We can assume that he has, or will." Jack dialed Howard, "Hey, Howard."

"Hey. Did you get her phone?" Howard asked.

“No, it was gone. I saw Mikhail Kazaki. He was the same guy I saw in the wine bar. He has the same accent and used the same name, Roma. He came back to her condo to change the locks.”

“He changed the locks?” Leena asked. Jack nodded to her.

“Ohhh, that’s not good. Not good at all. Now what?” Howard said.

“It doesn’t look to good for Leena. She’s been fired. She has no place to live.” Jack turned to Leena. “Do you have any money?”

“I have credit card from bank,” She replied.

“I’ll bet they turned that off too,” Jack said. Leena planted her face in her hands in despair. Jack spoke to Howard, “They cut her off totally. She doesn’t even have plane fare back to Moscow.”

“I don’t think she should go back to Moscow,” Howard said.

“Yeah, right.” Jack then turned to Leena. “How long is your visa good for?”

“I cannot stay in America. I am Russian national,” She replied.

“But what about your visa. We can buy time while things sort themselves out. How long are you allowed to stay?”

“Two years,” She replied.

“Two years!” Jack said. Leena nodded. Jack said to Howard, “Her visa is good for up to two years. The question is, what to do in the meantime?”

"In the short term, we all need to lay low. Mikhail is going to figure out that we know and that is a problem," Howard said.

Chapter 56 – Mikhail Calls Dmitri

As Dmitri exited the plane at the Moscow airport his phone rang, “Dmitri here.”

“It’s Mikhail.”

“I just landed. The flight was horrible, didn’t sleep at all. My head is pounding. What do you want?”

“The Sovcomflot operation,” Mikhail said.

“Right, and the gold and everything. Last month,” Dmitri said.

“It’s been compromised,” Mikhail said.

“What do you mean?”

“Interpol has arrest warrants out for me and Anton.”

Dmitri shouted into the phone, “HOW THE HELL DID THIS HAPPEN?”

Mikhail flinched, but his voice remained calm. “Not sure. Anton exposed me and himself to a woman on the boat. He took my mask and removed his. Perhaps someone escaped.”

A pause followed.

“ANTON! THAT PIECE OF SHIT. WHERE THE HELL IS HE?I WANT HIS FUCKING HEAD!”

“He is at the bottom of the Mediterranean Sea.”

“So you got rid of him already. Good. Maybe it is time for you to come home and disappear for a while,” Dmitri said

“Well, there are some loose ends here in California.”

"SHIT! What are you talking about?" Dmitri asked.

"Do you remember the Jew at the seminar?"

"Yes, what about him?"

"His name is Howard Goldman," Mikhail said.

"So what?" Dmitri asked.

"He knows about Sovcomflot and he has seen you and me together."

"This just gets worse and worse. I should never have gone to California just to see my mistress. Stupid letting my dick rule my life. Does Leena know? She saw us together," Dmitri said.

"They both know," Mikhail said.

"SHIT! DOES ANYONE ELSE KNOW?"

"A man whose name is Jack Hooker, an American," Mikhail said.

"Jack Hooker? I have heard this name. She knows him, doesn't she? Are they together?" Dmitri asked.

"No."

After a short silence Dmitri spoke, "There's no choice. Take her out. I want her to disappear. Do not touch the Americans. That would make this spin out of control. I just want her out. Just get rid of her, understand?"

"Yes," Mikhail replied.

Dmitri hung up.

Dmitri's administrator poked her head into his office. "Your next meeting is here."

"Okay, give me two minutes and then show them in."

Dmitri took a mirror from his desk, studied his face and upon finding a blemish on his nose, took a bottle of skin tone from his desk. He put a little on his finger tip, then dabbed at the blemish, painting it away.

My dick is more trouble than it's worth.

Chapter 57 - Fraternity Sanctuary

Leena and Jack watched television in the safety of Jack's room. "Leena, are you hungry. Do you feel like Indian food?" Leena nodded. "How about some Samosas, Aloo Panack, and Tandori Chicken?"

"Sounds wonderful, but we cannot leave, Jack. We are 'hiding out', as you say."

"Let me take care of this." Jack dialed his phone.

"Amber Dhara, best Indian Food in Palo Alto," a voice answered.

"Hi, I want an order to go."

"I am sorry, but the kitchen has just closed."

"Hey, is this Mohan?" Jack asked. Mohan was born in the U.S., but his parents emigrated from India. He was a brilliant student and bound for Medical School. His father was an engineer, but his extended family ran Amber Dhara. Mohan was the first Indian-American Jack had ever known. He was a good friend; a close friend. "Mohan, it's Jack Hooker."

"Hey, it's the Hook. What can I do for you?"

"Feed me. I'm starving."

"Of course, we will feed you, my good friend. What would you like?" Mohan warmly replied.

Jack ordered food and then prepared to leave. "Where you

are going, Jack?" Leena asked.

"To pick up the food. You wait here, okay?"

"I am scared, Jack. What if Mikhail comes?"

"Hmmm, good question. Okay, come with me," Jack said.

"What if he is watching fraternity and sees us leave?" Leena asked.

"Oh, well, I have a little secret. Only the elite fraternity brothers know."

"Elite fraternity brothers? I am sorry, Jack, but there is no such thing," Leena replied.

"Well, within Frat World there is. Let's go," Jack said.

It was near eleven o'clock on a school night and the fraternity was quiet. Leena and Jack slipped out of his room and scampered down the second floor hallway until they came to a door near the very end that had a combination lock. Jack punched numbers into the door lock, opened the door, and they disappeared inside. Jack lit the room with his cell phone flashlight. The closet had a furnace that rumbled away, a couple of buckets, mops, brooms, a shelf that held poisons, cleaning fluids, and a few tools. He gave his light to Leena. "Hold my light, shine it here." He moved the shelf. Behind it was a rectangular metal plate held onto the wall with four screws. He took a screw driver from the shelf, removed the screws, and slid the plate to the side revealing a passageway with rickety stairs that led downward into darkness. A musty smell filled the closet. Spiders and webs criss-crossed the passage, which was too low to stand in. "May I have the light?" he asked. "Follow me." Jack used a stick to clear the webs as they descended. The stairs led to a large room that was filled with boxes, shelves, and a couple of antique toys. He moved a shelf from a wall. Behind it was another passage. "Come."

"What is this place?" Leena asked.

"A secret passage. The house was built by a rich guy a long time ago. He went berserk and murdered his daughter and probably his wife. They found the daughter's body in the bathroom on the third floor, but never found the wife. Maybe he buried her down here someplace. Scary, isn't it?"

"This is horrible, Jack." Leena grabbed his arm.

"Yeah, and it smells bad. Look!" Jack pointed at the skeletal remains of a rat. Leena grabbed his arm. "At least, no one can see us come and go. Almost no one knows about the passage. We can use it safely. No one will know."

They crouched as they walked. At the end of the short tunnel was a second door which he opened and they stepped outside. He led her to his car which was parked in an alley and hidden under a car covering. He pulled off the car covering and they folded it and Jack tossed it into the trunk. "Let's go."

Leena and Jack returned to his room with the food, using the passage to re-enter Sigma Chi. "The passage gives me the creeps, Leena."

"What are creeps? Such a funny sounding word."

"Makes me scared, uncomfortable."

"It is cold and scary and the spiders. I am glad to be in your room." Leena shuddered.

The two sat on the floor, opened the to-go bags, and scooped small piles of rice, curry, and tandoori chicken onto paper plates. They shared a large Kingfisher beer.

"Kind of hot. I like hot," Jack said.

"Oh well, Jack, this is not really hot at all. I have been to India and the food is wonderful, but when you ask for hot, it cannot be eaten by a western person. Your mouth hurts with this food. May I have a piece of naan?"

They ate slowly and in silence until they had their fill. Jack put the leftovers in a small refrigerator. He and Leena took the plates to the bathroom, which at one in the morning was deserted. They tossed out the plates and brushed their teeth.

"I need a shower, Jack. I feel dirty and I am smelling bad."

"I think you smell delicious, like a pretty flower with a touch of curry. I don't think we should risk taking a shower here."

"Why not, Jack? It would be kind of sexy." Before he knew it, she shed her clothing and stepped into the shower.

"Yikes!" Jack said. "Okay, let's make it quick." They soaped each other and then Leena grabbed him, pressing her slippery body against his.

"What is this, Mister Hooker?" She gave him a sly look as she took hold of his excitement.

They kissed while she slid her body over him.

"No, no, Leena. Let's go back to my room. I want privacy. I will have Leena for dessert. I want to take my time and savor each morsel," he growled.

"Yes, Mister Hooker."

They scampered naked and wet, back to his room.

Chapter 58 – Afterglow

The two lay on his bed, spent and satisfied. "Do you mind if I smoke, Mister Hooker?" Leena asked.

"Nope, go ahead. You know, I am wide-awake. Don't think I can sleep."

"I am too nervous to sleep, Jack. What is time?"

"After two. Want to watch a movie?"

"Okay, what movie?"

"How about *Chinatown*? It is a classic American movie."

"I have heard. Roman Polanski movie with Jack Nicolson and Faye Dunaway. I have never seen this *Chinatown* movie. What is it about?"

"Bad guys in Los Angeles and a detective. Sort of a good guy. Sort of a sleazy guy. A little bit like an anti-hero."

"Anti-hero? Well I like Roman Polanski movies. Have you seen The Pianist about this Jewish musician hiding during World War Two?"

"Yep."

"I love the way he shoots movies, the colors, the scenery, the characters. Let's watch this *Chinatown* movie."

He opened a small case of DVDs, found *Chinatown*, put it into a DVD player, and then returned to the bed to snuggle with Leena while they watched. About forty-five minutes into the movie, the beautiful Evelyn Mulwray and detective Jake Gittes fall into bed. Afterwards, Evelyn takes care of Jake's nostril that was slit open by a thug earlier in the movie.

Leena looked at Jack's face. "This bandage on your lip is dirty, Jack. I think you should put new one. I can change it. You have another bandage?"

"Yeah, okay." He retrieved his dopp kit and handed it to her.

"Here, Jack, a clean one. Here is iodine to preventing infection." He flinched while she peeled away the dirty bandage and dabbed the cut with iodine. She applied a new bandage and kissed him and then he kissed her. Soon they were aroused. They made love again to the strains of Chinatown. Afterwards, they fell asleep.

Jack started awake at hearing a rustling sound by the door. He looked at the clock; five o'clock on the nose. He sat up and saw an envelope on the floor by the door. *Not again! Shit.* He slid out of bed, tip-toed to the envelope, squatted down, and opened it. A photo slipped out and fell to the floor. It was a photo of Leena, naked, kneeling, blind folded, arms tied behind her back. A note on the back said, "She is for sale. Interested?"

What the fuck! He tried to speak, but his voice had gone. Suddenly, the door flew open knocking him hard in the head and onto the floor. There stood Mikhail Kazaki, towering over him. "NOOOOOO!" He sat straight up in bed.

"Jack! Jack! Jack! Wake up. You are having bad dream."

Leena held him. “It is okay now. See? Just a bad dream.”

Perspiration dripped from his clammy face. “I dreamt they had captured you and then Kazaki burst through the door.” He ran his fingers through his hair. “I don’t think I can sleep anymore. I’m getting up.”

“I can sleep, Jack. I am going back to sleep.”

“Okay.” He bent over and kissed her temple. She closed her eyes.

Jack grabbed a towel and dopp kit and headed to the bathroom for a shower and very careful shave. He returned to his room, dressed, went downstairs to the kitchen and made coffee, settled on the patio outside, and stared blankly into space as he sipped. He heard the flop of the newspaper as it landed on the sidewalk in front of the fraternity. He went inside for a second cup and then ventured outside into the dark morning for the paper. From the Sigma Chi landing overlooking the street, he spotted the paper and began to descend the steps to fetch it when he saw the dark outline of a man sitting in a parked car. Jack froze. The man’s head turned and appeared to look at him and then ducked down. Jack ran back inside locked the front door and ran up the stairs to his room.

“Leena, Leena, he’s out there. I saw him.” He stood by the window looking out at the car.

Leena sat up. “Who? Is it Mikhail Kazaki?”

“I couldn’t see his face. It was too dark. Come here, look.”

The naked Leena left the bed and stood by Jack’s side. As

they looked they saw a man, dressed in black, wearing a ski mask, cross the street and climb the steps of the fraternity.

"Let's get out of here," Jack said. As Leena dressed, they heard someone try to open the locked fraternity door. Jack saw the man on the sidewalk looking up at the fraternity. Jack stepped away from the window.

"Quick! We have to leave, like now."

They grabbed a couple of bags and fled down the hall to the passageway.

Chapter 59 - Fear and Loathing

Rachel started awake. “Howard, pssst, Howard.” she whispered and shook him.

“Uhhhhhh.” Howard rolled over.

“Howard, wake up. I hear something.”

“What? I hear something too. Your voice. Now go back to sleep.” He pulled a pillow over his head.

“I hear a noise outside.”

“Huh? Well, go check it out. It’s probably a raccoon or something.”

“Howard, I’m scared.” She nudged him.

“What? God damn it! I’m trying to get a little sleep around here.”

“Shhhh. Listen.” Falling metal clanged as it hit patio concrete in the backyard.

Howard sat up and looked at Rachel. “Did you hear that?” Rachel nodded, wide-eyed. Howard pulled the blankets up to his chin. “Call the cops?”

“Nooo. Go see what it is. You know, ‘it could be just a raccoon’. Howard the coward. Go see.”

Howard put on a robe, stumbled into the living and stood by the book case that blocked the view to the back yard. He removed a couple of books and peered through. Two shapes stood on the patio, near the back door.

Holly Shit! He flew back to the bedroom, dove into bed, and pulled the covers over his head.

"What did you see?" Rachel whispered.

"There are two guys in the back yard." Someone knocked on the backdoor. "Yikes," Howard whispered.

Rachel jumped out of bed and grabbed a fire poker from the fire place as she tip-toed through the living room towards the backdoor. There was a second knock on the back door. She rushed to the door, flipped on the outside light, and peered through the peephole. "Jack? Leena? What are you doing here?"

"Let us in, we need to talk," Jack answered.

Rachel opened the door. "What's going on?"

Howard peeked around a corner. "Hooker? What the hell? It's a little after five."

"We need to talk. We need to figure this out. That Kazaki guy was out in front of Sigma Chi this morning. He's looking for us."

"You're shitting me," Howard said.

"I couldn't see the guy. He actually put on a ski mask. He tried to get into the frat. Dude, we're in deep shit."

"Time to run away," Howard said.

"Fight again another day? Yeah I agree. I'm scared shitless and I'm pissed off. I want to kick the shit out of this guy. And I want to hide. I'm torn. And this Dmitri character too, I want to kick his ass." Jack said.

"Right. You're going to attack this Mikhail guy. He'll kill you, you idiot. You don't want to tangle with these guys."

"Yes, I do. I want to kill those fuckers."

"Right, and become dead meat. Look, Kazaki is a pro and he'd make mincemeat out of you and Leena and me, for that matter."

"Yeah, I know it's a stupid impulse. Soooo instead, we're going to hide at our place in the woods near Portola State Park. That's where we're going." The park was in a Redwood Forest in the Santa Cruz Mountains, about one hour from Palo Alto. "We've already packed. We are going there now." Jack's father had bought a cabin years ago in the Middleton Tract, a small community of summer cabins developed by the Stanford luminaries in the 1930s. Jack's prize Moose Head, stolen from a rival fraternity, hung in the living room.

"With luck, he'll never find you there."

"God, I hope not. Before we all run and hide let's talk about this. We can't just hide. These guys aren't going to just give up and walk away. We have to do something," Jack replied.

Howard started a fire as they chatted. "You know, there is a string I can pull," Howard said.

"Must be big string, Howard." Leena said.

"It is. Here's what I'm thinking. I have a cousin in Russia, a distant cousin, someone I've never met face to face, but we have an email relationship. For years, I've known this guy. His name is Grigori Navalny."

"Oh well, Howard, I have heard of him. He is not very popular in the corporate world in Russia."

Howard raised his eyebrows. "I can't imagine he would be."

"I've never heard of him. Who is he?" Jack mumbled.

Leena leaned over into his arms and kissed him on the cheek. "Poor, Jack, you are always in the dark."

"I hate being the dumbest guy in the room," Jack complained.

"Yes, I'm sure you do." Howard grinned.

"I do not like you saying these insults to my boyfriend, Mister Jack Hooker." Leena lifted Jack's hand and kissed it.

"That's okay, Leena. Howard has a deep-seated need to abuse men who are taller and better looking. It's instinctual, impulsive."

Howard nodded. "Touché."

"So, who is this Grigori guy anyway?" Jack asked.

"Grigori runs a blog in Russia that exposes corruption in government and business. Let's go there now." Howard typed into the laptop. "Here, that's it." He handed the computer to Leena and Jack.

"It's Greek to me, or should I say Cyrillic. So, what does it say?"

Leena read the screen. "Oh, I have heard of this scandal. It is with Transneft and embezzling money."

"So tell me, what is Transneft?" Jack asked.

"I will tell you, Jack," Leena said, enthused. "It is an oil pipeline company. They are giving away ten percent of company profits to charities."

"Sooo, what's wrong with that?" Jack asked.

"They were not real charities, Jack. They were pretending charities for embezzling money. Navalny exposed the corruption. People went to jail. He does these things many times in Russia. But I think this Grigori man is tilting at windmills," Leena said.

"His blog makes a difference," Howard said.

"A small dent, Howard, a small dent only. And he is risking life. I do not think it is a smart thing," Leena said.

"I disagree," Howard said.

"I agree with Howard. So what's the idea?" Jack asked.

"We can expose Mikhail and Dmitri with Grigori's blog," Howard said. Leena became quiet.

Jack smiled at the idea of bringing down a big man like Dmitri, a guy who messed with his girlfriend. "Let's go for it. What do we have to do?"

"We need to show Grigori the criminal sketch, the story of the sex slaves, the transaction where Leena laundered for Dmitri, and that Kazaki is Dmitri's body guard. He can take it from there."

"I do not feel comfortable, Howard. I have known Dmitri for two years and he has been very good to me."

"He is a psychopath who launders money for people who traffic in sex slaves, and probably lots of other things. He just smacked you in the face and dumped you on the street. Dumping you was as easy as taking a dump and flushing a toilet," Howard said.

"Howard!" Rachel scolded.

"Okay, okay. Bad metaphor, yeah. Sorry, wrong metaphor." Howard shook his head, but then he continued, "You know what I mean, though. Seriously, your relationship is over, and now he has his thug looking for us."

"They'll turn you into road kill." Howard's voice curdled.

Howard laid out the evidence on the living room table; the sketch, NovoRisk personnel records, Rachel's patient, Mikhail Kazaki. "We are missing the proof of the transactions and Dmitri's connection to them. We have enough on Kazaki, but not Dmitri."

"Oh, I can get. I have email from Dmitri saying to move gold. My laptop is in the car."

"I'll get it," Jack said and left to get the laptop.

Chapter 60 - Fighting Back

A few minutes later, Leena had her laptop and retrieved the email. “See, it is here.” The three gathered around her laptop and read.

“That’s it? I can’t read it,” Jack said.

Howard read out loud, “Yep, that’s it, the smoking gun. The date is October second. It is from Dmitri and it says, ‘After moving the gold to the Geneva vault, have it moved to the Minsk branch in Belarus. Here are the vault numbers.’ Can you send this to Howard and myself, just to back it up.

“You know, Dmitri could have the email deleted. If he was careful, it’s already gone,” Howard said.

“I have idea, Howard. My friend in IT. She can get email and back it up, too. She is Tatiana. Here, let me send her email.” Leena typed away. “Oh, email is not working.”

“If you’re fired all your accounts and access are gone,” Jack said.

“How I contact her?” Leena asked.

“Create a Gmail account. It’s free. Go to Google. Here, let me show you,” Jack said. In a couple of minutes her account was set up. “Let me do this so I can get your emails on my phone.” He fiddled with his phone.“What is the password, Leena?”

“Mister Jack Hooker is password.” She smiled.

“Very original.” He pressed buttons on his phone. “Okay,

you're ready to go."

Leena typed an email to Tatiana.

'Hi Tatiana,

> I have some bad news. I am no longer with NovoRisk bank. It is breaking my heart, but there is nothing I can do about it. I do not feel like going into detail right now, I am too sad. I will tell you more when I am back in Moscow. Please don't mention this to anyone.
>
> I need a small favor. Do you see the attached email from Dmitri? Can you retrieve it from the email server, check whether it is still there and if so, send me a copy?

Your good friend, Leena'

"Okay, that is done." Leena sighed.

"A single email from Dmitri is pretty weak. I guess it's better than nothing. We'll see if Grigori thinks it is enough to post on his blog."

"Wait, Howard, I have other idea. I know head of Accounting at the bank."

"Head of Accounting? He's probably a crook, too," Jack said.

"No, no. I am sure he is not crook, Jack. He is very honest man. His name is Alexi Andreovich."

"Is he a friend or what? Please don't tell me he is another boyfriend," Jack said.

"He is not boyfriend. His is acquaintance and highly placed, third or fourth man at bank. I can give him email from Dmitri with vault numbers for gold and picture of Mikhail Kazaki. He is a worried man with a lot of paranoid feelings about the bank. He is kind of man who cannot resist looking into this email and things like that. Here let me send him." She composed a second email to Alexi.

'Hi Alexi,

> Dmitri fired me so I am no longer working at the bank. Before I go, I must alert you to some strange things that happened before he fired me. Please read the attached email from Dmitri. He asked me to perform an irregular transaction, moving 100kg of gold from our Geneva branch to Belarus. The vault/account numbers are in the email.
>
> I am concerned this transaction was illegal. At the time, I assumed the transaction was okay because Dmitri asked me to do it. Now I am worried.
>
> Also, see the attached URL to Interpol Web Site and the picture of Mikhail Kazaki. He is wanted by Interpol and works in security for Dmitri. He was involved in this gold transaction. And I performed a 'special' transaction for him on Oct 2. I transferred 300,000 Swiss francs to the Belgrade branch, into an account with his name. Here is the account number, 387-54308-4487

Thanks,
Leena Kiraskaya'

"There. That is done now, too," Leena said.

"Let's wait until we hear from your friends before we expose this on Grigori's blog."

"Agreed," Jack said.

"Can I smoke cigarette, Howard?" Leena asked.

"Of course, you can. Just go outside on the patio. Be sure and shut the door." Howard grimaced.

"Oh shits, Howard," Leena said.

"Sorry, I hate the smell and I don't want to get lung cancer."

Part III

Chapter 61 – Escape

"I know exactly where to hide from this guy," Jack said, as they fled Palo Alto feeling twinges of relief amid a flood of panic. They drove away, winding up Page Mill Road, up the bayside of the Santa Cruz Mountain Range, passing through hazy groves of pine and madrone, bursting out into warm sun light, and then plunging back into dense fog that crept down the mountain side on cat's feet.

Page Mill Road intersects Skyline Boulevard which runs along the ridge of the Santa Cruz Mountains from South San Francisco to Santa Cruz, ending in an old growth redwood forest. At the intersection, Jack pulled off the road and onto a patch of ground that was bordered by the two roads and a wall of Manzanita. "We're at the top. Let's check out the view of the bay."

He led her by the hand from the car to a spot with a clear view of the cities and freeways below from San Jose, to San Mateo.

Jack pointed. "There's Hoover Tower at Stanford." The monolith towered above the campus. It was crowned by a cupola which was adorned by a reddish sphere on top, like a cherry. Hoover Tower is a library of historical documents, left to Stanford by Herbert Hoover.

Leena piped up, "Oh well, Jack. Hoover was President during Great Depression. It is a library. He gave books and documents to the University. Before he was President."

"Really, I had no idea. How did you know that? You're so smart."

"Oh well," She emoted and raised a hand in the air. "I had tour of campus, how you say this, an Orientation Tour."

"You're so smart." He kissed her forehead and then said, "Let's go. Another twenty minutes and we'll be there."

He started the car, stopped at the intersection of Page Mill and Skyline and then crossed Skyline, where Page Mill became Alpine Road changing from wide and well-paved to narrow and twisty with worn patches of gravel. As the road descended into the folds of forested ridges and mountains, they passed green meadows, cows, shady groves, and a ranch house with horses, but not a single car.

Jack read a sign, "Portola State Park, two miles. We're almost there." The road arched to the left, forming a crescent around a meadow of high brown grass that separated a grove of oak trees from a forest of redwoods.

"We are going to a State Park?" Leena asked.

"No, no. We're going to our cabin in the woods. It's in a little community of cabins in the forest. You'll see. It's coming up."

He turned onto a nearly invisible one and a half lane-wide road that disappeared into the redwoods. He stopped at a wooden gate whose two-foot square wooden posts and eight inch beams were grey with age and spangled with moss. A sign on the gate read 'Slate Creek Road'. A chain wrapped around the posts and ran through eyehooks, securing it shut.

"It's the Middleton Tract. These guys called the Stanford Luminaries built cabins here eighty years ago. I think they were Masons or something like that. One of them was a guy named Sterling. He was the President of Stanford University in the 1940s. Another guy, Frederick Terman, had one too. I don't remember what he did," Jack said.

He lowered the window, letting in the smell of detritus, the buzz of insects, and melodious bird song. A riot of jays sounded an alarm, warning of the intrusion.

"He'll never find us here," Jack said.

He dialed the combination lock on the gate, opened it, drove through, and then secured it with the chain and lock. They continued down the road, which was pocked with holes and bumps. The car scrapped the pavement, letting out curdling screeches each time it bottomed out.

Jack winced. "OOOOOOO, that's painful."

A gigantic pickup truck with monstrous tires approached going the other way, driven by a man whose hair was pulled into a pony tail beneath an orange cap. The truck was silver and black, and had a gun rack with a rifle at the back of the cab. He wore mirrored sun glasses.

Watch out. Here comes the prison guard from Cool Hand

Luke, Jack thought as the theme to *Deliverance* played in his mind. He was a little afraid that the guy might just drive right over his Corvette, so he pulled off the road, his car screeching loudly and scraping on the pavement, embarrassing him.

As was the custom in the Middleton Tract, the driver stopped partially to greet, but mostly to inspect Jack, assess him, and perhaps protect. *He has a freaking shot gun,* Jack thought.

He leaned out the window to look down at Jack in his low lying Corvette "Wrong car for these parts," The man said. Jack nodded as the man eyed him and his Corvette silently. He then asked, "Where're ya headed?"

"I'm Jack Hooker. I'm heading to our place. The Hookers, back in the huckleberry."

The man went silent as he studied them. Jack tried to read his face, but saw only reflections in the mirror lenses of his glasses.

"Nice day we're having," Jack said nervously. The man didn't answer. Jack added, "Don't you think?" and swallowed.

"Had better, had worse. What are you doing here?"

"Right, we're just coming up to our place, just for the night." Jack said.

"Baton-board back in the Hucks, eh? Yeah, Hooker. I know your old man. How's he doing?"

"He's doing okay."

"Scientist. Right?" the man asked.

"Yep."

"Smart man, your dad. What about you?"

"Uh. I'm okay. In accounting."

"All right. Have a good day." Satisfied, the man drove on.

Jack continued gingerly up the bumpy road. They crossed a wooden bridge that spanned a brook. "We used to fish for trout down there in that creek, sometimes all day long, moving from hollow to hollow. It was at least ten years ago. Jeeze, where does time go? Let's take a look, stretch our legs." He stopped the car.

They ambled down a dirt path to the wet sand bar and gravel that bordered the stream. The water gurgled through a maze of boulders, slowed, and then disappeared around a bend into the red woods.

They inhaled the cool air of the forest, fragrant with creek algae and ever-greens. Jack recognized some of the rocks that he used as stepping stones as a kid.

A frog jump into the creek, making a splash that rippled across the slow moving water. The hum of the forest replaced the din of the city, a pleasant change that calmed them. Jack skipped a stone across the water. Leena tried, but missed the water completely. She tried again.

"Let's go," Jack said and they climbed up to the road and drove off.

He turned down an unpaved path bulldozed through the huckleberries. "This is ours." He gestured at the trees. "We have six acres. It's covered with red woods, madrone trees, huckleberry bushes, and ferns."

As he rounded a bend, the shiny aluminum cabin roof

appeared above the shrubs. The bushes cleared and the entire structure came it view. They jumped out and walked across the clearing towards the cabin.

Leena looked at the quaint cabin. It was made of red wood that had faded to grey. Wooden steps led up to the porch, which ran the length of the front of the cabin. The porch had a four-foot-high railing that traced the perimeter.

"It was built in the 1930s," Jack said.

They climbed the steps. From the vantage point of the porch, they surveyed the clearing in front which made a rectangular yard about a quarter acre, bordered by an impenetrable wall of huckleberry. Huge redwoods rose through the 'hucks' making a canopy overhead, standing in quiet watch over the forest, as though waiting for something to happen with a patience only known to trees. The yard was covered by a damp mat of needles and leaves that crunched underfoot.

"The woods are lovely, dark and deep, aren't they?" he asked and then unlocked the front door. They entered into the main room which served both as kitchen and living room. The air in the cabin was musty and smelled of burned wood. Directly in front, as they entered, was a large counter top that extended from the wall on the left into the room by six feet.

"We sat on the stools and ate at that counter."

On the other side of the counter, in the left corner, was an old wood burning stove that came from a time when wood burning stoves warmed homes and cooked food.

The rustic French windows of the main room were made of small panes in columns of four; the floor was hardwood lacquered and polished, twenty by fifteen feet with a throw rug; with chairs semi-circled around an iron fireplace that sat in the center of the room. It was painted black and its black metal chimney rose between the open rafters through the ceiling. A stuffed moose head with antlers looked down from over the eating counter.

"Jack, you did not shoot that animal?" She gasped and pointed to the enormous stuffed head of a moose that greeted them.

"Actually, I stole it." Jack grinned and then told her about how he had 'rescued' the moose head from a rival fraternity.

"It's freezing in here," Jack said. "I'm getting some wood for a fire. Just wait here."

Jack returned with kindling and logs which he placed in the fireplace. "There are two bedrooms. We'll sleep in the one facing the front." He lit the fire, which soon crackled away. "That should do it." The smell of smoke and warm air filled the room.

"The cabin doesn't have electricity, so we have to use kerosene lamps for light." He removed the glass lamp chimney lit the wick, and adjusted the flame.

"Hoh, Jack, I am feeling so bad, hold me." Leena sat on a sofa by the fire. He joined her. They sat in the warming sanctuary, safe and sound, but upset and afraid.

Darkness fell. The moon and stars blinked through the canopy. An owl hooted in the dark forest which was followed by a responsive hoot from a second owl. A third hooter joined. The hooting grew, peaked, and then faded away into the gentle hum of crickets.

Then they heard the distinctive crunch of forest leaves beneath walking feet in the darkness outside.

Leena grabbed Jack. "He is coming. I hear him in the woods."

Just after she spoke, the crunching stopped. "He heard me. He is stalking us," Leena whispered.

Minutes of silence followed, and then the crunching renewed, in the front, to the left, beyond the wall of hucks that bordered the yard. "He is coming, Jack."

Then they heard a second set of footsteps that came from behind, also on the west side.

"He is surrounding us," she said and grabbed Jack's arm.

Jack smiled. "That's a raccoon. They're coming for food. That's all."

Soon, they heard paws clicking on the porch floor outside.

"Come." Jack took a lamp and led Leena out on to the porch and into the cold night air. A raccoon appeared and approached, stopping ten feet away. "Told you. We used to bring dog biscuits for them." The raccoon came a little closer. "Sorry, little guy, I don't have anything for you."

They went back into the cabin and huddled on the couch until Leena fell asleep. Jack nudged her awake. "Let's get into bed."

Chapter 62 – Morning

The raucous caws of stellar jays awakened Leena and Jack. Jack rolled over to check his phone for the time and accidentally raised the blankets filling the bed with freezing air.

"Oh my Gods! It is cold in this cabin, Jack." Leena hugged him from the back.

He held up his phone. "It's a little after six-thirty." He rolled back under the covers, buried his head into her neck and rested.

Leena sat up and looked out through the paned glass, across the porch and onto the yard. She saw a circular fire pit and a picnic table with logs as chairs. A stellar Jay popped onto the porch rail, looking villainous in his black hood and crest. He reigned supreme over the yard, which hushed obediently as he twitched from pose to pose with flits and flutters, taking a step, stopping to caw, taking a bow, then another step, stopping to preen, bending over to rub his beak on the rail as though sharpening a sword, and then returning to attention to caw loudly, reminding all that this was his forest.

A second Jay challenged him, landed on a branch overhead and cawed. An onslaught of caws followed.

"Christ, listen to that racket," Jack complained.

"I am cold, Jack."

"Come here, Angel, here's a little warmth, a little love, luv." He put his arms around her.

She snuggled into him. “A fire is what I am having on my mind, Mister Hooker.”

“Fire? Yeah, okay, a fire.” He rolled naked out of bed, startling the Jay who flew away.

Cold air struck his body. “Jezuss it’s freezing out here. Yeah we need a fire.”

He walked to the living area, knelt by the fireplace, crumbled newspapers and put them in. Leena pulled on a robe and joined him, putting kindling on the crumbled paper.

Jack lit the fire and then strategically placed logs on the fire as it grew into a blaze. They went back to bed and waited for the warmth of the fire.

“I want to check in with Goldman,” Jack said. He dialed his phone. “Howard?”

“Hey, Jack, are you in the woods?”

“Yeah, hiding in the woods at the cabin,” Jack said.

“Rachel wants to call the police,” Howard said.

“Call the police? Forget that. Don’t do that. I think this whole thing is going to blow over.”

Howard called to Rachel, “Rachel, let’s wait and see. This could disappear in a few days or so. Let’s hold off.”

Jack could hear Rachel in the background, “I’m calling the police anyway.”

“Shit, can’t you get her under control,” Jack said to Howard.

“Uh, right, under control, her? I don’t think so. She has a

mind of her own, you know," Howard said.

"She is usually the only one with any common sense around here."

"She wants to call the police," Howard said.

"Okay, so this time she's wrong. Listen, I'm turning off my phone to save the battery. There's no electricity here. Nothing else to report," Jack said.

"'Nothing else to report'. Very official sounding. Are you in the FBI or something?" Howard asked.

"'Bye."

Mikhail sat in the darkness of his room puzzling over recent events, analyzing what went wrong. He had been slow to detect that things were amiss. He hadn't reported that Leena and Jack were together. His behavior confused him, troubled him. *It is Leena, her blonde hair.*

She briefly appeared like a vision in his mind, her voice, her face, her eyes, her hair, and then she vanished. Her image was replaced by excruciating pangs of nausea that clenched his viscera; beads of sweat formed on his face, he felt cold and shivered uncontrollably. A tunnel formed around his vision; his heart pounded. He felt like he was being pulled into a hole, painfully smothering.

He arose from the couch, began to stagger towards the bedroom, but lost consciousness and collapsed, his head smacking the tile floor with a loud crack that no one heard.

He felt a cool breeze on his face as he flew through

darkness in utter silence, as though he was vapor, a mere tingle of dust, speeding along. Before him, the blackness swirled, broke into fragments of vision accompanied by a roar that sounded like a stereo speaker at full volume on all frequencies. A dream played in his mind that showed a snowy field grayed by the ash of burnt bodies, skulls, bones; a mass grave. It was next to a slew of frozen black mud. Yellow sludge dribbled from a pipe.

Then his cell phone pinged, fragmenting his dream, waking him. It announced the arrival of a text message which showed the latitude/longitude coordinate of Jack's last cell phone call. He Googled the coordinates and found a map of the Middleton tract. He now knew where they were.

Chapter 63 – Exploring the Forest

The mild scent of burning wood spread through the cabin, bringing with it the warmth of the fire. Jack climbed back into bed and nuzzled Leena. She turned towards him, pressed her naked body up against his, shaping her body to his, fitting like a puzzle piece, settling into him.

They lay like this for minutes, arousing him to full wakefulness, but before things could progress she stretched her arms overhead and flexed her legs, forming an X with her body, going taught for a moment, and then she hopped out of bed. “I want to go looking around in the forest.”

“Oooooohhhhh.” Jack stretched. “How about later?” He pulled the blankets over his head.

Leena dressed and then hit him with a pillow. ”I want to explore. Are you coming with me?” She walked out onto the porch.

“Shit.” He sat up and looked through the paned window and across the porch onto the cabin yard at the fire pit which reminded him of his childhood: Saturday afternoons, hotdogs, beans heated in a can on the grill, and the crisp tan char of roasted marshmallows. He put on his Nikes and walked outside, onto the deck of the cabin without putting on anything else.

Leena gasped, but then laughed as he pranced around on

the deck in the privacy of the woods. He went back into the cabin, slipped on gym shorts and a dyed tee-shirt he loved. The shirt had a brain, grey, drab, with a caption that read, '*Your Brain*'. It sat next to a tie-dyed, rainbow colored brain in a beach chair, wearing shades with a caption that read, '*This is your brain in California.*'

"Let's go. We'll take the Cabin Trail. It's in the back." The Cabin Trail began in the backyard, on the south side of the cabin, and rose a hundred feet to the top of a ridge. The trail then curved to the north, running along the west side of the property line, along the ridge.

He took her by the hand and led her up the Cabin Trail, which wound its way through undergrowth, passing fallen trees, pale white in decay with orange toadstools and patches of moss. The trail traversed the ridge side, rising towards the top, tipping downhill to the right, towards the cabin, which they could not see through the dense forest.

A hundred feet up the trail, they came to a redwood tree stump, ten-feet-tall, standing on the downhill side of the trail. It was hidden behind a wall of huckleberry bushes which stood five feet themselves. The stump was charred and hallowed out, like a cylinder. The stump stood watch over its former body; a redwood that had fallen at least a century earlier. It lay on the ground bordered by huckleberries. A monument to the slow passage of time in the forest.

"This was my fort. Let's take a look through the bushes, through the burrow, under the bushes. Come with me." He crawled on his hands and knees under the wall of bushes to the backside of the stump. Leena followed.

The cylinder of the stump opened in the back, and there was a small platform on top of the stump large enough to stand on. Crude steps, little more than wood hammered into the side of the stump, led to the top of the fort. They climbed to the platform from where they could clearly view the trail below.

"We played capture the flag when I was a kid. Once they captured me here and took me prisoner. I was the king and they were the barbarians. They won that day."

He momentarily recalled making love on a blanket at the base of the stump, when he was eighteen, to a sixteen-year-old girl who was on fire with lust.

"There's a short cut through the woods. See the fallen tree?" he pointed to the fallen redwood. "Right through the bushes, to the top of the ridge. We would just walk along the fallen tree and then…" He snapped his fingers. "I'm there in no time. This is my forest. I know every inch; each trail, each stump, each hiding place."

Jack brushed away a layer of redwood needles from the floor of the fort, revealing a stick, two feet long, two inches thick; it had a knot on one end.

"See this? One of my weapons." He picked it up. "It was my club, like a hammer. Did you know that the weapon of choice on the Russian Steppe, four thousand years ago, was clubs, often made of copper? It was the Copper Age."

"What you are talking about? Four thousand years ago, copper clubs?"

The club still fit his hand. It was still solid. "You know, the Indo-Europeans of the Russian Steppe and Thor's Hammer."

"I don't know what you are talking about, Jack."

"I am the Horrible One," he growled.

She folded her arms and said, "You are an idiot, Jack."

He held the club over his head and shouted "I AM THE HORRIBILE ONE AND THIS IS MY FOREST!" His voice echoed through the woods.

"Do you think I scared anyone?" He asked. She laughed.

They descended from the fort and tumbled up the trail, a quarter of a mile or so, until they reached a T intersection with the Bridge Trail. The Bridge Trail ran along the ridge on the west side of the cabin. It marked the edge of Jack's land. The forest canopy here was so dense that there was no sunlight and nothing grew. The forest floor was bare, clear and open, allowing them to see a distance through the woods. Heading left, the trail sloped upward along the ridge and led deeper into the forest. Straight ahead, the ridge dropped away swiftly into a deep ravine. There was no path across the ravine.

Taking the Bridge Trail right, they headed down the ridge, along the property line and passed the Bridge Tree, a huge redwood that had fallen across the ravine. From the Bridge Tree, the path continued and looped back down to the front yard of the cabin.

They took the Bridge Trail right until they came to a fork.

"The path leads back to the front of the cabin. We're going this way to the Bridge Tree." He pointed left towards the ravine.

She looked towards the cabin and saw the roof faintly shimmer through the undergrowth of bushes.

He pointed to a break on the bush. "It's that fallen tree, from the fort." She nodded.

The Bridge Tree was a fallen redwood eight-feet in diameter. It stretched across the ravine like a bridge. The redwood stood above a creek bed that flowed only during heavy storms. Sometime, long ago, during a once-in-a-century storm perhaps, the creek eroded away the earth and stone, toppling the tree.

"It is sad to see a fallen tree, Jack."

The thick red bark on the top side of the tree showed no signs of decay and shoots of green sprouted from the tree, reaching upwards towards the sun.

"It fell but it is still alive. Don't be sad."

He led her by the hand across the ravine on the gigantic tree. The tree continued for another two hundred feet on the other side of the ravine. Jack and Leena walked along the fallen tree until it became too small. They jumped down and continued through the forest clearing until they came to a tiny field of clover, thirty feet in diameter, nourished by the rich forest floor and a small patch of sunlight.

Jack stopped and sat on a log and opened the backpack. "Water?" he offered.

She nodded and took the bottle from his hand. "It is so beautiful here. I want to take a rest here," she said.

She took a blanket from the backpack, spread it over the clover, stripped and lay naked in the sun.

Jack took off his clothes and joined her on the blanket. They felt the warmth of the sun on their bare skin.

Chapter 64 – Forest Nymph

Spent, indolent, and a little sticky, she lay on her back looking up at the dense roof of branches while he whistled *Norwegian Wood* and wove the clover into a crown that he placed on her head.

"A wreath for my Princess."

He lay down next to her, slipped his arm beneath her neck, cradled her head, and then petted her hair with his left hand. He brought his lips to her face and pressed them against her cheek. He raised his head so he could examine the warm curves of her nude body while stroking her right side with the open palm of his hand, dragging his fingers over her breast, across her stomach, to her thigh where it stopped, turned and tickled its way back up to her shoulder; his fingers like spider's legs.

"Hoh, Jack! What are we going to do," she whimpered, bringing him out of his reverie.

"Oh. Yeah. I would say that things don't look to good right now. What about Stanford? Will the bank keep paying?" he asked.

"No, it will not. I have savings. I have a lot of money."

"How much?"

"Enough. Tuition and apartment are paid for, I have plane ticket home when I am going home."

"That sounds like a plan. So stay on at Stanford. You know

they changed the locks on your apartment, so maybe you can't stay there anymore. Maybe you should stay with me?"

"That would not be looking good for me, Jack. Maybe I can stay with Rachel." She paused, and then said, "Maybe it is not so bad. I am having some good friends in Moscow. I can call them. They will help me find job."

"What about this Mikhail guy?"

"Oh well." She waved her hand with a flourish, dismissing the problem. "He will go away."

"If he catches us, what do you think he will do?"

"He would not dare touch me," she said.

"If he touches my love, I will kill him," he growled like a wolf. He put his forehead up to hers and blinked into her eyes.

He then said, "Yeah, I think things will blow over. Hungry? Wanna get something to eat?"

"Yes."

After eating, they decided to head back to the cabin. She slipped on her pants and shirt, folded her undergarments and put them in the bag. He put on his shorts and Nikes and put his shirt in the bag.

They left the clover and sunlight for the shade of the woods and crunched their way towards the Bridge Tree. They noted the new sprouts growing out of pieces of the fallen redwood, resurrecting the mother tree, which continued in the form of many younger trees. Some would become firmly rooted in the slowly shifting soil.

Chapter 65 – Crossing the Ravine

They crossed the steady redwood bridge tree, climbed back up to the Bridge Trail, and continued down the ridge towards the front yard of the cabin. As they descended, the silver aluminum roof came into view, flickering through the undergrowth. Then the bushes and trees parted, opening into a clear view of the entire front yard. They saw Mikhail standing on the porch. He had smashed open the door.

"That fucker! Let's get out of here." They fled back up the path.

Mikhail heard their footsteps and saw movement on the hillside. He ran across the porch, down the stairs, and towards the solid wall of huckleberries where he stopped, looking for a way through.

Jack and Leena ran up the trail to the fork that branched off to the Bridge Tree. "Follow the trail back towards the back side of the cabin. Go up the ridge and circle back down. I am going to cross the Bridge Tree and draw him over it. Wait until you hear me shout, then go back to the cabin and call the police."

They parted. Leena jogged up the trail and disappeared into the woods. Jack sat on the Bridge Tree on the far side of the ravine and waited for Mikhail.

Mikhail paced back and forth until he found the trail overgrown with bushes, but clear enough to follow. He began to cautiously walk up it, stopping, listening for clues, hearing nothing, continuing further, stopping again, and peering into the bush.

Jack heard Mikhail's halting steps climb towards the Bridge Tree and his heart pounded, stomach squirmed, and chest rose and fell as he panted.

And then he saw Mikhail carefully come into view and stop where the brush cleared into the open floor of the ridge. He surveyed the ravine, then the forest on the other side, spotting the fallen redwood bridge, his eyes continuing up the ravine and to the Ridge Trail that disappeared over a rise.

"THERE HE IS!" Jack shouted.

Mikhail's head swiveled, searching the forest, stopping when he spotted Jack on the Bridge Tree. He raised a gun. Jack scrambled across the Bridge Tree. Mikhail fired and the bullet whizzed past Jack's shoulder, hitting a tree that grew next to the Bridge Tree. The impact of the bullet jettisoned a cloud of splinters, one of which—not much larger than a toothpick—impaled Jack's left eye, pinning the lid to his eyeball.

"OWWWWWW,FUCK!" He tumbled off the tree and took cover behind the tree. "Oh my God! Oh my God! I'm blind, I'm blind, I'm blind!"

Kneeling, he leaned back against the Bridge Tree, put his hand to his face, and found the tiny stake in his eye. A knot twisted in his stomach and he felt like vomiting.

"Now I'm a fucking blind man. Fuck, fuck, fuck. I can't

believe it."

He pulled the wooden needle from his eye, releasing a steady flow of blood that covered his hand and ran down his cheek. The lid was shut tight, swollen and throbbing. He studied the blood on his hand with his good eye while his panic slowly turned to rage. "I'M GONNA KILL THAT FUCKER!"

He stood and shouted across the ravine, taunting Mikhail, drawing him away from Leena. "HI, MIKHAIL! WE KNOW ALL ABOUT YOU, AND THE SEX SLAVES, AND THE MONEY, AND SO DOES INTERPOL. YOU'RE DEAD MEAT, BUDDY! AND THEY KNOW YOU'RE HERE! I JUST CALLED THEM!" he bluffed. "YOU'RE JUST AN ERRAND BOY. A LITTLE GUY, RUNNING ERRANDS FOR *MISTER BIG CHEESE, CHESNAKOV*. WE KNOW!"

Mikhail faced Jack, measured the risk of crossing the Bridge Tree and decided to take another shot. He took aim at Jack.

Jack waved, making himself an even more attractive target, but before Mikhail could squeeze the trigger, Leena shouted, "HE IS GOING TO KILL US, JACK! RUN!"

"RUNNNN, LEENA! RUNNNN LIKE HELL!"

Mikhail ran up the Bridge Trail in the direction of Leena's voice.

"THAT FUCKER, THAT MOTHER FUCKER! I'M GOING TO KILL THAT MOTHER FUCKER!" Jack howled. A half-blind, insane rage engulfed him, extinguishing fear, causing his glands to inject an overdose of testosterone. He jumped onto the Bridge Tree and charged.

Leena turned left at the fork and headed back to the cabin. As she hurried along, the overgrowth narrowed the path and then opened it, allowing her to bound down the trail until a branch became entangled in her legs and she tumbled to the ground.

Panic set in and she froze on the trail floor. *I cannot go to cabin. He will find me.*

Then she saw an opening under the wall of bushes, just large enough to hide in. She rolled in and froze.

Mikhail continued to stalk, following the subtle foot prints; broken twigs and overturned detritus dark with moisture, until he found the sitzmark of her fall; a streak on the forest floor. He stopped, crouched, and scanned the forest until he saw the faint colors of her clothing through bush. He had found her.

Mikhail froze until he was sure she hadn't detected him. He was too far away to attack and would have to slowly approach, and then surprise her when he was close enough. By gradually slithering his feet along the forest floor, slightly beneath the leaves, he was able to move quietly towards her. Soon he was within thirty feet.

Suddenly, a stellar Jay dive-bombed, cackling like a machine gun and landed on a widow-maker the jutted out of a redwood, just above Mikhail's head. A second joined, landing in a madrone.

Leena looked towards the birds and saw Mikhail's outline through the bush, below the Jays. She gasped and jumped to her feet.

He charged her and threw a haymaker that connected with her head, knocking her to the ground.

"JACK! HE IS HURTING ME!" she screamed.

Mikhail stood over her, drew his pistol and aimed.

"JACK! HE IS GOING TO SHOOT ME!"

Mikhail hesitated. He couldn't pull the trigger.

Why? After easily executing so many others, he couldn't shoot Leena, who sobbed while on her hands and knees.

What is it? It was the blonde hair. It blocked him because it reminded him of Sasha, his sister who had died so long ago.

And then the sounds and images of Sasha came rushing back, flooding in his mind. He saw her naked, helpless, running from bullies on the play yard at the orphanage.

"Ilya is coming, he is hurting me." The desolate orphanage flooded his mind, intoxicating him with pathos and he froze. It all came back to him; yanking a stick from the fence, fearlessly charging Ilya, clubbing him into submission, then the plague that took Sasha's life, her ashes in the snow and the mass grave. He saw an image of snow with embedded skulls. He couldn't shoot.

Chapter 66 – The Wrath of Cyclops

Jack sprinted along the fallen tree, the short-cut to the Bridge Trail, cutting through the thick undergrowth. He arrived at the fort, climbed to the top, took the club, and raised it over his head. He saw Mikhail standing over Leena, gun in hand. He leapt from the redwood tree stump, taking aim at Mikhail's head.

Mikhail heard the rustle of Jack's feet and turned to see him in midair and took aim.

Jack shifted his target from Mikhail's head and brought the club down on Mikhail's right shoulder, breaking his collarbone. Mikhail cried out and dropped the gun. His shoulder slumped downward, his arm dangling and useless.

Jack fell to the ground, got back to his feet and charged Mikhail holding the club overhead.

Mikhail kicked Jack in the groin and Jack crumbled to the ground. He then pulled a knife with his good hand, pounced on Jack, and began pressing it towards Jack's face. Jack held Mikhail's wrist with both hands, pushing the knife away, but Mikhail leaned forward, bringing his weight down on the knife. The knife slowly approached Jack's face, moving towards his right eye. Mikhail then kneed Jack in the abdomen, knocking out all his air. Jack released his grip on Mikhail's hand.

The knife plunged towards Jack's face, but he turned his

head to the side as the knife passed by. To Mikhail's complete surprise, Jack bit into Mikhail's wrist, sinking in his teeth, fastening himself to it like a rabid beast. Blood flowed across Jack's face, into his mouth, and down his throat. Mikhail's blood fed Jack's frenzy.

Mikhail dropped the knife and stood, lifting Jack with his left arm. He shook his arm, but Jack's mouth held fast. He kneed Jack in the chest, but the bite didn't break.

Jack wrapped his arms around Mikhail's legs and lunged forward, tumbling Mikhail onto his back. He released the bite, jumped onto Mikhail's chest, and before Mikhail could blink, jabbed him in the left eye with his index and middle fingers, blinding him.

Mikhail bellowed in pain, rolled to one side and staggered to his feet.

Jack tumbled off, found his club and began slowly circling Mikhail, who backed away, his good arm coiled ready to swing. Jack's frantic panting whipped up the saliva and blood in his mouth, making a red form that slid down his chin.

Jack came at Mikhail with the club swinging, missing, and swinging again as Mikhail bobbed and weaved in slow retreat.

Jack charged, taking two steps towards Mikhail, club raised overhead.

Mikhail kicked, but Jack anticipating the kick, stood clear, and followed the kick with a blow to Mikhail's head, which cracked loudly. His next blow landed on the broken right shoulder.

Mikhail howled in pain and staggered backwards. Before he could steady himself, Jack landed another blow on the crown of his head, then a second, then a third. Mikhail fell to his knees and looked at Jack with astonished resignation.

Blood covered Jack's face, ran down his neck and soaked his shirt. He spent a brief moment looking at the pitiful, kneeling Mikhail, but the beast in him was unmoved. He landed a fourth blow and then a fifth; blows Mikhail didn't resist. He toppled over.

Still firmly in the grip of mania, Jack jumped on Mikhail, straddled his abdomen, raised the club with both hands and brought it down on Mikhail's head again and again and again.

"YOU FUCKER! YOU MOTHER FUCKER! YOU PIECE OF SHIT!" He beat Mikhail with uncontrollable rage until his forehead cracked down the middle, indenting, causing his eyes to look at each other cross-eyed. A reddish white tissue leaked out from his head.

Jack stopped and stared into the dead eyes of the fallen foe. "YOU ARE DEAD NOW!" he taunted the inert corpse. "You are dead, but I am not dead."

He rose to his feet and stared at Leena with his rabid right eye and red foaming mouth.

He felt faint, lost his balance, dipped to the left and side-stepped to regain his balance. He looked at Mikhail's broken head and leaking brains, which were now covered with insects that wallowed in the warm soup of blood and tissue.

Jack's wild look faded away. He looked at the blood on his

hands. “What the fuck!” The orgy of insects feeding on Mikhail’s open eyes and the metallic taste of blood sickened him. Overcome by excruciating nausea, he fell to his knees and vomited up bile from his empty stomach.

After the spasms ceased, he rolled onto his back and stared up at the green ceiling of the forest with his one good eye. The cool forest vapor soothed his throbbing wounds. A buzz of endorphins tingled and his ears rang. The fury, panic, and the beast in him ebbed away.

He rose to his feet, lost his balance and collapsed. Leena came to him. “Jack, we are okay. He is dead, but we are okay.”

“I’m not so okay. I feel pretty fucked up, actually.”

She took his hand and helped him to his feet. He put his arm around her shoulder and used her for support. Together, they stumbled back to the Cabin, settled onto the couch in the main room by the fireplace and called 9-1-1.

Chapter 67 – 911

"A man has been chasing us in the forest and trying to kill us. He was shooting at us!" Leena frantically shouted into Jack's cell to the 9-1-1 operator.

"We are at cabin in the forest." Leena turned to Jack. "Jack, what is address?"

He raised his hand, requesting the phone. She gave it to him.

"Hi," he wheezed, sputtered, and cleared his throat. "We are in the Middleton Tract, next to Portola State Park. A man has been killed."

"Killed! Shot?" the operator asked.

"No, beaten to death," Jack said.

"What?"

"Beaten to death, skull fractured."

"Jeezus, anyone else injured?" the operator asked.

"Yeah, me. My eye was impaled."

"Eye injury?"

"Right," Jack said.

"Right Eye?" the operator asked.

"Wrong eye. Left eye. Why?"

"Just curious. Paramedics will be there in ten minutes."

"Take off your shirt, Jack," Leena said, "It is having blood and smelling bad." She put the shirt outside on the porch where it soon attracted flying insects of all sorts.

She found a towel, soap and a large bowl which she filled with cold water. She brought them to the couch where Jack rested and began gently washing the blood from his face and chest. She made a cold compress which she laid across the swollen eye. Jack fell into a deep sleep.

Jack awoke to the heavy sound of clumping boots on the porch. The boots entered the cabin, pounding the wooden floor. His right eye blinked open and he saw three concerned faces huddled above, looking down. They were Leena and two paramedics, one of whom was blonde, blue-eyed, with an elongated head that extended from a longer than average neck. The second was black haired, brown-eyed and dark; a Latino.

He closed his eye and listened to them speak.

"Blood pressure is very low, forty-five over sixty. Pulse is around fifty, you're really dehydrated. I'm going to give you some fluids. You're going to feel a little pinch on your arm. He goes to the hospital after this."

"We need to wait for the police."

"She's fine," the gringo said. "A little scared, dehydrated, hungry. I gave her some water and a Snicker's bar."

"Your eye is a mess," the Latino said.

"Ow, shit!" Jack cried out as the paramedic padded it with disinfecting gauze.

"A stick was sticking in his eye," Leena said.

"GODDAMN! THAT HURTS!" Jack cried out as the paramedic spread apart the swollen lid.

"Yeah, I can see where it entered." He studied the bright red point of entry, which coagulated into a viscous scab.

The gringo said, "It looks pretty bad. I've seen this injury a couple of times. Kids playing with sticks."

"So, give it to me straight, Doc," Jack said, grimacing.

"Looks bad. You need a real doctor."

Jack went limp, becoming catatonic.

The paramedic injected him. "Demerol. It'll reduce the pain."

A deep, comatic sleep took possession of Jack.

Chapter 68 – The Police

Jack came to, hearing Leena telling the police about their ordeal. "This man, Mikhail Kazaki, he is criminal. He tried to kill us. He has gun to be killing us," Leena said.

"Where is he?" one officer asked.

"He is dead," Leena said.

"Where's the body?"

"In the forest. I can show you," she said.

Jack piped up. "Show them the Bridge Tree. He fired at me. The bullet hit a tree on the other side of the ravine and a piece of wood lodged in my eye. Shit!"

"He's awake."

Jack looked up and saw an African-American with a police officer. "I'm agent Slade, with the FBI. Do you feel up to some questions?"

"Ohhh, I feel cloud-like right now, like I'm floating. Answer some questions. Okay, why not. Shoot."

"We gave him some Demerol. He's been sleeping. He sounds a little punchy," a paramedic said.

"I've been Demerolized," Jack punned poorly.

"Right," Agent Slade side-stepped the pun. "So what happened today?"

"Today, today, today." A smile came to his face as he

remembered making love to Leena on a bed of clovers. He skipped that part.

"Well, we came here because we knew that Mikhail Kazaki was after us. We knew he was a criminal and he knew we knew. In fact, we knew he knew we knew."

“Right. And he pursued you?”

“Yesterday morning he showed up at my fraternity looking for us. We split. Came here to hide. Soooo, today we went for a hike and were returning when he appeared. We fled. He fired a shot at me, which struck a tree. A large piece of wood lodged in my eye. IT HURT LIKE HELL!”

“Mikhail is working for CEO of NovoRisk Bank in Moscow, Dmitri Chesnakov. They are laundering money,” Leena said with breathless anxiety. “Dmitri was my boss. He sent me to Stanford to study.”

“Okay, okay, slow down. Let’s get back to what happened today,” Slade said.

“After he shot at me, he chased Leena up the trail.”

“Then what?”

Leena said, “I fell down and hiding, but he found me and hit me. I fell down again and he pointed gun at me, but he did not shoot me because Jack jumped on him and knocked him down.”

“Yeah, I jumped on him and broke his right shoulder, he dropped the gun. We fought. He tried to poke me in the face with a knife. I beat him over the head with a club. I was so pissed I just kept beating him. Look, the guy almost killed us and he blinded me. I was pissed and scared."

"Is this the guy?" Slade showed Jack his cell with which he had dialed up a picture of Kazaki.

Leena looked at the picture, "Yes. That is him. That is Mikhail Kazaki."

"Okay, wanted by Interpol in connection with a sex slavery ring," Agent Slade mumbled as he quickly read the text with the picture of Kazaki.

"He also works for the CEO of NovoRisk bank, in security," Jack added.

"Yeah. Why would he want to kill you two?" Slade asked. "And how did you happen to find out about this? With the sex slaves and everything?"

"I was working with Dmitri at NovoRisk Bank. I was, how you say this, protégée," Leena said.

"And you worked closely with him?"

"Yes, almost every day and I was travelling with him, he was my boss, too."

"When did you first see Kazaki?"

"He and Dmitri came to seminar in San Francisco. I was at seminar too, as part of NovoRisk business, but Dmitri was calling him Petrov."

"Petrov what?"

"I do not know last name. He is same man as Mikhail Kazaki. He is in personnel records at bank, in security. I looked it up online."

Slade spoke to the officer, "Call the airport. Find out when Dmitri Chesnakov went through customs and in which states. If there's nothing in the Bay Area, see if he went through customs on the east coast, you know, one of the New York airports. Also check if he came with Mikhail Kazaki or perhaps someone who went by the name of Petrov. Call me when you find something." He hung up.

Slade turned to Leena and asked, "So, what are you doing in America, Miss…?"

"Miss Kiraskaya. Please, calling me Leena. I came to Stanford to study Risk Management. I worked at NovoRisk bank in Russia."

"Have you contacted Chesnakov? I mean, if you know him so well. What does he have to say about this?"

"He fired me. We did not have chance to talk."

"Why did he fire you?"

Leena gave him a superior look. "That is not your business, Mister Slade."

"It is very much my business. And if you want a, 'get out of jail free card', you better cooperate."

"What is,'get out of jail card'?" she asked.

"Just answer the questions, Leena."

"I am having nothing to hide, Agent Slade," she huffed.

"You seem to be a pretty lucky girl, travelling with the CEO, sent to Stanford, his protégé. How well did you know him?"

"I did not know about all these crimes, Agent Slade."

Slade paused, rocked back slightly as he took a breath and then asked, "Were you having an affair with Chesnakov?"

Leena blushed and said, "No, we were not having affair. I was his girl, but now I am with Jack Hooker. This is why he fired me." She then stared into Slater's face, slightly mortified. "It is none of your business, Agent Slater."

"Jealousy," Slade said and Leena nodded.

"I did not know about crimes. I did not know," Leena blurted out. Agent Slade studied her face with a skeptical eye.

"His body is in the woods?" the agent asked.

"Maybe a hundred yards or so. Leena can show you the way," Jack said.

"Let's go get him," Agent Slade said to the paramedics, one of whom grabbed a body bag. "You two stay here. Keep two eyes on him," he said to the officer and remaining paramedic.

"Two against one, not fair." Jack was stoned and silly.

Leena led Agent Slade and the paramedic into the woods while Jack slept.

She led to the gruesome site where they shooed away flies and wasps to get a clear look at Kazaki's face. "God. What did he do to him? His forehead is beaten in. His nose is smashed," Slade said.

"He was like wild animal," Leena said. "And we were scared of him. He could get us again."

The officer retrieved the gun and club. "Here, the gun's been fired, looks like one time. This club is covered with blood."

He put the weapons in evidence bags and zipped them shut.

"Bag him and take him to forensics. Leena, can you show me this tree with the bullet Hooker mentioned?"

"Jack. Jack," Leena said, gently nudging him. She caressed his face.

He awoke, opened his eye and, through a fog, saw Leena's warm, affectionate face. He felt calm, content, and tranquil until he hear Agent Slade's jarring voice. "So, Hooker. We have Kazaki's body and we're taking him to forensics. We found the gun and your club. You killed this guy, right?"

"Self-defense," Jack mumbled. His rising pulse pulled him out of the comfort of semi-consciousness until his was alert. The pain rushed in. "Oh my God. My whole body feels bruised."

Leena thought she saw his eye injury throb.

Slade met Jack's obstinate, one-eyed stare. "I understand. It looks like it probably was self-defense. Do you feel up to making a short statement?"

Jack tried to raise his head and sighed painfully. "I feel like dirt."

"I'll make it short. You want to go to the hospital after this or to jail?"

"Hospital."

"Okay, I need a statement." Slade switched on the recorder on his cell phone, read Jack his rights and then questioned him for half an hour. When he was done, he said, "Take him to trauma care. Check the eye. Leena, you are coming with us. We have a few more questions."

The paramedics lifted Jack onto a gurney. Leena walked with him out of the cabin to the ambulance.

"I am missing you, Jack," she caressed his face, then kissed his cheek. She watched as they loaded him into the ambulance and shut the doors. He fell asleep.

"The MRI shows damage to the retina that may never heal. It could become a blind spot." The doctor wore magnifying spectacles as he stared at the MRI Image. "It's lower, right of center. About the size of a pencil eraser. You could call it a permanent disability."

Jack listened with his eye patched, hunched over in the hospital bed, looking at the doctor with his right eye, and panting with anxiety while digesting the bad news. "THAT SUCKSSSSS!"

"Agreed. It sucks, but you aren't blind at all. Just a blind spot." The doctor tried to soften the blow. "You're healthy enough to go home. I think Slade is going to check you out today. Come back in a week to change bandages."

The doctor left and Howard and Rachel poked their heads in. "The Hook," Howard said. Rachel carried flowers. "Or should I say Cap'n Hook now that you have an eye patch?" He saluted childishly.

"Funny," Jack grimaced.

"Where shall I put the flowers?" Rachel asked.

"Kind of you, Rachel. I appreciate it. I think there's a vase in the lower cabinet." Jack gestured towards a dresser.

Rachel found the vase, filled it with water, arranged the flowers, and set it on the dresser. “There.”

“Very nice.”

“So, how do you feel?”

“How do I look?”

“Like shit.”

“Thanks, ‘How weird’, I can always depend upon Howard for bullshit.”

“Have you looked in a mirror?”

“No. I’ve avoided it.”

“Here, I brought this in case you were curious.” He held up a hand mirror.

A neat patch covered Jack’s left eye, beneath which lay a deep purple bruise that tapered off, becoming blue, and then yellow. A scatter of small cuts and scabs peppered his face. “I look like a mutant monster. I could scare people.”

“We told Agent Slade everything, my patient, her escape. He interviewed her and she identified the corpse. He isn’t going to hold any of us. He’s done. He’s closing the books.”

“Have you seen Leena?” Jack asked.

Howard looked at Rachel, who looked back, sighed and then broke more bad news. “They sent her back to Moscow.”

“You’re kidding?”

“Nope, not kidding. She’s back in Russia. We didn’t even have a chance to see her before she was sent home,” Rachel said.

Jack sank into silence.

"So, we also brought this." Rachel held up a bag of candy. "Honeycomb."

"Will she be safe?" Jack asked.

"She is returning to a protection program. Russia is kind of a crazy place, but they want law and order there, too. Witness Protection. She has to disappear."

"Are they going after Chesnakov?"

"Not in the U.S. That is a totally Russian affair," Howard answered.

Jack sulked in silence.

Agent Slade visited Jack in the hospital. "So, Hooker, I got the whole story from Howard Goldman, Rachel Katz, and Leena. Leena went back. She's in witness protection custody."

Jack's arms, upper thighs, calves, and abdomen ached as he stood in front of Sigma Chi. He dialed Leena and heard, "The number you dialed is no longer in service at this time." He sent an email that bounced back. His texts hadn't been delivered. She was gone.

He gave up, at least for the moment, and firmly gripped the handrail of the steps leading up to the front door.

Greg stood outside at the top of the steps. "DUUUUUDE, we read about you in the papers. What the fuck happened?" Greg came down to Jack and helped him with the steps.

And then they heard from the living room inside the frat, "HEY, IT'S THE HOOK! HE'S BACK!" This was followed by a murmur that buzzed through the house and the sound of feet bounding down stairs. A couple of heads poked through the door, came outside onto the landing at the top of the steps, and began to jabber.

"JACK. OH MY GOD!"

"Jesus! Look at that patch!"

"Look at that bruise!"

"And all those cuts!"

They were joined by a third and then fourth, who added their jabber.

"Cap'n Hook."

"He can hardly move."

"Walking like an old man."

And then a voice spoke that silenced the jabbering. "You murdered a man, Hook." It was Bob, the Insolent Voice of the Brotherhood of Evil.

"It was self-defense," Greg said. "Self-defense is not murder."

"How'd you do it?" Bob asked.

Jack ignored the question and continued to the top of the steps. He then said, "I'm moving out."

"Well, we won't miss you."

"Feel a little safer," Jack said to Bob and then stopped and faced him. He looked into Bob's eyes, which darted away from Jack's stare. Jack exhaled, rocked his head very slightly and said, "I beat him to death with a club." He waited for a response from the Insolent Voice in the hush of conforming frat boys.

To some, he would be a hero, to others a foe, but the story of Jack Hooker, Leena, and the death of Mikhail Kazaki would become woven into the tapestry of Sigma Chi's oral tradition.

Dmitri sat in his corner office, above the streets of Moscow reading about the death of a Russian National and international wanted criminal, Mikhail Kazaki. He turned towards the window and tapped his fingers on his pursed lips and wondered whether he was at risk. He knew they would tie Kazaki to him, but he had friends in high places that would stop any legal action or anything published in the press. He had nothing to worry about.

A young brunette knocked on his door. "Come in Tasha. Sit."

The twenty-eight-year-old sat facing Dmitri.

"We have an opening for a junior executive in the Risk Management department. Your superiors feel you would be perfect for the position. Are you interested?"

Jack sat in his Corvette, a little woozy on Vicodin, and played with his phone. The impulse to call her pestered him, reminding him of Leena, every few minutes. He brought up a picture of her, then another picture, then a third. Then his calendar pinged a reminder. *What?*

He brought up the reminder and there was attached a short video, from Leena. He started it.

It was her smiling face and crooked smile, pulled to one side, and cocked eyebrows that together suggested a mirthful coquette was about to say something witty, to tease, to sting or to flatter, but her moistened eyes betrayed the sadness of farewell.

"So, Mister Jack Hooker." She stopped as her face cracked with real sorrow. A tear ran down her cheek as she paused, cleared her voice, and continued in a very soft, vulnerable voice. "I am loving you, Jack." She paused again. "And I do not want to go home, but now I must go now. I must disappear. I will be hiding."

She looked into the lens of the camera. "I am loving you, Jack." She kissed the lens of the camera. That was the end of the video.

www.ingramcontent.com/pod-product-compliance
Lightning Source LLC
Chambersburg PA
CBHW032133190626
46814CB00005BA/1679